Praise for
Regret the Dark Hour

"Richard Hood's *Regret the Dark Hour* is a search for Regional Truth and the ways memory, representation, and history intertwine to produce stories, interpretation, and character. This novel is a triumph—giving us the sound and flavor of prohibition-era East Tennessee, in a mix of voice, perception, and blindness embedded within the darkly tangled story of a family murder."

—Shelby Stephenson,
Poet Laureate of North Carolina and author

"*Regret the Dark Hour* calls up a story of betrayal, forbidden love, and familial violence in prohibition-era Appalachia. Hood's stunning and lyrical writing vividly captures the world of this forgotten time period. A beautiful debut and wonderful addition to southern noir."

—Jen Conley,
author of *Seven Ways to Get Rid of Harry*

REGRET THE

DARK HOUR

RICHARD HOOD

REGRET THE DARK HOUR

Down & Out Books
3959 Van Dyke Road, Suite 265
Lutz, FL 33558
DownAndOutBooks.com

The characters and events in this book are fictitious. Any similarity to real persons, living or dead, is coincidental and not intended by the author.

Cover photo by Richard Hood
Cover design by Lance Wright

ISBN: 1-64396-028-8
ISBN-13: 978-1-64396-028-9

To my father, Glay Morgan Hood
(Fall Branch, Tennessee, age 101)
and my aunt, Opal Hood Leedy
(Fall Branch, Tennessee, age 109).
They lived these tales.

CHAPTER ONE

FALSE DAWN

—WILDWOOD FLOWER—

Oh he taught me to love him and promised to love,
To cherish me over all others above,
Now my poor heart is wondering no misery can tell,
He left me no warning, no word of farewell.

Oh he taught me to love him and called me his flower,
That was blooming to cheer him through life's weary hour,
How I long to see him and regret the dark hour,
He's gone and neglected his frail wildwood flower.

—Carter Family, 1927

i.

Nole Darlen hadn't even thought about pulling the trigger.

The sound, the flashback, the acrid odor—all were so sudden and strong that there was no room for individual sense-impression. Instead, he felt one overwhelming impact, neither hearing, touch, smell but a compound of all senses, so that he tasted the thunderous sound—a coppery pulse of flavor on the roof of his mouth—and heard the rising smell of burnt powder, too loud, like a clashing of brass. And only later, in memory, he saw the bullet's impact punching the body into a stretched upward leap and crumpling it to the floor. He felt the breaking of the chair as a febrile crinkling, barely audible in the echoing throb of the gun blast. He saw the body land with a *fuffing*, like a rug being shaken out.

He really hadn't known he was going to fire just then and certainly hadn't anticipated the crash of effect, and so he stood, overwhelmed, for a moment. The pistol, which had kicked up and back from the firing, was suspended in his raised hand, just at his ear, as though he were listening carefully to the chamber. He was still smiling wryly at that last bit of conversation, the ludicrous challenge: *You wouldn't dare.*

Then he made a small sound, incomprehensible, even to himself. A groaned syllable of some sort. And threw the gun to the floor as realization swept over him, pushing him furious and frightened through the crudely framed doorway. And out into the deep night.

His first few frenzied steps faulted in the gluey spring mud, sending his body forward and throwing him to shockingly cold, wet earth. The fall increased his terror, and he wrenched himself upright, running again—this time with an exaggerated, high-stepping hop, thrusting and pulling his feet into and out of the grasping muck.

He ran about ten yards this way, then stopped, stock-still. He made that same single-syllable sound and turned, wrenching his feet about and lurching back into the shed. He dropped to his hands and knees and scrabbled around on the hardpacked floor for the Colt revolver. Tucking the cold, heavy piece into the waist of his pants, he arose and left the shed again, this time walking bent forward with a grim determination, like a soldier moving through hostile fire, following some drilled command: one foot then the other, dogged and deliberate, through the mud and out onto the grassy clearing around the house, which brooded heavily over him. Then he began to run, out of the clear, across the graveled lane, past his tethered horse, and into the deepness of the invisible woods. He stopped, still, again, as the pitched darkness flooded over him.

"The sonofabitch. The sonofabitch. Sonofabitch," Nole breathed, as though he were chanting some bizarre mantra. He drew the heavy Colt and held it at his side. Then he ran again, down the steep trail, until his foot kicked against a root and he was flung down once more, this time onto the hard, dropping path. He felt the cold earth, then a burning abrasion on forearms and knees, and he slumped, letting his entire weight fall flat on the ground, lying outstretched and still, the pistol clutched in his hand, now flung out straight over his head but actually pointing downward on the cold, stony slope. He rasped out the same small sound a third time, struggling to regain his wind.

Nothing could have prepared him for this, any of this, in spite of plans and avowals. It was as though the blast of the pistol were something that had happened to him, not something he had willed, done, caused to occur. This time yesterday he hadn't even known the pistol existed, much less that it would determine his actions so decisively today. And so he had yet to consider how any of this could fit into a sequence of events, actions, and consequences. He had forgotten entirely about his father, whom he had just shot—the body piled onto the floor of that flimsy shed on the splinters of a caned chair that had broken with the sound of crumpling paper. Now, the man did not exist at all, as though the entire day, the shed, the gun itself had been blotted out by that flash, and so Nole's hand no longer held pistol or weapon but only a cold, unnameable weight pressing the back of his fist against the pebbly ground.

Once, when Nole was a child, his father had made him a bullroarer out of a piece of horn and a thong. And he had wound it and pulled it, wound it and pulled it, all day long, fascinated by the strange elasticity that came not from rawhide or horn but from their interaction with his own hands as he pulled outward and felt the toy draw back the other way, against him. And then he would draw it out again and let it pull him back, like a surge and release, flow and counterflow, as though all the rigid, hard things in the world had become elastic and were tugging and swaying, accompanied by a deep sonorous hum. And what he recalled most vividly was lying in his bed, that night, and he could feel the movement still, in his hands, sore and blistered from the rub of the thong, but still seeming to draw and strain and give back in to the thrumming of the bullroarer, moving through the middle night of sleep, dream, roll, and turn.

And the next day, Nole had been out in the barn, where his father had sent him to fetch gloves and fence wire. And he had pulled the bullroarer from his overalls and begun the hummed play. And forgotten the errand and his father and the world itself. Until the man had crashed through the door, shouting his name, and had snatched up the thong from his hands, unthreaded the piece of horn, and thrown it all out the bright square of the doorway. "Now you get to work," he'd said. And then cursed—"goddamn thing"—not cursing the boy, but the bullroarer, the toy he had made himself for his boy's amusement.

Nole thought of that moment as he lay stretched out on the trail. *Goddamn thing,* his father had said and flung away his own gift, made with the man's own hands from the things around the farm—the bone and the rawhide—and given to his son, who found it all so wondrous and magical, the stretch and rebound, blur and thrum. And stood now, empty-handed and surprised, in the cold floating dust of the barn.

Sometime later, thirty minutes or an hour, Nole uncurled himself from the chill ground and stood, rubbing his elbows and knees where the hot sting of his fall needled the skin. Down the hill, beyond the screen of woods, the stream rumpled and slapped. He tensed, hearing a sound like a whistle, then relaxed, hearing the echo of creeksound off the hillsides. He stretched his arms over his head, realizing he was stiff and sore, as though he'd been climbing a mountain or pitching hay all day long. "'Stead of killin' Daddy," he said aloud. He felt a wash of regret followed by a blotting of bitterness and anger. He turned, tucking pistol into waistband, and walked slowly up the trail, back to the lane, past the still horse, to where he could see the looming bulk of the house across the way. Behind it and off to the left leaned the pale blur he knew was the shed. He looked again at the huge house and its turret, a picture cut from a magazine and pasted against the black scrapbook paper of the sky. "His goddamn house," he said, aloud again. "His wife. His reward." He sniffed. "I reckon I finally showed him." He turned toward the shed. "Hell," he said dismissively. "Get on up."

So he retraced his steps, across the soft grass of the lawn surrounding the big house, bigger than anything in this county, outside of town anyway, and everybody wondered what four people could find to do to fill up a house that large, when most folks raised families of ten or twelve or even more in their little places, put together out of chink and daub and fresh boards from the sawmill, still smelling of the hot blade and slapped up in some impossible extra time between setting out and suckering and threshing, canning, cutting, grading. And hog killing. *It's cold enough to kill hogs. Cold enough...* He went on by the house without looking up at it, straight and deliberate, back through the muck around the shed and into the door.

The lamp was still lit, throwing an amber wave over the interior. It looked to him like a place he had never seen before, and he found himself actually searching its fifteen-by-fifteen-foot space as though he were looking for some small object—a coin or a flat pick, fallen out of his pocket—and not anything the size of a dead man. But his eyes gradually stopped wandering and settled on the bulk, in darkly stained overalls, humped and twisted over the remains of the pine chair, blood dropping thickly from a shattered rowel.

"What in hell's he got a chair out here for anyhow?" he said.

There was a lot of blood, very dark, as though deep holes had been torn in the scene—the packed dirt floor, what was left of the chair. The body itself glinted slightly around a great torn blackness in its very center.

"Deader'n hell," he said. "Deader'n hell."

And suddenly he found he was crying. He felt no real sadness, felt hardly anything at all except the run of tears down his face.

He stooped and grabbed the dead man's leg, pulling it to pivot the body around. Then he picked up both feet, kicking away the dripping remains of the chair, and began dragging his father's body across the shed toward the door.

It took all of an hour for him to wrestle the lifeless form through the mud and over the grassy sward. He stopped every once in a while and let tears fall, the way a man will sometimes turn his face up to feel the falling rain. Then he shook off the sensation and went back to work, pulling the dead man around to the front of the house. When he reached the porch steps, he let the feet fall free. They hit the boards of the steps with a resonant THOOM that caused him to start and rub his hands nervously up and down the hips of his dark pants. He wiped a sleeve across his wet face, then he sat on the steps. He rose and pulled the awkward, heavy pistol from his waist. He sat again, laying the cooling pistol on the wooden step beside him. He was breathing heavily. The body was sprawled out, arms above its head, feet resting incongruously on the second step of the porch riser. Nole looked at it, felt an urge to cry again. *No*, he thought. *He ruined everything. The son of a bitch.* He hacked wetly and spat directly on his father's body, stood up and took the feet once more. He pulled them around, pivoting the body again, walking the legs down the steps and around, so the head now faced the house. He moved along to the steps and then bent and lurched the body upward, holding it beneath the arms.

Drawing the body up the steps was a matter of hefting and shrugging the weight as high as possible and then heaving it, tossing it down and upward. Then bending, hooking the armpits again, hefting and heaving again. His hands were sticky with blood by the time he had the body solidly on the porch. He stepped back down three stairs and sat, again, catching his breath, rubbing his cold, sticky hands along his rough thighs.

He thought of fights he'd had as a young boy, the fists swinging wildly and striking into a thin, bony young body just like his own but belonging to any one of any number of boys from these hills. He would be shouting with fury, trying to hurt the other, teeth clenched tight, fists swinging, frustrated that his puny arms could only do so little damage, feeling the terrible purple explosion when fist connected with nose. He remembered realizing, later, that this had been, in fact, *murderous rage*, and that he had been prohibited from committing actual homicide only by lack of size and weight. *So this is what it feels like to want to kill someone*, he had thought, remembering the frustration, the need to push harder and crueler than he actually could, the gritted teeth. But it wasn't like that at all, this actual act, this murder. He had felt no rage, no clenching, pushing need. As if it had been somebody else, not Nole Darlen: some stranger who happened by and decided—just passing the time, he supposed—to kill this man. It had been like an afterthought, almost casual, the finger tightening on the trigger. And that was all there was. And this was murder?

"Well, well," he said.

He stood again, walked to the heavy front door and opened it, swung it in. He couldn't have said why he was doing all this, dragging his father's murdered body back to the house. Perhaps he felt the mansion itself was the only fitting memorial to the man. Or perhaps he had some obscure impulse to compose the scene for those who might find it. He couldn't have said.

He returned to the body and went to work, lifting the feet again this time, drawing the body across the porch and over the threshold, into the dark hallway. Again he let the legs fall, and this time they made a lighter *thlack* against the polished hardwood floor. He turned and opened a door on his left, across from the big, curving walnut staircase. Bent again, lifted legs again, and drew the form into the small side room, where he dragged the body around again, head-forward. Hooked armpits and hefted again, raising and throw-dropping the bloody corpse onto the narrow bed. Rubbed hands again on overalls and stepped back out into the hall. He pushed the door shut and walked back outside to the front steps. He stepped down, slightly dazed, until his feet touched ground. Then he lowered himself, sitting on the second step, and stared vacantly at the pale light just visible over the hill to the east toward the Hobbes place.

ii.

Burlton Hobbes had been dreaming but knew it was a gunshot even before he came fully awake. He sat abruptly up in bed as the last *skewing* echoes dropped over the hills.

"What in the name..." he said and drew himself the rest of the way out of bed, scrabbling for lamp and matches.

"Burr-el," his wife muttered, stretching an arm out across his side of the bed, searching, still asleep.

"Maydie, git up outen bed. I done heard a gunshot yonder."

"Hmmm?" she said.

"Maydie. Git on up. They's somebody a'shootin' a gun yonder."

"A gun?" she said, rolling away, struggling to remain asleep. "What? A gun? I don't hear nothin'."

He fumbled a match from the box, struck it on the wall, and lit the tallow candle by the bed. The room threw itself into shape around the couple and the bed: a heavy, carved dresser with a pale lace runner on its top; a series of homespun frocks hanging from hooks on the side wall; the silver-blue glazed warp reflected off the window's waved surface. Just visible in the doorway, snuffing curiously from the darkened hall, a dog's long muzzle appeared.

Burlton had already drawn up his overalls, bunched and

tucked the tail of his nightshirt into the waist, and hooked them up. He moved into the doorway, his body's momentum turning the dog ahead of him. "'Tchout, Hoover," he said. The dog was a pale blur leading him through the short back hall. "Put some shoes on, Burl," his wife muttered. But he was already out the door. "Heavenly days, Burl." Then, a whisper, "Hush, you'll wake the young'uns."

He left the house, the dog snuffing and scampering ahead of him, into the deep night, thinking, *It's a sight colder'n I'd thought. Well, now, that gunshot'd carry right far in this cold. No tellin' where it mayt've gone off. But now, what in hell is anybody firin' off a gun this time of night? Must be plumb midnight. Ain't huntin' nothin' at midnight, leastways not without dogs. Just kids raisin' hell, I reckon. Billy Wade and me, we'd go out of a night and shoot a time or two, just to hear it go pop. Surely she isn't... It couldn't have nothin' to do with her...*

My lord, it's been a rough day, with all that tellin' Maydie, tryin' to tell. Who'd ever imagined such a thing? I be durned. Well. I'd like to catch that boy at somethin' over here, give him a taste of what he give Jem. I was just talkin' about that to Rose today. Yesterday. What a terr'ble thing.

I don't know. I don't know but what this is all fixin' to get worse and worse.

Well. Nothin' goin' on out here. Just some kids, I reckon. I'll just clomber up and see what's to see and go on back to bed. It's colder 'n a pump handle out here.

He topped the curve of the hill and looked across at the big house, its peaked roofline at his eye level. He squatted, buttocks to heels, and watched the grainy dark landscape, surveying the rich man's property. He felt no envy or anger, but he couldn't escape a certain curiosity each time he looked upon the incongruous size of the dwelling. *Ain't it strange that she mayt've lived right there? Right over the hill? But look at that durn place. Enough for a army of folks. What in hell anybody need with a place like that?*

* * *

He'd had this same conversation two years ago at the diner across from the tobacco warehouse where he'd just laid out his crop. Three of them, sitting stiffly at the bare wood table, eating chili and cornbread. Drinking buttermilk.

"This here's the best damn part of farmin', I'd say," Donny Gooden said and wiped his sleeve across his reddened mouth.

"Good chili, ain't it?" Burlton said. He took up a piece of cornbread and broke it into his glass of buttermilk. Pushed it around slowly with his spoon. "You think it's worth all that work out in the patch, all year long, raisin' a crop takes you thirteen months to get up?"

"May not be worth it, but it's a hell of a sight better than doin' all that work and not gettin' the chili, now, ain't it?" Donny had said.

"I'd a heap druther stay to home and not do the work," said Tom Gooden. "Chili or no chili."

"I reckon," Burlton said, eating the sodden cornbread, the milk dribbling down his chin.

The door *skreyed* open and a thin man in overalls entered. He was wall-eyed, and this gave the left side of his face a bulging, glaring, slightly mad expression, while, on the right, he appeared genially intelligent. Although he worked shifts at the paper mill, he seemed comfortable with the farmers, drawn to them, and he usually found his way to the warehouse at auction time, where he could be seen moving lazily about, talking, telling stories, passing on the news, which he seemed to know more precisely, and more thoroughly, than most. Burlton knew him about as well as the others, which was to say he saw him with the season, and, also like the others, was pleased when he appeared.

"Haddy, Hogeye," Donny said.

"Haddy, boys," Hogeye said. "You all doin' all right?"

"All right as gettin' right," said Burlton. "No more than usual."

"That cornbread looks like home," Hogeye said, sliding up a rope-seated chair. "I believe I'll have me a chunk." Through the streaked picture window, the men watched a new yellow automobile roll up to the warehouse and swing in diagonally to park. The mules and horses shuddered and stamped. Then, as though on some command or practiced drill, they slid haunches to the side and dropped their ears back, standing stock still.

"Who the hell..." said Tom.

"Darlen. Carl Darlen. Who the hell else? That ain't no Ford," Hogeye said. The car's rear door swung open and a tall man in an ecru linen suit unfurled himself. He stood, looking vaguely about the street. Pulled something out of his pocket. From that distance, they couldn't see what it was until they saw him dip his head into cupped hands and saw the blue smoke from the cigarette.

"What's he doin' into town? Oughtn't he to be out to Blair's Creek a'buildin' another mansion house, maybe to put his chickens in?" said Tom. "Why the hell he build such a big house anyways? Ain't got a goddamn thing to put in it but his own little family. Anyhow, you look down inside that ice cream suit and he's just a damn farm boy like the rest of us."

"Maybe his wife made him to do it," Donny said. "Wouldn't be the first time a man's wife done..."

"She didn't have nothin' to do with it," Burlton said, sharply. "Weren't none of her. Besides..."

They turned and looked at him quizzically.

"That's all right, now, keep your shirt on, Burl," Donny said.

"Well, now I suppose he had to do somethin' with all that money," said Hogeye. "Didn't he? Don't you figure? First off, he finds hisself with half the land in the Holston Valley, just a'fallin' into his lap when his daddy dies, and what's he a'goin' to do with it? It's too big to farm and it's done already been timbered right down to the ground. He mayt could wait and give it to his kids, except he ain't got but two, and one of 'em's a girl and the other one, Nole, he ain't interested in nothin' sets as still as a piece of land does. If he can't bet on it nor dance with it nor throw it down his throat, he ain't a'goin' to want it, is he?

"So here comes these couple of big shots with a bank in each pocket, talkin' all about *the magic city* and how this here town'll be the *cradle of the new South* and all such. And they's pleased to represent the whatchallit development corporation and they's all a fixin' to give him more money'n he's ever dreamed of just to get the title to that river bottom where they's a'goin' to build two or three of them magical factories.

"But I believe they found out they was wrong on one count. It weren't more money'n he'd ever dreamed of. Because he refused to sell. So I believe he was already a'dreamin' of a heap more money'n what they'd put in that first offer, now, weren't he? I bet them big shots thought, here's a hick, we can hand him a shiny penny and he'll reckon it's a whole dollar. So ain't no point in payin' this hayseed any more than he wants to take, now is there? So I reckon they kindly low-balled him on that offer, thinkin' he'd snup it up and they'd have their factory and most of both of them banks still a'rattlin' around in they pockets. But he fooled them.

"Yessir. He just says, 'Thank you kindly, but I believe I'll just set still on this here acreage until a feller comes along with a offer that's worth spendin' five or ten seconds of my precious time a'thinkin' it over.' And then he sets back and waited on them to notch her up a mite more.

"And when they come back right away and tried to give him almost twice what they done offered at first, well he knowed then how much that there land mayt be worth. So he just said, 'Thank ye kindly,' again and set back and waited some more. It must've felt like growin' punkins to him: nothin' much to do but just set there on the porch and watch 'em vine out and bud up, and they'll just keep on a'gettin' bigger and bigger until you got more punkins than you could thow a cat at. Like all he had to do was set around and that money'd just keep on gettin' bigger, until he had more of it than he had punkins even. More'n he knowed what he was a'goin' to do with it.

"So one day them two must've come by and I reckon they'd finally mentioned a price that's higher than he'd ever dreamed of after all, and so he didn't have nothin' to do but just sell it.

"So then, just like that feller with the punkins, he's got a whole lot of somethin' he don't need and can't figure what in hell to do with all of it. Which ain't much of a fix with punkins because you can just leave 'em set and the rot'll take care of 'em. But you cain't do that with money, can you? Particularly if you mayt be a mite of a penny pincher, kindly. Because it won't set out in a field and get soft while nobody's watchin'. Because money attracts attention, and folks won't let it set around long enough to rot like. You see? So he's in a fix now. He done got shed of all that land he didn't know what to do with, but now he's got a load of money he knows even less what to do with than he done the land."

"So he builds him a big old box to keep it in." Burlton tipped up his glass, letting the last of the sourysweet buttermilk drip into his mouth.

"I reckon," said Hogeye.

iii.

The sound of the gunshot had soaked out into a chill night, not unusual for this time of year in these jumbled Tennessee foothills. By dawn, there would be ice on the mountains, and they would stand gray and lacy over the rolling land. Chimney Top rose by itself, shadowing the farms along Blair's Creek as the cold of deep night began to set in. The creek rang and snapped, sounding trebly and thin. In a month's time, it would burble and curl, rounded and deep. The cows and horses snuffed steamy clouds from their wet nostrils and the hogs rolled deeper into their muck, seeking the warmth in the wet ooze. It was late March, and tomorrow would be bright and kind with that coating of warm clement breath over everything, bringing up the smell and feel, the suck and pulse of the wet season, closing you into the land, wrapping the hills around you, no longer the wide, dry winter but now the embracing body of spring.

But the nights were still cold and sharp, of the stiff dead year. It was yet winter just a few hundred feet overhead. The trees on Chimney Top were bare and hard. Only the rounded hills showed the pale yellow of leaf and birth, the affable dabs of redbud, the coming fulgence. Resurrection. It would be warm, liquid day soon. But the nights remained bitter and edged.

It was setting time, when the tobacco seedlings were laid out under the long, narrow strips of canvas, where they would develop through the spring. The beds had been burned in the winter, and the small plants would stay covered for the season, to be cradled in shadow until early summer. Then would begin the laborious process of planting—the whole family in linked motion, as though performing some ancient rite—father carrying the big basket of plants and dropping one after another, every foot or so onto the harrowed, red soil. Mother following, scooping a cupped hole and setting the pale green shoot while Sissie came behind with the cedar water bucket and dipper. Finally, Brother would firm and tamp down the wet soil around the small, lonely-looking plant. And on and on, filling out the fields with the strange crop—demanding, back-breaking, completely inedible...poisonous, in fact—upon which depended the family's entire hope for cash flow of any sort.

Then a summer of suckering, worming, spraying arsenic of lead, watching for black shank and blue mold, working in the gummy, harsh leaves, in the hot sun, the most tortuous labor anyone could have devised for making a little money, raising a crop.

In autumn, the family would again enter the field together, this time to cut and split the stalks, slide the sticks on the sled and drag them to the barn, where they'd be hung to cure until grading time. Then Father would sit at the board, grading each leaf, while Momma and children tied off the hands of long red, short red, lugs—all the grades—into the baskets for the day's trip to the auction to see whether this year's crop would tide us over until the next, which we had already been working for a month. Nobody wondered *Why are we doing this?* They accepted, acquiescing, because tobacco farming was no different from living, like something that happened to you, something you found yourself doing, year in and year out.

Fifteen miles to the north, the Holston River had slapped and warbled to the same tune of season and cycle for uncounted centuries. Then, five years ago, machines had come and gnawed into the river, and now the canalized channels led off the fork of the river at the north end of a long, flat stretch of tangled undergrowth called Long Island. Angled sluices, like grasping fingers, greedily framed the rising industrial complex, rumbling and smoking beneath bulges of cloud—not the marks of seasonal turn but, in fact, themselves immune to solstice or equinox. Here, the billowing outpourings of turbine and smokestack enclosed like sulfurous swaddling the infant wood-distillation factories and brickworks and paper mills, resting on the Roalton bottomland where Carl Darlen had been born and bred, had planted and plowed, wed, and raised daughter and son. And then this same Carl Darlen had sold the entire stretch of rich bottom—island and all—to the eager developers of factory and planned city, so that he had to move fifteen miles further south to flee from the modernization he had as much as ushered in. Roalton, once a sleepy tobacco warehouse center, had become a thriving modern city. Only the southern third of Long Island remained as it had been, tangled and dense with swamp willow.

So Darlen had come to Blair's Creek, out into these foothills, and built this absurdly incompatible mansion in a land of cabins and mud where he now lay shot to death by the son who had traveled those same fifteen miles, tonight, for the purpose of pulling the trigger.

On this March night at Burlton Hobbes's place, in the cold early hours, Sarie Gill shifted and rolled over in the bed she shared with Janey, who tucked herself into the hollow of warmth left behind, curled into her younger sister's heat, the moist child's odor. Janey's own body was tacky with warmth, but her nose, peeked above the feather tick, tasted the hard, tangy air. She curled her hand into a light fist and tucked it between her thighs, brushed the other hand up to the mounded center and cupped herself. Slept.

iv.

Burlton squatted in the chill of the night, watching the Darlen house, his memory still echoing with the gunshot he knew he had heard. But nothing stirred. He sniffled, reached into the bib pocket of his overalls, and pulled out a twist of tobacco, considered it a moment, then replaced it, stood, and turned his back on the gigantic house.

"Naw," he said aloud. "No point in hangin' around out here. Ain't nothin' to see. Where'd that dog get to? Hoover!" He whistled sharply and started down the hill.

It wasn't until he began to walk back that he realized how cold he'd been. He began to move in a stiff-legged strut, descending the steep slope. When he was about halfway down, he discovered Hoover walking at his side, carrying a stick in his mouth. As usual, the dog seemed to tote his prize thoughtfully, as though it had some secret value. They hurried on down and back into the house. Man and dog headed straight to the dark kitchen as if responding to a single will.

"Phewboy, it's a cold 'un," Burlton said, drawing a rope-bottomed chair out from the worn oak table. He turned the chair about and sat, lifting his bare feet up and cupping their cold, callused weight, one in each hand.

"Phew, boy." He let go of his feet and extended them outward toward the iron stove that still radiated a dry, tangy heat. The dog moved to the darkened corner, flopped wetly to the floor, rolled, and scrubbed his back against the boards, then settled out on his side, his usual spot for the night. He slid his head around and gnawed desultorily on the stick he'd fetched in from the cold.

"You comin' on to bed?" Burlton's wife said. She stood at the door and held up a flickering tallow candle, tinting her pale flannel gown a dim ochre. Her hair was undone and hung long and gray over her shoulder and down her side, beyond the great swell of hip. The gown was unbuttoned from the neck, forming a deep, creased cleavage, the plump chest shadowed blue in the candlelight. "Or you want me to light the lamp?"

"No, Maydie. Let's get on to bed," Burlton grunted, getting up. The dog lifted his head a bare inch, nearly invisible in the shadowed corner, surveying man and woman gravely. Then he dropped back down and exhaled a loud sigh.

She led the way back into the room and lay the candle down on a small, dark table on his side of the bed. She went around the bed and made a light *heez* sound as she climbed under the quilts on her side. Meanwhile, the man sat on his side, picked up the candle, and blew it out. He swung his legs around onto the bed and lay still as Maydie tossed the quilts over his body. She lay back down, turning heavily, her back to him.

"You find them fellers shootin'?" Maydie said

"Not a dern thing," he said.

V.

Nole Darlen, the thin young man who had just killed his own father, sat on the steps of the big house, shivering slowly. He was thinking, oddly, about watching his mother do the wash on some nameless Wednesday of his childhood. He would want to help, and she would let him scoop up a gob of the wheat-flour paste from the pan and throw it in the hot kettle. And then he would sit and watch as she dipped the white clothes and linens into the boiling starch. She would be hot and wet, her brow a shining silver curve, her taut body stuck to a patched dress, arms pushing and thrusting thinly at the mass in the pot. He thought she was beautiful.

And he would help her lay the clothes out on the bright grass to dry, feeling the cold friction of the wet cloth, the after-image cooled by the wind on the back of his hand. And when they were all finished, he would look at the multi-shaped patches of clothing spread across the curved grass, already bespeaking *human*, seeing the form, the wearer, already apparent in the puffed breast of shirt, or pale concavity of shift, draped across the ground. *Mamma. Mamma.*

"Hell," Nole said and stood up, stretching his body, feeling again the ache of his effort in arms, shoulders, buttocks. "Hell."

The sky was lightening. He had told himself, much earlier,

that he would sit until dawn, and he had looked across at the shadow that was his horse, thinking, *When I can see all four of her legs, when I can distinguish them, it'll be gettin' on day and time to get on out of here.* And he had begun staring at the deep stain of horse-shadow and waited. But then he had got to thinking about his mother and the washing and had lost track of the horse. And so now he didn't even look to see, but rose up and moved through the thin light, across the grass to the gate, and along the lane to where his horse was tied, by the other gate. She swung her head around to look as he approached, then wafted herself back and stood still again.

"Git," he said sharply, mounting and starting off the horse all in one movement, one moment of time, so that he seemed not to have drawn himself up onto the horse so much as to have merged his movement with the forward curve of the already-moving larger animal. The horse cloppered and side-stepped, dancing in place for a quick second, and then gathered and moved off along the lane slowly, up the hill, toward the glinting dawn.

At the Hobbes house, Janey Gill had awakened in the side room, as usual, just before sunrise. Unlike the others, she and her sister slept under the feather tick because she liked the warmth and the contrast between the soft, fluffed feel above and the harsher scrub of the straw tick below. She rolled onto her back and slid her bare feet off the bed and out from under the tick, like a girl walking carefully into cold water, testing the air, trying out the feel on her skin. Then she drew out her arms and lifted them straight upward, stretching her upper body, feeling the slow turning of her side, the even ribs patterning her skin, and then the smooth curve of flank and hip. She didn't bother to notice the two others—the older cousin and younger sister—still sleeping in the bed. They were no more to her than the heavy rolled blankets that served for pillows. Easy enough to ignore girls, bedding, the room itself, as suffused with interest in the flexing turn of her own body as she was.

I'm certain of it, she thought slowly. *And I'm a'tellin' him today. He'll be happy, I reckon.*

She swung her legs to the floor and rose in one motion, moving quickly across the pale board floor toward the broken scrap of mirror on the wall. Then she spoke aloud, quietly, to the dawning air. "And if he ain't, well, that's a mite of wishin' you had the meatskin 'stead of the cracklins, ain't it?" She was wearing a thin cotton shift that didn't so much cover her body as it illuminated the swell of her hips, her curved thighs, the shadowed sloping valley between, in a kind of moving, fluid frame, as though she were walking in a surrounding fog or ether, making her form appear to be more on display than it would have been had she strolled across the room naked. She reached the mirror and swung her head up and around so as to slide the image in the small glass along her length in what was less an appraisal than an appreciation. "Nole Darlen, my darlin'," she breathed at the lissome image in the silvered glass. She was young and sinuously beautiful, and she knew it.

"Janey Gill," her aunt called through the door. "You fixin' to milk?" The edged sharpness of the voice stirred the two remaining sleepers who began to tumble and toss themselves out of the bed.

"'M on my way, Aunt Maydie," Janey said to the mirror. She made one last sweep with her eye and then turned away, drawing the pale haze of shift over her head and dropping it carelessly to the floor. Naked, she pulled a soft cotton shirt off the wall and swam her arms into it. Buttoned it. Reached a pair of overalls from their hook and stepped into them. She heard her uncle clomping out of the room and into the kitchen.

She had been bound out to aunt and uncle ten years ago, when their own children were all grown and left the home place and, although it was probably a better life than she possibly could have had at the old place, with her parents and all the other kids, she resented it all, bitterly, with the deep, scalding antipathy of a seventeen-year-old: a blend of sheer selfish pride and sad despair. The teenager's credo: *I'm so bad, so bad, even God cannot redeem me.*

She had worked for them, aunt and uncle, doing their chores on their farm every day, and they required her to watch her sister as though they had no responsibility for that little one, but only for Janey, and yet their concern for her somehow included the imperative that Janey be the constant medium of contact with little Sarie. *What is Sarie up to, Janey? Janey! Did you see what Sarie done, Janey? Why in the world can't you keep her out of trouble?* Janey Gill would awake in the night, hearing her aunt's cutting voice, a constant counterpoint even in her sleep, always in mid-harangue, shrilling indecipherable words in that rhythm of desperate nagging she had come to know like the graggle of the guineas, the nicker of old Taft, the screek of the backdoor.

"What in the world you got into, Hoover?" she heard Uncle Burlton bellow from the kitchen. "Good Lord. Hoover! Git on outen that!" he boomed.

And now, on top of that, they had tried to forbid her seeing Nole Darlen—*Nole Darlen, my darlin'*—she said to herself as she tucked up her hair on the way out to the mud hall and door. "Did you'uns get your sister outen the bed?" her aunt called from the bedroom. Well, they hadn't been able to do it, had they?

"I'm a'milkin,'" Janey Gill responded, throwing the words over her shoulder as she banged out the door and flounced across the yard, scattering the chickens, their *bluckbluck bluck bluck* a coda to her answer.

"Get on, Hoover," Uncle Burlton said, entering the kitchen. As the dog uncurled slowly from his corner by the stove, Burlton stopped short and stared, puzzled. "What's all this mess?" he said. "What in the world you got into, Hoover?" He bent and picked up the stick Hoover had been gnawing in the dark corner last night. "Well, I be damned," he said. "Well, looky here. Looky here."

vi.

The Darlen mansion had been built three years ago and, in addition to being the only multiple-story dwelling in this part of the county, it was the first private residence to be built by outsiders: by a carpenter and crew from the city. Folks from all along Blair's Creek, from the entire part of that country—Lick Branch, and Dane's Fork, all around Chimney Top—would come and watch the building, standing quiet and shy and patient in the lane as the men from elsewhere drew up the lumber off the big truck and hammered and sawed into the bright air.

It had not taken long, for a house of that size, and when they finished in early September, and built shed and barn, springhouse and smokehouse, people would stop as they rode by, and look on the entire homestead that had been nothing at all just a few months ago, and shake their heads, mutter "Lord, Lord" or some such thing. And ride on.

But that hadn't quite been everything. Because truck and crew and all returned a week later and set to work digging a huge pit out in the back.

"What in hell's he a'doin' yonder?" folks would ask Burlton, who lived nearest to the new place, just over the hill to the east. Burlton had developed something of a tangential celebrity because of this proximity, and he was looked upon by all as the first source of authentic knowledge about the details of the entire outlandish project. When someone would say, "It's got a great big old carved stairway inside, and I got that right from the horse's mouth," that meant they'd heard about the staircase direct from Burlton. And so you could count on it. So when the crew began to dig an enormous hole out behind the house, everyone came to Burlton to find out what it was.

"It's the privy," he said gravely.

They looked at him a moment, perhaps awaiting the glint announcing that he was kidding, or wondering why he might be putting them on in this way. But he didn't alter his calm, absorbed, entirely serious expression.

"It's whut?" said Ned Lacey. "Whut privy?"

"It's the privy," Burlton said again. He offered no further explanation, and this confirmed their earlier suspicions: he was putting them on.

"You thank we don't know the difference between a privy pit and a gravel quarry?" said Ned's brother, Haines. "And that yonder favors the quarry over any privy pit I ever seen. So what in the hell is it, Burl?"

"It's the privy," he said a third time, with absolutely no alteration of inflection or expression, calm, grave, patient.

"Who in hell'd dig a privy the size of a durn tank?" said Haines. Burlton reached into his bib pocket and pulled out a twist. He snapped the Barlow knife open with his thumb.

"I believe the feller's name is Carl Darlen," he said, and cut himself a chaw.

So word rang along hills and valleys, and everyone strolled on up again to stand in the lane and watch as the crew dug the pit and fashioned frame and shingle to an outhouse nearly the size of most folks' homes along Blair Creek.

"She's got a great big perch with eight holes on her," Burlton told them. "All rasped and beveled out. And a lid on each hole.

And paper-rollers on the wall."

"Eight holes!" they said. "What in the hell's anybody want with eight holes in a durn privy? He fixin' to hold church in it?"

"Don't blame me," said Burlton. "I'm just a'tellin' you all what's yonder. I ain't buildin' it nor livin' in it, neither. But I believe he done decided to build him a house big enough to do whatever he's a'fixin' to do just as much and as many times as he's a'fixin' to do it. Seems like to me."

But that wasn't everything, either. Because a week later, a T-model truck turned up, loaded down with sacks of cement and piles of lath. And the two men in the truck, strangers again, built a form and mixed up concrete and constructed an odd two-level bench out front, near the narrow cart track that ran from the barn, past the house, and out to the lane.

"Now what in hell's *that*?" they asked. But even Burlton didn't know this time. Until he saw it used, a week later, when the family appeared.

"It's a gittin' up place," he told them. "They marches the horse or the buggy or what have you up to it for the gals to git on. That's what it is, a gittin' up place."

But Burlton hadn't known then that what he had seen had been final departure, not arrival at all. He had taken to spending a little time each day at the top of the rounded hill separating his little farm from the construction site, watching intently, wondering each time, *What in the world would a feller want with a place like that?* as the structure slowly took shape and the Darlen family, man and wife and the two fully grown children, had come out at odd times, usually separately, as though they followed some scheduled rotation, to watch the building of the enormous new house. But this time, wife, son, and daughter had come for a moment to see the finished place, mansion and bright red barn (the only painted outbuilding around the Chimney Top area, either), the eight-hole privy. They had come that final day, and then left. And the mother, at least, had never returned, refusing flatly to inhabit the huge house, and living

29

alone, instead, in an apartment in town. If she had a reason for renouncing the new home, no one ever found out what it was. And so Carl Darlen lived there all alone, in one small room on the ground floor, the grown children coming out once in a while to spend a day or two, then going back to their own separate lives.

And even when mother and children had come out to watch the building progress, it had been as though they led separate existences, disconnected and indifferent to each other, linked only to the slow raising of the house, which each had come in turn to witness.

"What kind of a family is that?" Burlton had said aloud one day from his viewpoint on the hill.

On the earlier occasions, he had watched Nole, whom he had seen before, heard about, earlier—a drinker and hell-raiser about town—and whom Burlton could tell was a fool even from a distance: the thin, jumpy young man ordering the workers around as though he really believed they were afraid of him. Then Nole would throw himself onto his horse, trying to look rakish, but succeeding only in jerking his mount's head around too harshly, kicking it too brutally, and would ride off, alone, silently bidden good-riddance by everyone at the site the instant he disappeared over the curve of the hill.

The daughter appeared very infrequently. She was in her late teens and unremarkable, so that Burlton hardly noticed her sitting a small mare and squinting expressionlessly at the work going on before her, as though she were trying to read a map or find her way through across a foggy mountain top.

Burlton couldn't have said why he climbed up there each day to watch. Likely he was following the universal rural man's instinct for bashful curiosity. Later, though, he came to believe he had been waiting, patient and unexpectant, but deliberate and determined all the same, to see the other, the wife and mother. And afterward, he went each day to watch quietly and see if she might appear again. And again.

She had been around forty, though she looked younger, lean and angular, but with a kind of abiding beauty floating just beneath the surface, like the subtle coloration of a vein's blued beating beneath translucent skin. Burlton had first seen her very early one morning at the beginning of summer, when the house existed only as stone foundation and the bare beginnings of frame. She had been standing alone in front of the new construction, and he had been on top of the hill, squatting on his heels, watching her. She wore a deep blue dress, no bonnet, and her auburn hair tumbled thick and tightly waved, over her slim shoulders, to curl at her breast. At once, she stretched up her thin arms toward the sun, arching her entire body.

"My sweet Lord," Burlton had said.

CHAPTER TWO

DAYBREAK

Chicken in the breadpan, kickin' up dough,
Sally does your dog bite? "No sir, No."
Sally does your dog bite? "No sir, No.
Daddy cut his biter off a long time ago.

Sally in the garden siftin', siftin',
Sally in the garden siftin' sand,
What she going to do with the hog eye, hog eye?,
Sally's upstairs with a hog-eyed man.

—Pope's Mountaineer's, 1928

i.

Well I seen the whole Nole Darlen show, ever damn bit of it.
What I didn't see I could pert well figure out.
Nineteen and twenty-two I come down to Roalton to work
the mill. From that little old farm away back in the mountains,
where all my kin was still a'workin' away on them fields that
was so steep you couldn't get no mule nor plow onto 'em—you
had to break 'em by hand, spade and snaffled hoe. And a portion
of sweat, I'm a'tellin' you. Couple day's rain and the whole damn
crop'd wash down in the holler, you'd lost everthing.
I tell you, back there, you knew how to work. Didn't know
nothin' else. Suckerin' t'bacca, weedin' the corn lot—hunt and
trap, run the skins down the road, and get ten cents for 'em.
I was born with this here eyeball problem, makes the whole
left side of my face look stranger'n a spotted snipe. That big old
eyeball a'pokin' out and pointin' sideways, well it ain't a wonder
everbody calls me "Hogeye." Always has done. My given name,
it's Clandell Blankenship, but you won't hear nobody call it
from one week to the next. It's just Hogeye this and Hogeye
that. It don't bother me none. Not a bad name, after all. They's
a hell of a lot worse.
Oh, when I was a little feller it'd sometimes make me kindly
prickly, you know, the other kids a yellin', "Sal's upstairs with

37

a hog-eyed man." Hell, I didn't even know what a upstairs was, much less why Sal mayt kindly be goin' there with the hog-eyed man. But I knowed they was makin' fun, the way you can tell if anybody's a'takin' off on you. And somehow you can tell when they're a'talkin' about somethin' kindly low down, you know. That Sal thing, that's from a old dance tune, it's called Hogeye, too. Has another part, "Sally in the garden siftin' sand." Don't ask me.

I reckon that was what made me to kindly stay by myself, you know. To this day, I ain't got no wife nor family, and I kindly likes to set and watch other folks. It ain't bashfulness; I ain't backward that way, not at all. The opposite, I reckon. I'll tell folks about what's a'goin' on around the place, you know. Folks kindly comes to me, it seems, to find out what they's all up to. Well, that's because I been a'settin' on watchin' whilst they're all a'carryin' on. I know what's up.

Sometimes I wished I didn't.

Anyways, back up on that mountain farm, I never figured they was any reason to look any farther than the next knob. I reckon I thought the whole world was mountains and dirt, guinea hens and hog pens, and folks yonder was as busy tryin' to grow crops as we was here, so why take the time to clomber on over there if it was the same as over here. You know?

But then come the war, and I signed up and saw a sight more than I ever dreamed they was to see. And spent some time when I wasn't a'tuggin' on a t'bacca plant, so I kindly got to see they was folks that didn't do that all the time, didn't work so damn hard just to get enough so they can keep workin', you know?

And about that same time here come the factories into Roalton, and fellers got to scourin' around these mountains a'huntin' workers and I heard they was payin' a good wage for men to just kindly stir the pulp around the paper mill. And I'll tell you what, that sounded a heck of a sight better to me than workin' in a crop ever day of your life, just to keep on a'workin'. Gettin' covered with t'bacca gum ever time you step out the door, or breakin' your back tryin' to bust up a hillside so you can plant some corn that ain't a'goin' to amount to anything anyways. So I figured I could get me a place in town and go to work for the mill and take things as they come, do some trappin' and take her easy for once in my life.

So I took me a job. Went to work with a bunch of other fellers that was about like me, just rawboned country boys a'wantin' the hell off the farm. Got me a room over by Twelve Corners and took to tryin' to learn to be a city boy. Workin' for money. Ain't that somethin'? When, back home, nobody had two nickels to rub together? We sure didn't work for money, up home. Not to speak of. A little t'bacca money was all the cash crop we had. That and whatever hides you could trap for a few Indian Heads. Anyways, I figured I'd give the town a try.

I don't know, though. It's like you never quite get the mountain out of you nor the town into you enough to actually be one or the other. It was a pert easy life, sure enough, workin' them shifts like that. But I believe I'd lost my mind if I didn't get out nights and set me a trap or two along the river, catch me a muskrat or two, just to keep a mite of home with me, so to speak.

And then things got to happenin' that would kindly sour you to the city life, you know. Make you wish you was back home with nothin' to worry about but the work. The bosses was always tellin' us bein' at the mill was "livin' in the bright day of progress," somethin' like that. Well, that may be. But I ain't so sure this here New South is all it's cracked up to be. I think it kindly twists things up, so you don't know what's what no more, and you don't even know you've got cambered until it's too late. And then you look around and the whole damn show is just a'goin' on its way and ain't nothin' you can do about it anyways.

I reckon if I hadn't been settin' there in Ketterling's in spring of nineteen and thirty-two, when Nole Darlen got his hands on that gun, I'd not have seen any of it. I'd be a'gettin' up and goin' to the plant and not thinkin' anything of it, while all that was goin' on—Nole and Jem and Merv Craishot, and then Nole's daddy and Burl Hobbes and all—and me thinkin' I'm just a'settin' in the sunshine of progress, while all around me these folks is a'hurtin' one another and we're all just a'smilin' and lettin' on that everything's just fine and dandy. Makes you wonder why they calls it "the bright day of progress" when it ain't nothin' but pretty god damned dark. Seems like to me.

Well, some stories is sadder than others.

ii.

Burlton Hobbes had looked down from his hilltop and watched the Darlen woman that morning, three years ago, as she stood in front of the new brick foundation, a stack of raw boards beside her. She opened her lifted hands and spread her fingers taut over her stretching form. He fumbled at the bib pocket of his overalls, then desisted. Sat still.

She looked up toward him, her arms still stretched above her head. A hand came down to shade her eyes, then she stretched it back upward and waved. He started for a moment, as though he'd been caught at something. Then he stood and made a feeble, flapping response. Rubbed his hands on his overalls. She dropped her arms, spread out a hand and beckoned, a scooping gesture. He rose and descended the hill, trying not to look foolish as he jounced down the steep slope toward her. *Lordy, lordy, lordy,* he thought, frightened. *Ain't you a sight?* As he approached her, she pointed over his head, to the rounded hilltop he had just descended.

"Jocund dawn stands tiptoe on yon hill," she said and smiled. "Ain't it?"

He turned and looked back into the rising sun. *How'd she ever see me in all that sunlight?* "Haddy," he said.

"Howdy," she said. "But your name ain't Jocund Dawn I

don't reckon."

"No'm," he said. "Mine's Burlton." Her eyes were very blue.

"Well, Burlton, mine ain't Juliet, neither. I'm Raferty. But a heap of folks calls me Rosary. Like the beads? The rosary beads. You know? Rosary beads? I don't know how it is folks calls me Rosary, but there it is. You ever meet my son? I ain't the mother of our Lord, I'll tell you that much. It's a sight better'n Raferty, I reckon. Lord only knows where they got that name. Maybe with a weegee board. You ever see one of them weegee boards?"

"No'm," he said. *I believe she's crazy*, he thought. *She don't look crazy, but she acts it right certain. I ain't never heard no woman talk like that, not even to another woman. I reckon she's crazy.* Then he realized, with a rush of embarrassment, that she'd been talking, and he hadn't been listening. Then he recalled that he hadn't removed his broad-brimmed straw hat. He jerked it off his head and held it in front of his body with both hands, as though he were trying to give it to her.

"...but I couldn't tell you why, not in a hundred years," she was saying. "Could you?"

"I reckon not," he said.

They stood side by side in silence and squinted at the rising sun. *It's later'n I'd thought, if that sun's clear over the hill*, he thought. Now that she was silent, Burl wanted to hear her speak again. He could think of nothing to say, himself. They stood in the quiet morning air while he became gradually and uncomfortably aware of the compact presence of her body alongside his. She was perhaps an inch shorter, and her hair, falling in a mass of long waves, was thicker than it had looked from the hill. She looked to be about thirty-five, but her body had a childlike insouciance about it, a tight freedom. *My sweet Lord*, he thought again.

"You live on over the hill, yonder?" she asked him, shading her eyes again.

"Yes'm," he said. "Me and all my folks."

"I hope it don't make you too angered, all this building, this big house and all." She turned back and swept her eyes across the site, then looked at him again, a more expectant look this time. "I believe it would make me mad as a fyce dog to have some stranger ride in and throw down a big house in my part of the woods, kindly."

Burlton didn't know what to say. He found himself, oddly enough, saying, "Thank you." Then, flustered, "No. I didn't mean to say..."

She hushed him and said, "Yes." She smiled, very slightly, almost a question. Then said, "It's just fine. I'm glad to meet you." And held out her hand.

Ascending the hill, headed for home, he felt as though he had been visiting another universe, a world so totally unlike his he could only gradually move out of its strange geometry, its weird, sidelong gravity. And, mounting the slope, he selected and gazed at a stem of grass, a stone, then, looking wider, a tree. Stared at each in turn until it began to assume a familiar shape. The dog appeared at the crest of the hill. It paused for a split second, then flung itself down the slope toward him.

"Haddy there, Hoover. How you?" he said. His voice sounded strange, as though it had taken on a new timbre, or his hearing had altered, sensitized. The dog bounded on down the hill, where he saw it circle the woman twice, her lean body bending to greet it. She straightened and waved once more at Burlton as Hoover ran back up the hill to him. The dog sat, eagerly, marching in place with its front paws. The last few inches of its feathery tail swopped back and forth. Burlton bent and scratched it on the head. Behind the straggly ears.

"That woman is somethin' else again, you know that, Hoover?" he said. The dog bounded to a stand, circled once, and shot up the hill, stopping at the crown and looking back for him. Still feeling as though he were returning from another world, Burlton plodded upward toward his dog.

iii.

Hoover had first appeared the winter before, right in the middle
of the hog killing, and just a month after Burlton had lost his
favorite hound, Buchanan. The new dog had been there for
quite some time before Burlton had registered its presence. It
was sniffing around the pots and lapping the thick, steaming
blood splashed on the ground, a young bird dog, a lanky puppy,
white-haired, with thick blue ticking and straggly ears. He hadn't
seen it around before. It was just after he had dragged up the
big boar hog from the great steaming kettle and begun scraping
down the bristles, feeling the hot tang of the wet hairs against his
icy, wet hands. The dog had moved right up to him and begun
snuffling at his legs and feet.

"Git own outta here," he had jerked, kicking his heavy
brogan into the dog's soft middle, as it made a sharp *yhat* more
of surprise than pain and curved swiftly out of his reach.

"Where'd this dog come from? Go own," he spat. He
grabbed a handful of bristles and made a harsh throwing gesture
in the direction of the dog. "Janey Gill, get that dog outen here."
His niece made a run at the hound, raising a stick in the air,
while the dog curled in his haunches and bounded away. At the
bottom of the rise, it turned and dropped onto its fore-elbows,
its hindquarters rounded upward, tail arched over its back,

inviting a chase. Janey threw the stick at the animal, who snatched it up triumphantly. When no one responded, it turned and loped up the hill into the cold night.

A week later, it returned, whining at the back door.

"Whose dog is that?" Burlton had asked from the breakfast table, as his niece rose and went to the door. She opened it, and the puppy leapt into the house, scrabbling for the kitchen.

"What in the heavenly..." Burlton skidded back his chair, preparing to kick the puppy out of the room, when Janey Gill ran in, laughing. The other kids tumbled to the floor, and the puppy disappeared beneath their bodies, their reaching, petting hands.

"That's all right," Maydie said. "It's just a stray ole pup." She reached to the skillet and took out a chunk of cornbread, throwing it into the swarm of children. Burlton had a brief glimpse of the pup, snatching and bolting the bread, gulping and straining at the dry crust.

"Don't you feed that dog," he had said. "If you give it food..." But he was already looking it over, thinking about a name.

Now, reaching the top of the hill, he turned to his dog, saying, "Come up, Hoover," and descended thoughtfully, still feeling the afterpulse of the woman's near presence.

"She's a right smart of woman, I'll say that," he said, aloud.

iv.

Later, when they had become lovers, Burlton had remembered that first morning, and wondered. They must have been two different people to have talked so obliquely, like crossed, snarled hames. Now, he and Rosary would lie and speak in soft, deep concourse, telling each other, precisely and beautifully, things that had never before been named, made into words. Raised in the hardscrabble life of Blair's Creek, Burlton had never suspected there might be outlet for the strange voices, tugs, and urges he felt wrestling inside himself. He had always imagined these inner selves to be like the dark gnats that would sometimes swarm round when he was working with both hands, tightening barbed wire onto a locust post, or trying to keep the plow on line, slewing through the wet, sticky clay behind the lurching, swinging mule. Like gnats, they were to be suffered or brushed aside when you could spare a hand to grab off your hat and swing it wildly about your head, knowing in the very act that it would do no bit of good. That as soon as you pulled the damp, sweet-smelling straw crown back over your wet brow, the gnats would already have come back, floating and striking against your face with the slightest, tickling quiver—more like a tightening of your own skin into flush or into gooseflesh than any separate, external touch, any contact with other live creatures.

So he hadn't known until he met her, united with her, that these pricklings and swarmings, these interior voices and incitements, were anything to be marked, named, put into anything as composed and communicative as human speech. He had thought they were irritations, as pointless and countless as the gnats. Merely a cloud of obstacles, distracting him from the work. Or maybe a part of the work itself, integral to the difficulty of the labor, to be got through, over with, so he could eat and sleep. Certainly nothing to be dwelt upon, explored, eased around, the way he would ease apart her cool fingers with his, interlacing their hands so the warm, damp webs of flesh at the juncture of their fingers would meet and blend. Or their legs, their knees like soft, questing prods, sliding along and through, pressing thigh and thigh, like mouths seeking droplets. He had never known.

They met on Saturdays, or at other odd times that brought him to town, in mid-morning, and she would take him into her bed, where they would love, and then talk, in this new language, this concourse. Downtown, his wife and the kids would be walking up and down Broad Street, with the other folks from out in the country, watching each other stroll along, eating Brown Mules, looking into the store windows. The best day of all their hard, constrained lives. And he would be with Rosary, telling her about the voices struggling beneath his work-laden surface, about the little boy who would stretch up to reach the latch on the springhouse door and would feel something, some sad flicker, not so much in his mind, his head, as in his lungs, his stretched breathing.

"Own't know," he would say, lying on his back beside her. "Somepin lonely like. Like ratchin' up for that door latch was the saddest thing in the whole world. Or maybe the openin', goin' in to the dark cool where you could feel the water slooshin' through. You know, sometimes I'd get down and fetch up one of them crocks where the milk was, you know, in the water? And I'd look down in her, at the cream a-risin' up. Swirl her around a mite, to see it wave and slicken. And that was the saddest feelin' in the whole world.

"And comin' out, into the bright sun, that feelin', the sadness'd close up tight, like a nightshade, and I'd feel fine, happy almost. But down inside, away down in the cold, like them crocks of milk, it'd be a'rolled up and a'settin'. I could feel it. You know? It was down in there, like in my own springhouse, down inside, like. A'waitin' to come back up, rise up like that cream on the milk crock. Like it was sadness just a'waitin' for the next time you stepped into the dark. This make any sense to you? Because it shore don't to me." And he would laugh.

And she would run her palm along his chest and belly, or reach across him and draw herself in, settling his near shoulder between her small breasts.

"I reckon it ain't supposed to," she would say. And then she would tell him. How, a little girl, milking in the cold dawns, she would tuck her nose into the cow's belly, into the loose skin between leg and haunch. And she would breathe in as deeply as she could, taking in all of the cow she could.

"And I'd be a'smellin' of that cow and feelin' her pushin' back where I'd run my nose against the grain of her hair, drawin' in all the while her cowsmell. And it'd mix up and swirl with the sound and the feel of the milkin', the draw and squirt, you know, and the chinklin' of the milk into the pan. And all round, like it was kindly seepin' through the cowsmell, they'd be the soury smell of the milk itself. And it didn't smell nothin' at all like the cow. You know?"

And he would turn toward her and slide his hand over the small of her back, along the deep groove of her spine and into the bowl-shaped curve where the tight back curved upward to soft split buttocks. And he would feel himself rousing.

Or they would lie, tingling yet with the feel of each other's moisture, the sticky sweetness cooling in still air, and they would talk about the things they knew, together, from their separate childhoods. They found they both had loved the days when the threshers would come through, watching the work, the chugging of the steam engine and the smooth flowing belts, the young men working and shouting and laughing in synchronous tandem, perfectly meshed, like the cogwheels of the machine, so that the thresher itself began to appear to possess actual life, to respire and flex and pulse. So the engine was just the largest of all these threshers—men and machine called by the same name—chief among the crew of like-minded workers.

But most of all, they had loved the excitement of the evening, the crew eating with the family and staying over at the house. The men, weathered and tough on the surface, displayed a gentle easiness, telling long stories or passing the news or talking about the crop, the weather. But there were always one or two who paid special attention to the kids, graciously, as though aware of the aura of divine visitation surrounding them.

"Was one of them whittled me a cedar Indian whistle," Rosary said. There was a silence, then they both laughed, each inwardly supplying the response, without any need to say it aloud: *I believe he wished he hadn't after I'd done blowed on the thing for a hour and a half.* And laughing again, nudging one another's naked body, sharing the inner circle of remembrance.

"Mamma'd make a great big meal, ham and chicken and beef and about sixteen different kinds of pie, and we'd all scamper around a'makin' the beds up for them fellers."

"Pawpaw'd set the rocker and make jokes about how they was eatin' last year's threshin's and why'd he pay them fellers to come again this year, just to eat up what he'd done paid them for last year. And he'd say, 'I reckon I mayt kindly do without no threshin' next year, just to save on the upkeep,' and they'd all laugh."

"And one of them'd say, 'Well, don't worry. I'm fixin' to take it a mite easier on myself this year. Last year, you worked us like we was borrowed mules,' and they'd all laugh again."

The lovers talked together, speaking out the lines of the

same story, their voices interchangeable, communing, feeding one another, tasting the sacred wafer of memory.

And then Burl told of the time the engine exploded, just over at Lick Branch, killing three crewmen and a little boy. And how he had heard about this and unrolled the scene in his mind—the engine, overworked and worn, giving out at last in a roar of shattering power and torn defeat. The adults talked about how one of the men had been thrown thirty feet by the blast, and *scalded pink as a skun kitten*, and Burlton had stared at the air in horror and sadness.

"They was the same fellers that had just been through our place a week back," he told her. "They was two brothers killed, and I remembered them. But the other, I didn't know which one it was, and I was troubled about was it the feller that had sang me a silly song—taught it to me—about a drunk snake and a fisherman feller. And I didn't know if it was him or not. You see? Because I didn't know his name. I couldn't even have told you what he looked like. Hell, he looked like a thresher, you know? So there weren't no way to find out was he killed by the engine explosion. I couldn't ask nobody if the man that sang the funny song was dead, could I? So I never did know.

"I never thought nothin' about the kid that was killed. Little boy my own age. Didn't think a thing. Ain't that somethin'?"

And they squeezed hands and nudged one another's foot in a sharing of his sorrow and regret, rising acrid and sweet out of the long-ago boy who had so loved the threshers. And Burlton found himself singing, quietly, unsure, a high, thin line of the long-ago tune:

Frogs I think a dozen, he brought them to the bank,
There where I was a'fishin', to trade them in for a drink.

And he found himself crying, slowly and steadily, like long rain.

V.

She had been raised, like him, on a small foothills farm, though hers had been over near Limestone and her father, in addition to farming, had run a small store and had been a minor county official. His enterprises marked the family slightly higher in social rank than the folks Burlton had grown up around. As a result, the girls in her family of fifteen children—she was the youngest— had been relatively well-educated. Some, herself included, even attending the state teacher's college in Johnson City. It was during her initial semester there that she had met Carl Darlen.

For generations, Darlen's family had owned an enormous stretch of land along the Holsten River, around the little town of Roalton. Even at twenty-eight, he had outlived most of his siblings and come heir to vast stretches of river bottom, including the long sinuous snake of overgrown sandbar called Long Island. He lived on a small farm, in the middle of these holdings where, like everyone else, he raised tobacco, corn, and wheat. He also owned three span of cartage horses and two large wagons, with which he operated a small hauling business. And he was looking for a wife.

"There really weren't much to it," she told Burlton one quiet morning, early in the affair. "I reckon I was lookin' to get out of wherever I was at exactly the time when he was a'lookin' for someone to take home with him. I was nineteen, so it was gettin' past time, and he was twenty-eight, so it was gettin' time. And he was kindly the perfect man, you know: just exactly the sort of a man I was s'posed to marry. He was hard-workin', well enough off, serious, and good-lookin'. And I was good-enough-lookin' and graceful, and I could sew and cook and work in the field. Play some music and read, even knowed some poetry. *The high-wayman came riding, riding,* you know? Just the sort of woman he was supposed to take to wife. So I don't believe neither one of us thought too much about any of it. Next we knowed, we was man and wife, and I was out of that school, livin' with him over near Roalton. Just like that.

"I don't believe I ever got to know him. Still don't. He's a quiet man, serious-like, without much but plain work and business behind them eyes. Folks would call him a good, steady man. But..." Her voice trailed off, and they lay in silence awhile.

"But?" Burlton said at last.

"But they was somethin' mean-spirited about him. Like he'd be nice enough to you if he had to, you know. But he didn't *want* to. He didn't take no pleasure in niceness. And it was like he got a good feelin' out of knowin' it."

"Outen knowin' he didn't feel good about niceness," Burlton finished. "I reckon I know what you mean. Reckon I've known folks like that. Like he's kindly happy to know he ain't showed no kindness?"

"Somethin' like," she said. "You wouldn't—folks wouldn't—have noticed it. They'd call him 'serious,' or 'even-handed,' maybe. Without seein' he was holdin' back on purpose to feel he could do it. You know?" And Burlton squeezed her hand, tucked down by their legs.

"Then he sold the bottom and Roalton become the boom town, and he gotten all that money. And he had to build himself that big old house," she said. "And I watched it go up all summer, and then I saw that I had done stopped watchin' the house and taken to watchin' and see if you was goin' to come over that hilltop today. And I knew it was wrong. Besides, he wouldn't spend no more money on the things we needed if we was livin' in the big old mansion than he had down by Roalton. He never did. He held back thataway, too. So he wouldn't offer nothin' new to us except a big place to put all that emptiness in. You know? So I knew I couldn't never live in that place. Not with him. Not with anybody, I reckon. Not after I started watchin' for you."

"What in the world was you a'lookin' at when you looked at me?" Burlton asked her. "I ain't nothin' but a old farmer. I ain't got no money, nor anything like the tone he's got. Or you, neither." He nudged her leg with his own. "I'd say you're pretty much tone all over. Besides, I'm a mite few years older'n you, too, if you hadn't of noticed." And he nudged her leg again.

"I can't say it right," she said. "Here's Carl who ain't done a bad thing to me at all. Worked hard, took care of us, iffen it didn't cost him too much. But not with us, you know. And proud to be not with us. You know? And then he up and sold the land and it was like another step away from us. Then that big house. I'd come out and look at that house a'buildin' and I'd think, 'It ain't even real. It ain't got nothin' to do with this country or with any of these folks around here.' And I'd realize, 'He's proud of that, too.' You see? Proud to have a place that don't fit, don't belong to anywhere but him. Like he wasn't buildin' that house to live someplace, but to live no place. Just like he turned that bottom land into no place, sellin' it for them factories. He didn't take no pride in it. Not even in the money he got for it. He was proud to show he didn't need that land enough to care about sellin' it or not. Just like hisself. And so the more I saw him, the more I'd find myself a'feelin' like *I ain't seein' him at all.* You understand?"

"Nope," Burlton said. They both laughed, lightly. This time, she nudged him, and then reached down and squeezed his knee.

"And one time I was comin' back up the road from out here and I met him a'comin' the other way. And I thought for a minute he was goin' to ride ride past me, not even say a word. So I called his name, like a question: 'Carl?'

"And he looked at me and just gave a little snicker. And he wanted to know was they any other folks out a'lookin' at the house, today? And I realized he didn't care even about that house but only about folks lookin' at it. Knowin' he was the man could build it. And then he rode on. And next time I'd go out there and wonder, 'How am I a'goin' to live in a house that isn't even there? Isn't anything but that man's idea of himself?'

"And then I looked up and you was comin' down that hill, and I found myself thinking, 'I can see this one. Here's a man I can really look at and he's still here.' And so I got to lookin' at you for the pleasure of it. And I found out you was a'lookin' at me, too. And I felt like I could die from it.

"And now, sometimes I think about him out there. He lives in just that one little room down by the front. Don't use any of the rest of that great big ole house. And I wonder what he's a'thinkin'. But you know, I just couldn't make myself go out and live there with him. Never no more."

It was winter, but the day felt soft, like that first morning they had spoken together. She tucked herself around his firm body. "Do you think we're a'doin' wrong, Burl?"

He said nothing, but he thought, *I reckon it's wrong. I reckon it's all a sin, lovin' like this. Because it's the work and the sufferin' and all like that makes things right, ain't it? And if they's a world made for the workin' out of the Lord's plan, like they says, then it must be the workin' out that's right, the hard hot sweat in the t'bacca patch over and over. And not this. Not this, because this ain't a part of no plan, nor a part of the world nother. This here is kindly like a'gettin' away from the world and the patch and even God, too. I reckon. Because this here ain't somethin' I worked at. Wouldn't even know how to work at it. No. This here is a thing that just happened to me. Because they ain't nobody in this here bed but her and me. And so it ain't nothin' right about it, and I'd trade everthing I ever done in the t'bacca patch or anywhere's else in the world—or heaven too—for just one more mornin' like this.*

At length he spoke. "Mayt be wrong, Rosary, but it's me and you, and so if it's wrong, then I reckon we is wrong. So I reckon doin' wrong is just what we're supposed to be a'doin', bein' as how we must be wrong. Inside. Inside, you know? Because if it's wrong, it's the rightest thing I ever done, and so that mayt just be the proof perfect that I'm wrote down to be a sinner, seein' as how doin' wrong feels so right about me. You know?" And kissed her.

"I reckon they's plenty enough sins down here to worry about ours," he said.

vi.

Through the first summer, though, he hadn't much thought about her, after that strange, initial meeting in front of the yet-unbuilt mansion. At the most, perhaps, whenever he climbed to the top of the rounded hill, he would feel a brief surge, recall suddenly the strong sense of her bodily presence. But he hadn't known what this feeling was, hadn't bothered with it, any more than a twinge in his aging joints—he had turned fifty that past winter and he had begun to feel it—the encroachment of cold and stiffness, harbingers of decline and wear.

But he found himself stepping loosely down the hill whenever he would see her standing by as the construction of the house went along that summer. And he would stand next to her and listen to her talk, about the foolishness of the venture, the grand house built for no purpose whatever. She had become his source of information about the details of the emerging mansion, the stairway, and the privy. She told it all in a light, sardonic voice, tinged with an irony that seemed to be directed at herself, as though the biggest joke had been on her. Burlton had never met the husband, though he hadn't remarked the fact that he always saw Rosary there alone. It had just seemed natural, since he had never known her to be around anyone.

So he wasn't even very attentive when he saw her with the

family—the day he learned what the "gittin' up place" was. He squatted on the hill and watched Rosary and her daughter—a young woman in her twenties, she had her mother's angularity and strength but none of the undercurrent of soft beauty—as they stepped up the concrete block and mounted their horses. The younger woman called something back to the house, a tossed farewell or someone's name, and they rode off. There hadn't been much to it and, if he had thought about it at all, it would have been to notice that he hadn't been so awed, stricken, with her beauty this time. He'd been more interested in divining the secret of the concrete bench.

All in all, he had grown to look for her presence, off and on, over the hill, and he had accommodated the pleasure he took in seeing her without thinking it meant anything. It had become an irregular part of his life, pleasant and longed-for, but external, a flavor, like coming upon a bed of wild strawberries in the course of a normal day's work.

And then the house was completed, and she was gone. The incongruity of the situation never seemed to sink in, as he watched Darlen working around the place, dwarfed in his solitary smallness against the massive home, empty of the wife and family he had intended to put in it. Burlton just took her absence as a thing that had happened and left the thoughts of her behind, save for perhaps a pleasant late night's musing.

And this made the next meeting an even greater shock, be-cause he was overwhelmed, completely cast down, this next time, as soon as he saw her walk into this new setting: the long, booming shed of the tobacco warehouse in Roalton.

It was a late morning in later November, and he had brought his crop into town with the others. He had weighed in and registered, and loaded the baskets, and he was now working in the long, far lane, setting it all out. She had recognized him at once and had walked directly to him as he laid out his crop on the floor, straightening up the hands, checking each grade to see that it looked good, bright, and valuable.

He was lucky to have gotten this crop in. It had been a cold, blustery fall, with two early frosts. But he had timed everything right, getting it cut and cured and graded in spite of the cold. The patch was tucked into the flank of the hill, and he believed this had protected it some, kept a lot of cold spots off the leaves. And then with it so wet, he was worried about blue mold for the better part of September and October. "A dry season'll scare you to death, and a wet season'll kill you outright," Donny had said. But the dampness kept the leaves deep in case so the grading went easily, with no need to pack down the tobacco overnight. The kids were most all grown, so they could tie hands and heft the heavy loads while he stayed at the bench, grading. All things considered, it had been a surprisingly good year.

"It's snowin' outside," she said to him, untying a wet scarf and shaking it down at her side, then leaning down and lifting out a hand of his long red grade. "How's your crop?" She sniffed the leaves.

He was tongue-tied. He stared at her, wondering, his eye drawn to a tiny pearl of water on her lashes. He could think of nothing to say. Then he saw another droplet at the base of her neck, curving its way toward the hollow above her clean, notched collarbone. The glistening line along her skin filled him with dread confusion. He was transfixed, while inside the voices shouted and wrangled, filling his face with a deep, red flush.

"You doin' okay?" she asked, fingering the leaf. Then she reached up and drew her fingers along her neck, clearing off the droplet. *Thank the Lord*, he thought. She lifted the tobacco toward her face, peering closely at the leaf.

"You see the colors? All the colors?" he said. *Now why in the heavens did you say that? You idiot. What in hell are you talking about?* But he couldn't stop himself. He listened, amazed, hearing his own voice, talking, as he rambled on.

"They's all the colors in the world in that grade," he said. "They calls it 'long red,' but you look into it and you see they's purple and yaller and gray. Even pink," he heard himself say.

He was appalled.

But she was looking at him with a new interest. She gazed him up and down and then held out the hand of tobacco, raising it, the way someone would look at a painting.

"I don't see no pink," she said. "But I..."

"In the shadin's, in the veins, there, where it turns," he said, unable still to stop himself. *What in the hell? She's a'goin' to think you're crazy as a hooped snake.*

She looked, then turned an exploring eye back to him, as though now it was Burlton himself who was the painting. He was miserable. But, mercifully, she dropped her eyes, then turned and put the tobacco back down into the basket.

"I weren't meanin' you..." he began, but she hushed him by placing a finger across his lips. Her hands were callused, but the contact was soft, as though the touch came from beneath the skin, from the liquid flesh itself. He felt a tugging feeling, deep in his body, then a pooling sensation, strange and warm. He blinked.

"You fixin' to have any dinner?" she asked.

So they walked across the street together—it was snowing thickly now—and sat in the hash house and watched Burlton fumble with his food, thinking, *O my sweet Lord* again. It had been well before dinnertime when they had first come in, and so they had had coffee and she had talked, but it was tense, awkward, even her voice sounding strained and misplaced. Then they had ordered food, more to have something to do than for any urge, desire to eat, that either one felt.

He tucked his chin into his chest when Donny and the others clomped in, talking noisily. They saw Burlton and Rosary and stopped talking. Stopped moving at all.

"Afternoon, fellers," Rosary said.

"Haddy, ma'am," Donny said. He sidestepped across the room to a table, followed carefully by the two others, Tom and

Haines. Burlton felt the blood swelling into his face again, his ears prickling. "Haddy, Burl," Donny said.

"Haddy," he said. He examined his chili. Then Rosary slid her hand across the table and nudged his. Tapped lightly with her index finger. Again that callused softness.

"It's all right," she whispered. "It ain't nothin'."

And somehow he found himself settling into the chair, feeling relaxed and pleased. He picked up the block of cornbread and broke it into his milk. Ate slurpily.

"It's a heap of snow," he said to the entire room. Rosary smiled and picked up her own cornbread. Broke the bread into her buttermilk. *Well, I'll be damned*, he thought. *I'll be damned.* He peered across at her, a new look. She was mashing the bread around with her spoon. *Well no wonder she sounded so crazy. I was, too. I'll be damned.* For the first time, he regarded her as someone—an actual person—he might actually come to know.

"Keeps up lak this ain't none of we'uns goin' home t'night," said Tom. They were still staring at Rosary, but it didn't matter to Burlton. He was fine. Relaxed. *It ain't nothin'.* He watched her faintly and listened to the talk.

"No, I reckon it's a night in the warehouse for us'uns. Lessen you makes a million on your crop today, sleeps in the boardin' house."

"Tommy al'ays sleeps in the boa'din' house, I b'lieve."

"Well, I ain't a'goin' to sleep on no wood floor in no warehouse. They can have my damn crop afore I'll do that. I don't see how you'uns does it. Sleepin' on them boards."

"That's all right. Don't matter none to me iffen you sleep in the damn wagon bed."

"Excuse me a minute," Rosary said, scooting out her chair. "I'll be back in two shakes." She straightened and walked across the room, through the swinging doors at the back, into the kitchen.

"Who in the world's that gal, Burl?" Donny said.

"Raferty Darlen," Burlton said. "My neighbor. You know,

grat big house yonder."

"Now I recall you a'sayin' she weren't livin' out there regular. That she done left and stayed on in to town."

"That's a fact," said Burlton. "But I done met her last summer, when they was buildin' the place. So I reckon I know her as a neighbor, even iffen she ain't. She's a right nice woman."

"Purty as a new calf," Tom said. "What'd you say her name was?"

But the door swung open and they hushed instantly, each man dipping his spoon into his chili, so it looked as though they had all responded to a single command. Rosary moved across the room and sat again.

"You wantin' some pie?" she said. "Or you 'bout set?" She reached her hand across again and nudged Burlton's. He looked at her. She nudged again, so he opened his hand. And she pushed a folded paper into his dry, hard palm. He could feel something small and metallic folded within the cool paper.

"Ain't nobody goin' home tonight," Tom said. "Rah me, look at her come down out there."

"Set," Burlton said, tucking the paper into his bib pocket.

Later, after she'd left, when he was in the warehouse awaiting the buyers, he drew the paper out of his pocket and unfolded it. Inside was a key.

23 Pineola St., the paper said.

CHAPTER THREE

MORNING

We know young men are bold and free,
Beware, oh take care,
The'll tell you they're friends, but they're false, you see,
Beware Oh take care.

They smoke they chew, they wear fine shoes,
Beware, oh take care,
And in their pocket is a bottle of booze,
Beware, oh take care.
Beware, young ladies, they're fooling you,
Trust them not, they're fooling you,
Beware, young ladies, they're fooling you,
Beware, oh take care.

Around their necks they wear a guard,
Beware, oh take care,
And in their pocket is a deck of cards,
Beware, oh take care.

They put their hands up to their hearts,
They sigh, oh they sigh,
They say they love no one but you,
They lie, oh they lie.
Beware, young ladies, they're fooling you,
Trust them not, they're fooling you,
Beware, young ladies, they're fooling you,
Beware, oh take care.

—Blind Alfred Reed, 1931

i.

On the morning before he killed his father, Nole Darlen awoke late. He was hungover and bleary, and he lay in the bed on his back, rubbing his temples and trying to remember. He rolled over on his side, then sprang out of bed suddenly and ran to the dirty window; he flung it open and leaned out, vomiting loudly into the alley.

"Shit," he said, wiping his mouth. He heaved forward and retched again, moaned, and pushed his fists into his temples.

He drew himself back into the room and began to walk toward the bed, rubbing both hands against his temples. His feet tangled with the corduroy jacket he'd worn last night and had abandoned in a clump on the floor. Now the jacket nearly pulled him down, and he cursed viciously as he picked it up and flung it into a corner. When he straightened up, his head throbbing louder, he saw a black pistol lying on the dresser, doubled in the mirror that was swung lopsily downward. It was a heavy Colt revolver. He didn't recall ever having seen it before.

He didn't remember that he had been at Ketterling's, very late, and there had been something Ketterling called "Scotch." Nole had been already drunk when he walked in the door of the smoky room. And, this morning, he had only a vague, vertiginous sensation that something had happened there. That he'd done something he was going to wish he hadn't done. But he had no idea what it was, and he hadn't begun to connect the shattered sensation, the violent retching, with the strange pistol. Not yet.

Ketterling's was no more than an old, paneled storage room opening onto an alley behind Twelve Corners, in the heart of the new "Magic City." There were in fact quite a few rooms like Ketterling's: "blind pigs," scattered around the alleys in this new boom town, providing alcohol for the young men who'd been drawn into the factories and mills, and a little extra cash for the bootleggers who ran them, selling the surplus or odd bottle that hadn't gone to a larger establishment. Ketterling's was typical: its cheap pine tongue-and-groove wainscot was stained and yellowed, and there was nothing whatever on the walls except, near the door, three nails for hanging coats. The room was lit by four scorched coal-oil lanterns hanging from the identically paneled, identically filthy ceiling, one lamp in each corner of the approximately square room. The wood above each lamp was blackened with soot, so that section of ceiling appeared not to exist at all, but to have been sawn into curves at each corner of the room, the lanterns suspended from sheer nothingness.

There were six or seven cheap wooden chairs with sagged-out cane bottoms and a pasteboard card table standing on three legs, its fourth corner propped up by a thin lath of poplar. The stick's bottom end had been whittled to a point and driven into the dirt floor. Three men were sitting at the table, drinking from round clay cups and holding greasy blue playing cards while one threw a bill into the center of the table. The men were not drunk—they had come to play cards, not to fight—and they were carefully sipping mild homebrew of the kind made from malt syrup in an old churn, in any of a hundred identical foothills farmsteads just like the ones they had left in order to come to town, to "work reg'lar," for a wage and to pay for their beer.

Earlier that night, Nole had attended a gathering of musicians, just outside town, in the ancient Sulfur Springs Old Regular Church. The sacred location notwithstanding, the music had been fueled by two jars of white liquor, settled not very discretely behind the opened lids of guitar and banjo cases. Nole had brought—and, though he didn't recall it, had left—his guitar, a new Washburn. He had consumed great swollen mouthfuls of the corn liquor until, after he had slewed his guitar around and crashed it into the headstock of Carlton Bowman's banjo, he had been firmly asked to leave. Cursing musicians, church, and banjos in particular, he had stumbled out the door and mounted his horse on the second try.

"That's a feller ain't got enough on his hands," said Will Taylor. "He gawged your banjar, Carlton?"

"Naw, it's okay," Carlton said. "Mayt help it a mite to git knocked around some. As it is, it don' know how t'play but about half these tunes. You think that Darlen boy goin' t' be all right?"

A newcomer, a fiddler named Warren, spat delicately onto the church floor and rubbed the gob out with his boot. "It's a heap of improvement to have him the hell outen here, I'd say that. That boy dranks corn likker like he's a'tryin' to chase the water down the crick. You fellers know him, hey?"

"Know him good enough to wish I hadn't," Carlton said. "Nole Darlen. His gran'daddy used to own about half this county. All that propitty along the river, where they's puttin' up them big fact'ries. Long Island, where that ambush, that Jem and Merv Craishot business was, a few years back? You remember that?"

"That was a bad business," said Warren.

"They's folks say Nole Darlen was kindly involved with that Craishot gal," Will Taylor said. "What was her name? Merv? They say could be he had somethin' to do with all that bidnits."

"Well that was a right bad business, sure as can be," Simkins said.

"Anyways," Carlton said, "Carl—that's Nole's daddy—done

69

sold all that land and built him a grat big house out to Blair's. Bigger'n your barn and the bird's nest atop of it, both."

"Nole lives clear out to Blair's Creek? Whut's he a'doin' in Sulfur Sprangs?"

"He don't rightly live there. His daddy does. But Nole, he just kindly visits out thataways once in a while. Ain't enough trouble out to Blair's to suit Nole. Nossir. He lives in town somewhere's, workin', you might call it, at the paper mill. His maw lives into Roalton herself. And his sis, somewhere in town."

"His maw?" said Simkins. "His maw don't live out to Blair's nother? Who in the hell is a'livin' out in that house that's so damn big?"

"I tole you. Daddy is," said Bowman. "Mawmy done gone out there a right smart whilst they was a'buildin' the place. But she never taken and moved out there. Don't go out there at all, nowadays, fur's I know. Lives in a little partyment in town. Nobody never knowed why. She just won't go out there and live with Daddy, no sir. Nole, he goes out there now and again. You reckon the ole man pays him to come out and use up some of all that space he done built, ain't got nobody to set in it?"

"I reckon," said another.

Nole had ridden straight to Ketterling's, where he found the three other paper-mill workers involved in their game of cards. He loudly demanded that he be dealt in.

"What hell kinder swill you got t' drank?" he asked Ketterling, who was sitting, as usual, under the lamp in the back corner. On the wall beside him, three boards had been aligned across piles of bricks to approximate shelves. Four or five whiskey "fifters," a handful of tiny four-ounce medicine bottles— "Jamaican Ginger"—and a fruit jar or two were placed randomly along the boards.

"Got some good Scotch, Nole boy," Ketterling said. His voice had a wiry, nasal, bleating quality, "like he's not had a breath of fresh air in his whole life," a patron had once said.

"Haw mush?" Nole inquired.

"Fifty cent a bite."

"Hell," Nole said and fished three bills out of his jacket pocket. "Here. Gimme whatever that'd buy. And start me on up with a pop of that Jake."

"You wantin' it all at once or one at a time?" Ketterling asked, getting out of his chair and lining up with the bottles. He selected one, swirled it round, and peered into it. Took up one of the tiny containers of Ginger. Then he looked at Nole's eyes. "All right, all right," he said, handing Nole the bottles. "Just thought I'd ask."

Nole dragged back the free chair and dropped loosely into it, tipping up the four-ouncer and drinking with a gubbling snort. He tossed the empty bottle over his shoulder and wrenched at the cap on the "Scotch."

"Hell's a game?" he said.

"Shoot Red Dog."

"I'm in, goddammit," he slewed. "Whosha deal?"

"Bill's deal. Hogeye's deal went down, but he's got ten back. Pot's at fifteen. Dollar bet, a deuce beats a nine."

"You got some crackerjacks to play on?" another man asked. Under an ancient, turned-down felt hat, he had a wide, wall-eyed stare, and everybody called him "Hogeye." His real name was Blankenship, and he was of the huge clan of that name from over on the North Carolina side of the high mountains to the southeast of town. He had come to Roalton to work in the mills because, he said, he was "tired of eatin' possum with a goddamn trencher." Still, he trapped and hunted right along the river, just as though he were forty miles away in Shelton's Trace.

They all gazed at Nole.

He was at that stage of drunkenness, they knew, that would guarantee his losing a good deal of money, if he had any to lose. So they wanted him in the game as much as he did. But they also knew him well enough not to bother playing on his

IOU. *You mayt just as well taken a ten-dollar bill outen one of yer own pockets and tear it up into little pieces and stuff it into a hole somewheres fer all you'll ever see of any IOU of Nole's.*

"Ket, where zat money I guv you?" Nole demanded, tipping the chair back and then, losing purchase with his feet, dropping forward, his elbows landing hard on the flimsy table.

"Whoa now, watcher there," said Sid Stanley, grabbing for the bills and coins that had jumped and scattered along the tabletop. "You just git yer pins stuck in the ground now. You reckon you can set still to play a game of Shoot?"

"That money you give me is in your gullet," said Ketterling. "Whut ain't on yer shirt front. No. You ain't got no money, Nole."

So the game went on without him. He watched, blearily, as Bill Nelton dealt three cards apiece in front of Hogeye and Sid. Bill then set the deck on the table and said, "Hogeye?"

Hogeye picked up his cards and spread them. Then he folded them and lay them gently back onto the stained tabletop.

"Five," he said. He fluffed a bill onto the table at his front.

Bill rolled a card out of the deck face-up in front of Hogeye. It was a ten of diamonds.

"Hell fire and damn it all," Hogeye said and turned his hand up. "Had a spade king but not a dymond in the whole barn." Bill swooped the five into the pot.

"Sid?"

Sid picked up his hand. Peered at it as though trying to read a fine-print book. Then he looked over at Hogeye's discarded hand. "Whut's 'at b'sides the kang?" he asked.

"Sixer club," said Hogeye.

"Six-er-club," said Sid deliberately. He peered at his cards.

"You fixin' t' bet Siddy? Or you just a'waitin' t' see iffen them spots is a'gonna change?"

"I'm a'bettin', I'm a'bettin'," Sid said. "Ain't no law 'gainst lookin' at yer cards, is they?" He slid a small hand of change a few inches toward the pot.

"Whut in hell's that?" said Hogeye.

"Dollar," said Sid. No one spoke. Sid looked round the table. "It's a goddamn dollar. That's the bet, ain't it? A dollar? I wants to bet a dollar, I kin bet a dollar, cain't I? Dollar bet, goddamn it." He dropped his cards onto the table and folded his arms tightly.

Bill turned a card in front of Sid. "Fiver hearts to high pockets over thataway."

Sid gave a tight little giggle and reached forward to flip one card over. It was a two of hearts. Bill gave a sigh and slid a bill out of the pot to Sid.

"I got me a squinch," Sid said and flipped another card. Seven of hearts.

Bill laughed and slid another single out of the pot. "You're a'goin' to outlive us all, Siddy," he said. "Ain't no doubt about that."

Later the next morning, Hogeye told the story:

We was just a'playin' Shoot Red Dog, same's usual, and here come Nole Darlen with a snoot full. Buys him a bottle of that stuff Ket calls Scotch and drinks her down before you could spit on the stove. Had him a little Jake, too, I b'lieve. Then he sets there and watches us for a hour or so. Begs him another drink or two offen Ket. I don't know how old Ketterling don't starve to death hisself the way he gives that likker away to no count fellers like Nole Darlen. He's just too damn good-hearted to be in the bootleg-blind-pig bidnits, I'd say. Sid says Ket used to be a preacher up around Erwin, but I don't know. Says he went to sellin' likker when he found his wife up to the choir loft a'doin' Will the Weaver with the circuit rider. I don't know. Rule a thumb is iffen Siddy says it happened, you'd do best to lay your money agint it.

Anyways, we was just a'playin' Shoot whilst old Nole Darlen drank Ket's free likker and tried to see could he rock that chair just right so he mayt fall over the table and bust up the whole damn show. I weren't doin' too bad, nother. Got a rough start and let my deal go down to Bill right first, but then I got most all that back and picked up a deal from Sid on one hand. Made a big bet on a hunch. I had three suits and all high, so I reckoned I ought to just shoot for the pot and the deal both, once for all. And Sid, he makes a little skreech like and turns up a two er dymonds. And I says, "Well I kin beat that, Siddy." And threw down my dymond Queen. "And I don't need no squich," I said. I weren't tryin' to make no trouble, just to kid old Siddy a mite. Because, a course, that there pot was all he done had. Hell, he never bets enough to stuff up a chicken's ass, so iffen you kin run him on one big bet you'll clean him flat out. So I tuck all his bank and got me the deal back. And me and Bill was just a'goin' to play one to one like. Least that's whut we thought.

We hadn't paid no attention to that Darlen boy for quite a piece, I reckon. We was just playin' Shoot, you know, and he was skeezin' around over there a'tryin' to get Ket to hand him another bottle to pour down his throat. He'll get up outen that chair now and again and kindly noodle on over toward them shelves, and he'll say, "Mister Ketterling, you ain't a'goin' to let a good customer go dry, now, would you?"

So we wasn't a'thinkin' of Darlen the least bit.

Anyways, I'm a'dealin', and Sid says he wants me to give him cards. And I says, "You ain't got no money left, Sid. And iffen you thinks I'm a'goin' to honor your note with that feller droolin' around over there just a'dyin' to start writin' out IOUs, well..."

"I gotta gun," Sid says.

"Whut in hell?" hollers Bill and jumps up outen his seat like Lazarus in the lifeboat. "Whut gun?" he says, kindly wild-eyed.

"Jesus Christ, Bill, set down," I says. "He ain't fixin' to shoot you with it. He's fixin' to pawn on it. Ain't you, Sid?"

"It's a good gun," he says and draws out that big Colt forty somepin another. Sets it right there in front of him. Whole damn table a'wobblin' from that big old six-shooter. "It's

worth a heap more 'n that pot," he says. "Got six rounds in her to boot. How much you give me for her?"

"Won't give you nothin' fer it," I says. "But iffen you want to bet me that how'tzer agint my bank—on one hand, now—I ain't a'goin' to tell you you can't," I says. "Iffen you're right sure you want to do that." I just couldn't believe Siddy'd bet anythin' was worth more'n a dry toot. But there it was. I figger maybe my givin' him a little kiddin' when he let his deal go down and I took that pot mayt of got him a little drasty. I don't know. After Darlen had done took out of there, and things had kindly settled down, Sid said he'd had a hunch he could just pick up that whole damn pot iffen he could find somepin to bet on it. Said he was just certain of it. Well, it was Nole Darlen done the pickin' up, I reckon.

Because we let Sid bet the gun. And I hauled out all the brass I'd brought and put it into the pot. Must've been thirty dollars with what I'd picked up tonight. And we weren't a'lookin' for no Nole Darlen, nother. We'd done forgot him, kindly like you forget how the privy smells once you been a'settin' in her long enough.

So we didn't pay no mind to Nole until he swoozed on over there and reached out just as quick as a yallerjacket and snatched up that gun. Well, that got our attention, I tell you. Jesus. And Sid had just told everbody, Nole included, the thing was full of live slugs.

"Stand back 'ere," he says a'wavin' that gun around and sometime he's a'pointin' it at me and sometime at Ket and sometime at his own damn self. But nobody was a'goin' to move no matter where he pointed her, because he was a'weavin' around all over the place, and he'd just as like to blow your damn head off by accident as he was because he done pointed the thing at you. So we kindly backed right off.

"Settle down now, Nole, and let's put the iron down," says Ketterling, and you could see he was a'tryin' to sound firm like, but friendly, too, you know, got both hands held out like he's fixin' to push the wagon.

"Shet up," says Nole, and he kindly swangs back over toward Ket again. Then he taken a notice of me, and he says, "How'd you like I straighten up that eyeball for you?" Then he starts scoopin' up money offen the table and stuffin' it into his coat until he leans too far into her and he kicks that there poplar branch out from under her and down goes the table and what's left of the money, and that right there like to scare me to death because I thought he was a'goin' to shoot me just tryin' to get hisself straightened back up.

But he leans that pistol hand on Sid's shoulder, with the barrel kindly pokin' Sid in the nose. And Siddy a'lookin' like a sinner on a Sunday mornin'. And Nole, he rightens hisself and then commences to backin' on out of there, a'wavin' that gun in our gen'ral direction. And then he's out the door.

Everbody kindly lets out a breath. Whew boy.

"You want me to go and grab him whilst he's a'tryin' to get on his horse?" I says.

"Hell no," says Ketterling. "Ain't nobody goin' out there 'til he rides that horse off or shoots it, one. He's just as like to do one as the other, and I don't want nobody but that horse of his'n out there to catch any bullets he mayt start to thowin' around. Damn luck he didn't plug one of us in here. What in hell was you thinkin' showin' a gun to that no-good..."

"There he goes yonder," says Sid, and we can hear the clippityclop a'fadin' down the alley and the sound kindly widenin' out when he comes to the street, you know. "You want me to go get the law?"

"The law?" says Ket. "What in hell you think you're a'settin' in, a church?" Then he gives out with a big old sigh like he's done tuckered plum out with the whole damn thing, Nole and Siddy and Shoot Red Dog and the whole damn blind-pig bidnits, too, and anything else you mayt want to thow in there. "No, Sid, let's just leave the law outen this iffen you don't mind too damn much, thank you," he says.

ii.

Most Saturdays, morning found Burlton Hobbes and his entire household walking up and down Broad Street in Roalton. Indistinguishable from any of the scores of country families enjoying identical days in any of a hundred small cities from Virginia to Alabama, the Hobbeses sauntered and looked round, met friends and chattered, bought themselves small treats, and enjoyed their day out of all proportion to the actual tangible delights they sampled.

The Saturday ritual engaged the entire family in concentric circles of togetherness, from immediate to extended relations and upward through ringed individual communities—Lick Branch and Blair's Creek and Hodgsen's Bend and outward to the deep mountain villages, Shelton's Trace and Camp Ten and Grayson's Knob—to the circle that encompassed them all: farmer's, country people, folks. They were outlanders come into town and acting like tourists on their first day in Paris, just as they would act next week and the next, able, somehow, to wring excitement and pleasure out of every step up or down the center of the same place they'd been last week.

Paradoxically, the family also rehearsed, each week, the fragmenting, centrifugal pull of separation—the splintering and attenuation that comes to every family, without exception—

with the crevasses and fault lines imposed, one after another, by the ticks of time itself. Because as family-oriented as all of this seemed, each group of parents and offspring would begin to discharge separate persons almost immediately, like sparks from a cloud chamber. Kids would dash off to find their friends and would begin a day-long shuttling from one group to another and back again. The older children—like teenagers at any spot anywhere on the earth's surface—would find the family circle a grotesque embarrassment and affront, and would instantly move outward to its far perimeter, hoping against hope to appear as sophisticated townspeople and, instead, desperate and despairing, would shout too loudly and strut with an air at once haughty and inconceivably awkward, seething as they erupted out of their children's bodies and into the cold, curved space of adulthood.

Then Daddy and Mawmy would split, the one to do "business"—and there was tacit agreement that the word would suffice for whatever he wanted to do that day—and the other to do "shopping," with the same umbrella policy covering her activities. Not that their behavior would differ very much, the one from the other. He would find a place to "set and chaw" with others like him, passing the time in laconic revolt against the long days of grueling, sweating labor, the inevitable lacerations from barbed wire, the bruises from the long wooden handles thrusting into his soft belly when the plow strikes another heavy root. Now he would squat in the shade with the others, luxuriating in nothingness, enjoying the lush laziness, the sheer pleasure of answering another's question a matter of whole minutes after it was asked, both men delighting in the long-lapsed interval like they were savoring a rare and succulent morsel. And she would find a similar group and engage in similar rebellion against the long, hot hours of scrabble and struggle, the searing metallic heat of the stove, the chaffing gnaw of Red Seal lye compounding with the abrasive washboard to toughen and warp her hands, and the years upon years of pregnancy—her normal state from age sixteen to forty-five, if she lived that long—followed each time by the horrific ordeal of birthing, which the attending doctor or midwife would pronounce "successful" if baby and mother happened to survive in any condition at all, everyone, herself and her husband included, expecting even the most normal delivery to be life-threatening to mother and child alike.

And so the women would have coffee and talk, or stand in their go-to-town dresses, out front of Woolworth's, and talk. Only the women's talk would be fast, sharp, and shrill because, for her, it wasn't so much the toil—which, compounded by the pregnancies, was a sight more grueling than the mind-numbing labor required of her husband—as it was the loneliness. Because her work was confined into smaller spaces than his: in kitchen, chicken house, vegetable garden. She was surrounded at all times by children, it is true, but their presence set the seal on her aloneness. So her only relief, aside from the welcome exhausted breakdown after each pregnancy, was the Saturday trip to town. And here, because she had only this brief day to recreate a week's worth of adult, human interchange, the talk was rapid and persistent, the women pouring out and soaking up an effervescence of contact, and converse, and character itself.

The Hobbes family had followed this timeless pattern year upon year, and still did, with one notable exception. Burlton's "business" no longer carried him to set and chaw among the others at warehouse or grain mill. Now he spent a longer period in the morning with wife and family—the four children who remained in his household—and he insisted they all meet together at eleven, at Donna's cafe, for a family lunch. He didn't mean to be caddish or conniving in this: he genuinely felt sorry for the time he took away from his wife and his family to spend with Rosary. So he treated them to a hot lunch and dessert at Donna's every week. From there, they would split apart in the usual manner, except that Burlton would wend his way toward Pineola Street, where Rosary awaited him.

Saturdays this spring were no different from the others, except that Janey Gill did not always show up at the café. There was some concern that she might be out somewhere with "the wrong feller," again, but there was an equal and unanimous sentiment against letting the whims of a rampaging teenager spoil the day in town. So they had their grilled sandwiches and Dr Peppers and "just let Janey run her own traps." Afterward, Burlton walked deliberately away from Broad Street and continued east toward Twelve Corners, where he turned south, walked two blocks to Pineola, and turned east again. It was a narrow, shaded street of small houses—identical, white bungalows—with, at the end of the first block, a three-story brick apartment building, a faded green canvas awning extending from the front entrance. By now, two-and-a-half years into the affair, he had his own door key.

Rosary lived on the third floor in a small efficiency, a bit cluttered with books, magazines, plants. There were four silhouetted landscape scenes of the sort produced by farm equipment manufacturers, each showing a bucolic background behind the black-enamel cut-out of steam engine or thresher or, in one, the new hand-operated clothes washer, a pert-nosed and heavy-skirted woman blackly turning the crank.

The bed would always be made, covers turned smoothly back on the near side—a delicate invitation, like a light caress along his arm. She would be sitting at the table, dressed in a loose gown, with two cups before her, the rich smell of the brewing coffee blending with the bitter metallic odor of the hot ring.

That first afternoon, the day of the warehouse and the snowstorm, he had let himself into the building, his breath held, feeling as though he were somehow trespassing, not on the moral conventions of sex and marriage, but on the bricked stateliness of the structure itself, as though his life surrounded by sawn boards, planked and framed and chinked houses and shed, had unfitted him for entry into this heavy, dim place. Whereas she seemed to fit here. Even though she, too, was of the hills and farmsteads, she seemed to belong more closely to the thick, dark air and the narrow hallway, the intricate, carpeted stairways, as though somehow she had escaped into her rightful place. Or perhaps the distinction derived from her very femaleness, flowing into the chambered corridors and the apartment itself, until she became the space, so that she enclosed the air, where he, the male, was surrounded by it. *But not Maydie*, he thought. *Ain't no place for Maydie by a far piece.*

It had been a fumbling and awkward affair, that first day. Burlton had known nothing to do but to stand in the middle of the room and tell her "it's snowin'" and then "it sure is a'snowin' out there" and hold out the slip of paper she'd given him with the address hastily scrawled across it, as though to excuse, authorize, his presence there. Until Rosary broke the tension by the simple expedient of curving her arm around his waist, pulling her body to his, and sliding her hand up his back, spreading her fingers wide to transmit by the very simplicity of the gesture the compounding, complex messages of desire. He was kissing her before he had time even to decide to respond, and the tension, the hesitancy, of a split second earlier, was replaced by an insistent hurry. Their bodies, so remote a moment before, now sought intimacy, contact, an embedded imminence that erased all the details of clothing or courtesy, modesty or morality in the swell and spread of sheer touching.

And the long, good talking afterward seemed an integral part of the loving, because the press of their bodies—the wet, hot encompassment of the female, the surrounded, searching push of the male—brought forth the fundamental fluidity of recollection and desire, expressing thick droplets of memory into the liquid emergence of their flesh. And so the entire act of opening and penetration and release was only the preparation, oiling the curved surfaces of body and mind so memory and converse might glide forth from these lubricious interiors.

And now, today, two-and-a-half years later, the talking had become entirely commingled with the touch, their voices speaking deep contact the moment he appeared in the room, so that now her words were a caress, his touch an explanation.

iii.

Nole Darlen couldn't quite place the pistol he'd found sitting on his dresser this bleared, hungover morning. And he certainly could never have imagined this day would end in Blair's Creek, much less that it would resolve into the flash and back thrust of the pistol shot, the toppling of his father's body over the brittle and incongruous chair, the pools of blood and the thick, viscous mud. He would never have imagined himself engaged already in the experiences that would draw these hours along until they would accumulate in one instant that would explode outward, extend suddenly, into the critical day of his life.

At the same time, he didn't feel as though everything was usual on this morning, as he thrust the pistol into the waistband of his pants, then stopped and removed the gun, placing it back on the dresser, and walked unevenly out the door. He didn't feel right. He was uneasy: frightened or anxious, angry or frustrated, he couldn't say. Perhaps it was only the hangover, the shaky susceptibility he had experienced many times before but had never been able to assimilate, so the feeling always seemed to place him outside the continuum of his own life. Like his dreams, his hangovers came often and vividly but, like dreams, only allowed themselves to be formulated outside of everyday experience, as the negations of event, occurrence, reality.

But not the drinking, the afternoons and long nights of shattered troublemaking. These were real enough to him. In fact, they were the central points around which he postulated his entire waking life, like a priest his breviary, or a hobo his timetable. He never used drunkenness as a mitigation of guilt, never a way to excuse his misbehavior. Rather the contrary: the violence or debauchery or merely shameful behavior of a night's carouse would not only serve to promote tomorrow night's intoxication, it would appear to him to vindicate last night's continual consumption. But the hangovers seemed suspended outside of the run of life, elapses of non-time, in which he inhabited a fluid, elastic world not his own.

So it might have been the hangover. But this time, whatever it was, it had obtruded on his day with an unexpected directness, as if he had awakened and discovered that the dream world had exchanged places with the real one, and now he was experiencing some elemental sort of phase shift—not a new world, since he knew the terrain, but a new relativism—like a bird must feel when its wings have been clipped, and though the world may remain the same, the bird itself is dislocated, out of place, out of relation with its own fundamental reality. Or as if he were walking around on the stage set of a play he had once seen. Everything so familiar, and so false.

Nole entered the street, the morning sun pressing against his eyes like weight on a bruised heel, and he stood for a moment, wondering what it was he had meant to do, where he was going. Something was expanding inside of him—that was the problem— some pressure, some terrible avulsion, as though his will and his body were being wrenched apart, so—like the bird, whirling and crashing on flightless wings—he couldn't distinguish the things he was doing from the things that were happening to him.

"Janey's coming, ten o'clock," he said, and he thought, *coffee*, and turned, heading for Twelve Corners, walking jerkily, his legs moving too fast, somehow, responding to impulses beyond his control. A wave of vertiginous pain struck at his temples, the nausea sweeping along in its wake, a clammy sweat breaking on his forehead. He stopped again. "God damn," he said.

Donna's was a narrow, smoky tunnel of a place. Out front, above the thin screened door, hung a metal tobacco advertisement with the block letters "EAT" pasted to its center. Inside, a stained counter ran back along the right, with its row of battered pine stools. At the near end, an oversized, ornate cash register glowed a dull greenish-gold. On the wall behind it hung a huge paper calendar depicting two rosy-cheeked little girls in flounced yellow dresses playing with a kitten, all of it soft-hued color-wash, in grotesquely inconsistent juxtaposition to the stark, primary blue and red of the blocked calendar pages themselves.

Four cheap deal tables occupied the strip of space remaining along the left.

The walls were nicotine-stained yellow-amber, washed several layers deep over an ancient robin's-egg blue. The resulting hue was like old dishwater, or an effect of some bilious ooze, not so much a color as an exudation, so that vision seemed to participate in the soury-sweet smell of grease and sweat and stale smoke. Two young men were at the middle table, talking with an older man at one of the stools, his right elbow on the counter, the hand continually stirring at a light tan cup of coffee while he turned the rest of his body toward the tables. He appeared to lean away from his own center of gravity, as if his hand had been caught fast by the coffee cup and he was trying to stir his way free, working steadily at loosing himself from an invisible cord around his wrist. Behind the counter stood a thin, red-haired woman in her forties. She would have been quite pretty in the fresh air, but she looked only inapt in this well of dinginess, like a cut-out in a soiled tablecloth, exposing the smooth, clean pinewood beneath. Her face and body were utterly expressionless. She appeared not to be there at all.

The three men peered at Nole Darlen's figure as it entered,

unrecognizable, a black absence in the bright, backlit rectangle of the doorway. They tracked his form as it moved on into the dim room. Gradually, the features took their place on his face, and the men, who had been leaning lightly forward, settled back again, looking at each other.

"Well, now," said the man at the counter. He was top-heavy, slew-gutted, on thin legs, and he had a broad, soft mouth, so that he looked like an anthropomorphic frog in a children's book. His name was Hutch Cantwell, and he ran a boom-and-bust coal and coke business in town. "Well, now," he said again.

Darlen appeared not to see them. He went no further than the first stool and sat. He felt as though he were shaking uncontrollably, as though they could all see it.

"Well, now, boys," Hutch said again. "If it idn't the feller his own self."

Darlen remained silent. The woman—Donna—moved over and stood in front of him, across the counter. She said nothing. She pulled a pad of paper from her hip pocket and drew a pencil out of her hair. She stood still.

"Chout, Donna," Hutch said. "He's a lady killer. Ain't he, boys?"

The other men laughed, low and quick.

"Ain't that right, Darlen? Ain't you a lady killer? A outlaw catcher and a lady killer?" Hutch spread a wide hand and gestured to the entire room. "This here's the feller hisself. Idn't it? Let's see...three, four year ago, now, weren't it? Yessir, here he is, the lady killer and the outlaw getter. Ain't it?" He laughed, sharp, loud. "S'matter, big boy? Got a mite of a headache this mornin'?" The other men laughed. The one at the counter stopped stirring his coffee and spun himself around the other way, looking down the counter at Nole, who sat still, staring straight ahead at Donna, while her expressionless eyes returned his gaze in unblinking apathy. The two of them, facing each other, could have been plaster figures in a store window for all the emotion either demonstrated. And yet both seemed taut, charged with suspense, a sheer, impassionate, waiting.

"What say, boy?" Hutch called. He laughed again into the senseless air. Donna and Nole stood, facing one another across the counter, unmoving, unreal, backlit against the smeared light of door and window that seemed to absorb the sound instantly, damping out reverberation, echo, so the laughter itself sounded metallic, cold, and lifeless.

"Coffee?" she said to Nole, posing pencil against order pad.

He drank his coffee against the low murmurs of the men's talk, the occasional outbursts of laughter. He wouldn't leave, wouldn't allow them to run him out, even though he knew they were still laughing at him, telling the story back and forth, the Jem Craishot thing, and Jem's sister, Nole's girl, Merv. And he thought of her, how she went off somewhere completely beyond his sight or reach, in those slopes around Chimney Top, where he was afraid to go now. *Goddamn*, he thought, drinking the scalding sour coffee, *ain't nothin' never goin' to lay still*, letting the hot liquid battle the rising waves of nausea and despair, the low churning of hangover and the murmur of ridicule and memory against the raw immediacy of each blistering swallow that focused everything on the lashing pain—tip of tongue and tender tissue of throat—as though the searing coffee could cauterize both the festering of last night's alcohol and today's gibing laughter. And the history of the event itself, the betrayal his father had forced upon him, ridiculed him into doing. *Nothin' never goin' to lay still. And it was all his fault.*

When he finished and stood, fishing a dime from his pocket, the murmured taunts ceased. He tossed the coin onto the counter, where the spingling sound of its wobbled landing seemed to ring with a volume out of all proportion to the thin, waggling source.

"Bring us s'more coffee down here, hon," Hutch said. Then the three men exploded in long, rolling guffaws as Nole made his way out the door, trying to move slowly, deliberately, but feeling impelled, pushed along by the swells of laughter booming behind. He told himself, *Not so fast! Not so damned fast!* And he felt that burning sensation, the one he'd known since childhood, the one that seemed in fact to arise from earliest memory, from his earliest consciousness, even, of self: the hot shame that would coalesce soon enough into heavy sorrow and that, sometime later, might find itself seething and bubbling. Because he would give anything not to be Nole Darlen, and not to have done as he had three years back.

iv.

"Mayt could be they oughter lock him up, give him somepin to think about," Burlton said, mentally checking the time of day, thinking, *plenty*. He and Rosary had been talking slowly and feelingly about her son, the deep weight of worry Nole caused her, and her own sense of Nole's profound wounds. How she thought more deeply about Nole than ever she had about the daughter, Mary, who, she said "is just a normal, regular girl, that never give me nothin' to worry about. I don't think about her twice a week, it seems. But Nole..." Her voice had quivered with care and concern.

This had surprised Burlton, at first, because he had never heard Nole Darlen spoken of in any terms other than derision or warning. It had never occurred to him to imagine there might be another series of feelings evoked by the wild, careless young man. Burlton had never considered that Nole Darlen might have thoughts, emotions, passions of any sort at all. Darlen was a rounder, and the description itself must mean—if it were to mean anything to be worth using at all—that Darlen was nothing else. He was a "rounder," a hoop snake, swallowing its own tail, purled and rolled, without further dimension: complete, change-less, a circle of irresolute, shiftless, pointlessness.

But now Rosary was telling Burlton something else, asking

him to expand not only the way he viewed Nole's character, but to change the thinking upon which his entire sense of *character* depended. And he wasn't sure he understood. Wasn't sure he wanted to understand.

"Oh he's a bad sort, Nole," she said. "Everbody says it. And I know it, too. They ain't any gettin' 'round it. He's a drunk and a rounder, and you can't trust him, can you?"

"Maybe 'bout as far as you could thow a shod mule," Burlton said.

"Well, I know it," Rosary said. "He ain't got a friend in the world. But everbody thinks it's because he don't care about a thing. Like he'd just as soon laugh at the whole world, tell 'em all to go to hell because it don't matter two cents to him."

"Seems like it," Burlton said. He rolled onto his back and twined his fingers together beneath his head. He pushed the heels of his hands against his skull in a circular massage. He felt good. "I seen him," he said. "And what I ain't seen, I done heard. But it ain't none of your fault. Ain't..."

"But that's not the thing," she continued, as though she hadn't heard him. She rolled her body toward him and spread her fingers on his chest. "It ain't that he don't care. No. I believe I know my own son, don't I? And he's got a right big problem, sure enough. But it ain't carelessness, Burl. I'm certain of that. I think he cares too much. He ain't arrogant. Not really. Oh, it looks a'plenty brash to folks. And you mayt could think I'm crazy, but I know it's because they ain't never felt as deep as he has. Really. And so they can't see sadness, the kind of sadness he has inside. I believe he's the lonesomest person I ever seen. He ain't got nobody but himself. And he don't like that feller."

"Sad," Burlton said. He wasn't asking or challenging. He sounded as though he'd never heard the word, as though he were trying it out, working out its sound and its connotative savor. "Sad," he said again. He covered her hand with his.

"Oh I know all of it," she said. "He rages and rousts around, doin' the awfullest things and just laughin' about 'em.

Goes out and gambles away his money like he'd be disappointed if he was actually to win somethin'. Throws away everthing anyone hands to him. And laughs. But I know my own boy. And it's sadness is what it is.

"I recall when he was a young'un, sometimes," she said. "I'd be out a'tendin' to the garden or doin' the wash, you know? And I'd turn round a row, or come round the lye firkin, come outen the springhouse, nother. And he'd be there a'settin' on the ground and just lookin'. Lookin' at me."

"Lookin' for what?" Burlton said.

"For I don't know. Don't know what. Like he was the only little boy in the whole world. Kindly like he knowed he was supposed to be playin' or runnin' around havin' fun, but it weren't no use. Or like he was just too busy bein' lonely to be able to play. Like they was too much of him and not enough of nobody nor nothing else. I don't know.

"I recall once when I made him up a little puppy-dog doll outen some scraps and things, just a little play-purty doggie, you know. And I could see he liked it. Loved it, really, when I handed it to him. Like he was purely tickled to have it, you know? And then a mite later, I seen him out by the shed. He was playin' at takin' the puppy around for a walk. He had it on a little piece of line, and he was just a'walkin' back and forth, a'pullin' that little ball of rags along the ground. And he couldn't do it right, somehow."

"Do it right?" Burlton said.

"It was like he didn't know how. Like he knew he was supposed to have fun with the thing, supposed to be enjoyin' it. But he didn't know how. And so he just kept a'walkin' back and forth, pulling it along, just that little boy, all by hisself. Like he was a'tryin' to do it right and like he thought maybe if he kept on at it, maybe it'd start to be fun—like it mayt kindly *commence* to be actual playin' if he'd just keep up a mite longer. And like maybe then he wouldn't be so lonesome. I don't know. It was the saddest thing I ever saw."

"So you reckon maybe it's the same thing now, don't you?" Burlton said. "You think it mayt be that he's still a'draggin' that play-purty of his'n around the lot, a'waitin' on it to start being fun. Don't you?"

"I don't know," she said.

"Like it mayt could be the corn likker and the gamblin' and the gals and all is just that old rag puppy. Ain't you?" he said. "And so mayt could be iffen he gets somebody mad enough at him to take a swang at him, maybe pistol-whoop on him, why at leastaways he'd be a'doin' somepin with somebody. So at leastaways you couldn't call it lonesome no more, even iffen it weren't dezactly what you'd call fun. Ain't it?"

"I don't know," she said. She rolled over again, onto her back, and tucked her hands behind her head, and they lay there, the two of them, in the exact same posture, which set off the differences of age and gender, the light turn of her breasts and the sated curve of his sex, his gray chest hair. They were both gazing at the ceiling, each feeling the other's presence more powerfully for not looking, that physical emanation, radiance any naked body emits when it finds itself proximate to another's bare flesh. Each could sense the turn of the other's hip, the hook of elbow, the axillary hollow—could feel the other far more vividly even than the self, because the self was only the mirror, the receptor, upon which the other pulsed this fulsome, unmistakable, naked presence. And so the self was entirely shaped and placed by the flow of this other, this sensual fleshly radiance. So lying there, not touching, not looking at one another, each could feel every minuscule dimple, every springing hair, every damp pudged crease of the other's skin.

"He used to would fight," she said. "He'd come on home all beat up and dirty, just a kid, but his knuckles'd be all scraped up and the tears in his eyes. And I couldn't tell was he feelin' mad or hurt or what. I knew whatever it was, he was feelin' it deep and full. Deep and full. But I'd never know what. And it was like not knowin' I'd let him down somehow or another.

Let him down when he needed me the most to know what it was he was a'feelin'.'"

"Because iffen you knowed, then it mayt be ragin' or hurtin' but it couldn't be lonesomeness. That it?" Burlton said. "Not iffen you knowed what it was, too? All right. I reckon so."

"Like if I was a'goin' to have made him a play-purty, I oughten at least to of showed him what to do with it. Oughten to of gone out there with him and played too. Drug the little thing around the lot with him some. Showed him. At least."

"Showed him what?" Burlton said.

"I don't know," she said.

"Because you surely couldn't have gone on them fistfights with him, could you? And you cain't go about gettin' drunk and tearin' up the patch, playin' cards and jumpin' on young gals with him, could you? And you really think anybody can show anybody anything about not bein' lonesome? Rose? And you cain't ask them other folks to put up with them shenanigans, can you? And even iffen you could, they ain't a'goin' to, not after he's done come back once or again. Is they?"

"I just wish they'd see he ain't a'doin' all that out of meanness. It's out of pain. It really is. And if they'd just take a mite of time to kindly look at him, try to understand him…"

"Sure enough, Rose. But I don't reckon anybody's a'goin' to spend they time a'tryin' to understand some young buck that's got his hand up your daughter's shift same time as he's a'drinkin' down the last of your likker. He don't give you a hell of a lot of chance to do any…"

"You know he's runnin' around with that niece of your'n?" she said.

"Was," he said. "But I done put a hobble on her."

"Did," she said. She stretched an arm down between them and patted his near thigh. Slid her hand up, then down. "You did."

He sighed deeply. "Now just what in hell does that mean? 'You did.' What 'you did?'"

"Means I bet you ain't checked that hobble in a good while.

What you thinkin'? You can't just hobble neither of them two. Oh I reckon you might could pen her up. And set there right out front of the stall door with your lantern and your shotgun. You mayt even could hire a neighbor to help you, to set over yonder and watch the back window. But ain't just no hobble goin' to work if you're just a'goin' to throw it on and leave her out in the lot. Hobbled or not."

He sat up. He watched her looking at him: his shaggy chest, the white hairs. The soft paunch. *She's thinkin' I'm purty old.* He sighed, again. "You think I'm a old fool."

She looked at him. Slid her eyes along his body. "I think you're a right handsome old fool," she said. "Purtiest boy I ever saw." She reached across his legs, drawing herself over him. Kissed the bulge of his belly. Nuzzled his lap. Then turned her head, resting her cheek in the hollow of his lap, pressed against him, touching. He laughed, deep and slow.

"Now wait right there," he said. "Let's not get to market before the mules does."

"Hmmm?" She rolled her head against him.

"Stop that. Wait up, now," he said. "What you mean cain't hobble?'" He grasped and stilled her hand, which had begun to smooth along his body.

"Lord, Burl. Honey," she said. "Just when did you throw on that hobble in the first place?"

"Own't know," he said, a touch cranky. "While back. And she done stayed right along with us, like I told her she had to."

"While back," she said, mimicking his peevish tone. She turned, slid up, and kissed his nipple. "She ain't standin' around you'uns right now. Where you reckon she is right now?"

"What?" Burl said. "What 'right now?'"

V.

On this same spring Saturday, Janey Gill had gone looking for Nole Darlen as soon as she could ease herself beyond the periphery of the family circle. She had threaded her way through the streets just to the north of Twelve Corners a few hours ahead of her uncle. Clearing the immediate Twelve Corners area, she dropped south to rejoin the main street and continued straight-on, into a neighborhood of square, boxlike buildings. Each of these structures had a store or a business showing its wares behind a large bleary front window while behind, or to the side of the building, an exposed wooden stairway ran steeply up to identical, small-windowed second floors. Most of these dreary upper stories were composed of rented rooms inhabited almost entirely by young, single men who worked in the mills or factories that had caused the emergence of the neighborhood in the first place. The narrow alleyways bracketing these buildings—whence the second-floor stairways rose—were the scenes of sporadic dice games or occasional romantic encounters and the short, slashing fights that sometimes followed both.

Janey walked to Nole's building, stood before the alleyway entrance, and looked sharply over her shoulder. *Well, let 'em ketch me, I'll be durned*, she thought, more for encouragement's than for truth's sake, and she entered the shaded passage, heading for the side stairway.

She had been here a handful of times in the time since this romance began. The first visit had caused all the trouble because Uncle Burlton had seen her coming up through Twelve Corners where he was standing on the far corner. *The old turtle has done followed me,* she thought, though that wasn't the case at all. In fact, when he saw her, his first impulse had been to hide himself. He realized, though, that she had likely been somewhere she shouldn't have been and, in part to turn the spotlight off himself, but also out of genuine avuncular concern, had crossed and confronted her.

"What you doin' away out yonder, Janey Gill?" Burlton asked her.

Her instinctive response had been antagonistic and, she realized later, this had cost her a great deal, where a humbled, beaten sorrow would have given her time and platform upon which to mount a thoroughly acceptable and totally fictional account of her doings. Instead, her answer was immediate, open, and aggressively truthful.

"I been to see somebody, what d'you care about it?" she said. She began to flounce satirically around him when he reached out and took her arm.

"Who you been seein' up thisaway? Ain't nobody up in them worker boys' town for no seventeen-year-old gal to be lookin' at. Who you a'seein' yonder?" he asked her.

She curled away from him petulantly. "Ain't none of..."

"You stay away from over yonder. Or iffen you can't, I'll make you to stay at home on Sat'd'y, you hear? You been a'lookin' for that Darlen boy and I done told you to let him be, didn't I?"

She had met Nole that summer of the house-raising, the same season of Burl's and Raferty's acquaintance and, though it had taken a few years, he had eventually worked his way into her mind and her body. He would see her working around the Hobbes place as he rode by on his infrequent trips to his father's, and he'd stop and call to her. She had been surprised and delighted at this notice from a pretty man like him, a town man, and she had taken to watching for him. For Nole's part, he began to reverse his priorities: using the presence of his father's place on Blair's Creek as an excuse to ride out and hunt down Janey Gill. That had been at first. Now she came to him, the way he had intended from the start.

After the confrontation with her uncle, she had felt compelled to stay away from his place for several weeks following that first visit. She had hated her uncle for it, and her Saturdays in town, transformed from wondrous holidays to torturous ordeals, found her slouching along beside her aunt, surly and seething, waiting. Waiting for the next week's trip and another day of those long hours of furious inactivity, compounded by her pent desires, her knowledge of what pleasures lay just beyond Twelve Corners, even more excruciating for the very will to overcome. Because she knew she could wait her uncle out, and she was determined to do it. So she inflicted the waiting upon herself, measuring out the weeks and augering his concern against his growing confidence, adding and subtracting the hypothetical hours until the Saturday would come when she could be certain of his complete carelessness.

So she'd been coming up here again for a number of weeks, meeting Nole Darlen in his room where, each time, he would push her onto his bed and take her, enthusiastically, gracelessly, even violently, without a hint of affection or tenderness. And she would get up and dress and go out, down the steep wooden stairway to the alley, completed, satisfied, and thoroughly in love. This was all she needed, these five minutes of furious sexual grappling, to ease her through a week of waiting—to make up for all those earlier weeks of biding and withholding—until next Saturday, when she would make herself available to him again.

And she was absolutely faithful to this weekly swelling and release of desire, the ensuing time in between charged with dreams and visions, not so much of the sexual action itself, or of his body, but of her own, her lean, supple, twisting flesh beneath his grasping hands, the exquisitely curved softness of buttocks and breasts beneath his pounding, impersonal hardness. It seemed to her to offer a total fulfillment of her own being, a vindication of her very place in the world, the precise space filled by her flesh, her embodiment *here* and *now*.

Where to Nole Darlen this was no more than a lucky happenstance, this pretty young girl climbing into his room from the alleyway every Saturday, to offer herself to his pleasure. Nole had changed his ways when he'd been with Merv Craishot, had found a temporary lapse in his loneliness, and had found a depth of intimacy he had never known. But it had all gone away, and since that time, he had reverted to type. His behavior with Janey Gill was a measure of how much he'd had with Merv, since the greedy, emotionless plunging of this new "love affair" showed how far back he'd fallen since Merv had gone away. Because Janie was nothing to him but a mirror of his own desires. He would think nothing of doing the same with another woman the same day, if he were lucky enough to find one and sober enough to perform. He paid no attention to Janey's own pleasure. He was barely aware of her presence as a sentient partner. He could not have told you the color of her eyes.

But this Saturday was to be different in so many ways. On this bright morning, Janey climbed the stairs and opened Nole's door to find him standing still in the very center of the room, his head flung back, one hand grasping and rubbing his forehead, the other holding a Colt revolver extended at his side. She felt an immediate urge to flee, to throw herself out the door and down those long stairs, to get away from this man, who she already knew could hurt her, had hurt her. And the presence of the pistol seemed a confirmation of the possibilities hinted at in his earlier roughness, the pounding violence of his sex.

And even this was confusing, because the threat and the promise had become intertwined, a part of the desire and release themselves. Because she came here at least in part for that roughness, the edge of fear that sharpened her own pleasure. So, at the very instant that she experienced the recoiling impulse to run away, she found herself quickening in physical anticipation of the violence itself, so that it seemed as though one Janey Gill were already running down the steps outside, while another Janey Gill was uncurling her sinuous, naked form beneath the barrel of that heavy pistol. And it was this second urge, the compulsion to give him her body, that won.

So she caught her breath and moved across the room toward him. "What you got there, Nole?" she said. She reached him and pushed herself against him, her right hand going to his shoulder, her left to his right elbow, above the gun hand. He stood still for a moment and then jerked back, as though he had only just now felt the press of her body. He swung the gun away from her in a sweeping arc, shouting, "You get on!" As soon as the sound came, he clapped his free hand to his forehead and squeezed, holding the throbbing temples together against the outward explosion of hangover, the pulses of pain. "God damn," he breathed. "God damn my soul."

And she went to him and moved herself against him. She had learned how to do this in that elemental school where beautiful young women learn to understand the music of their own movements, the growing presence of breast and hip serving as score, practice, and recital all together, as if the mere posses-sion of the instrument has carried with it the ability to play: the way she was playing now, pressing herself against him, the warm, insistent swell of breast and hip perfectly sufficient to arouse, and thence to cajole. And she knew that as long as she chose to maintain this least contact of breast-to-bicep, she would have his complete attention. And persuaded him to set the pistol aside, out of sight, into the top drawer of his bureau. And coaxed him onto the bed, where she rubbed his throbbing head, cooing to him and splashing herself against him, his arms straight at his sides, not reaching for her, but even so catching the soft plush of her body as she swept herself across him, leaving a series of warm pools on elbow, tricep, shoulder, the after-pressure of touch, like puddles irradiated by the rounded rays of hot sunlight now here, now there, fading slowly as he felt his own skin rebounding.

"Come on," she said as she leaned herself backward onto the bed, pulling him down with her. "Come on, Nole boy," and she unbuttoned her blouse and pulled his hand inside, anticipating the rough squeezing.

But he didn't grab at her, and what happened was so unforeseen, so stunningly improbable, it was a matter of several seconds before she could recognize it, put a name to it. *What's this? What's he doing?* she thought, feeling his hand curl and lie passively between her breasts, his head falling heavily onto her bosom and the choking sound she had never imagined hearing from him. She didn't know that he was burning with the humiliation, the outrage of his reception by the men at Donna's, that his wounds—the jeering references to Jem and Merv Craishot, his own hand in the downfall of both—were such that he, in fact, took no notice of her at all, so completely involved was he in his own regret and fury. And so it took a while, before she realized, recognized. And then *He's crying*, she thought. *He's really crying.*

And she would have been perfectly astounded to know what he was thinking just now. Because he was responding on a level far beyond the consciousness afforded her young body, as he wept and slavered against the cool skin on the resilient concavity of her breastbone, between the warm, soft curvings. Aroused as he was, completely beyond her comprehension. Thinking, *Mommy, Mommy, Mommy.*

vi.

Burlton was lying on his back again.

"You knew that Craishot boy? Jemmy? Jem Craishot?" he said. He heard the syllables of the name move out into the room in the timbre of his own voice, and he saw, as if suspended just below the ceiling, the young, *terrible young*, figure of the outlaw. *Jem*, he thought, as though trying to evoke a corresponding awareness on the part of the figure itself, the floating simulacrum of the good-looking kid, who stood in characteristic pose, slouching, hand on hip, head tilted almost sardonically: not so much cocky as winningly insouciant. *Jem*, as though he wanted to hear the boy thinking, too: *Uncle Burl. What's the word, Uncle Burl?* The way Jemmy always greeted everyone. *Somepin he picked up somewheres when he was just a tad, nine or ten, and he'd say it ever time he saw anybody, "What's the word?" I wonder if he said it to that sheriff. I reckon so.*

She had answered him, but he hadn't heard and she knew it, so she nudged him and rolled toward him, again, sliding her thigh up across his legs.

"I said of course I know him. Know who he is. Who don't know about Jem Craishot? The outlaw? What's he got..."

"I known him all his life," Burlton said. He looked again toward the ceiling and saw, this time, the child, towheaded and running, always running. The image seemed not so much suspended in the room as projected from it, shining through his pupils and thrown onto a screen inside him somewhere, against the back of his own skull. And then another, like the flip of a slide, the grown Jem, sitting in Burlton's kitchen. *Last time I ever did see him*, in the dim lampglow, shivering, scared, saying, *"They give me no choice, Burl, they give me no choice at all."* And this one, this shaking, scared young man—*terrible young, he's young yet, but I'll not set eyes on him never no more*—this the famous one, the celebrated outlaw. Not the happy kid or the laughing, slouching country boy, but this one: on the run, out of control, *"No choice, Uncle Burl, no choice at all."* This was the irony, because this quaking, frightened one was Jem Craishot, the one they all sang about…

There was a man in Tennessee, Jem Craishot was his name,
He got into bad company, and a murderer he became.

…and always, when he heard the song, he thought, *They don't know. Don't know who or what they're talkin' about, all them folks who thinks they can say or think anything they want about him now that he's a feller in a tune or on a newspaper. Like he's just there to be made up about. Like there ain't no Jem at all except the one they done decided they was a'goin' to tell us all about this time. And they think it's all just songs and dancin', 'stead of killin' and sadness. And Jem's sister, Merv, what about her? Don't nobody sing no songs about her. She's got nobody tryin' to remember her, does she? Not Jem, no more, and Nole Darlen, I reckon he kindly moved on, right that day, left her to hook her own rugs. Move on to the next niece of mine, I reckon. Lord help."*

"You knowed Jem Craishot?" she said. "I mean, you really knowed him?"

"He's my nephew," Burlton said. "I knowed him all his life. I held him in my arms whenever he was a baby. He and my boy, Claude, was great pals. They'd hunt and fish together, ramble together, you know. Jem, he'd be half the time livin' at our place, and Claude half the time over to Jem's. I know Jem by the back, I'd say." And he was thinking, *She don't know it, does she? Here she is a'tellin' how nobody don't understand her boy, Nole, and she don't even know. And do I tell her? Do I let her know what she can't do nothin' about nohow? What difference does it make anyways?* And he stilled himself. They lay together in silence for a minute or two, their hands touching, twining absently, clasping and dropping, then just the fingers tracing each other.

"Ain't that a thing?" she said at last. "I'd no more think Jem Craishot was ever a little boy than Jennings Bryant. But of course he was. He had to be a boy once, didn't he?" She laughed, lightly. "But you know, somehow you don't never think of him as anything but a bad man, you know? Big bad outlaw man."

"All right," Burlton said. "Ain't that just what I was sayin' about your boy? Now can you ever believe that anybody that's a'wrasslin' with your boy Nole or is a'tryin' to keep him off their girls. You believe they'd of thought Nole Darlen was ever that lonesome little boy?"

"I don't know," she said. "I reckon not."

But he was remembering again, the images thrown back against the concave inner curve at the back of his skull, and he was turning around inside, turning back on himself, to watch. And this time, it was Jemmy as an eight-year-old, beaming with pent excitement and pride and holding out the single-shot Remington his daddy had given him. And Burlton saw himself, hefting the short-stock carbine, feeling its balance, pronouncing it a *mighty fine rifle.* And hadn't thought anything of it.

Because how many kids is got a little rifle like that for huntin' rabbit and squirrel and whatnot? It weren't nothin' no different for Jemmy, least not that I ever seen. Fact is, most folks'd say a boy like Jemmy was no more likely to try and shoot somebody'n he was to shoot hisself. Because he was just a reg'lar kid. A mite reskier than some, I suppose, brighter'n most of 'em, that's sure. And he surely turned hisself into the best shot in the county, or anywheres else, I reckon. But he didn't use the knack for no crimes, did he? Took up trick shootin', a'travellin' with that show. So he weren't usin' guns in any way'd send him out to turn into no desperado, what they call him. No, sir.

And so he told her about Jem Craishot to keep from telling her the other things he knew, *and what that Hogeye feller downtown says, "I know Carl Darlen was in on it, too. I know Nole didn't do it without his daddy put him on to it, like I know corn don't grow without rain, and there ain't no need for me to prove it to nobody, least of all my own self."*

So Burlton told her Jem's story, lying there in the bright noontime, naked, feeling Rosary's presence, knowing he would have to arise and leave the room soon: he'd been here an hour and a half. But the knowing seemed to convey a kind of leisure, a sense of pure lapse, since from now until that moment, that tick of the clock at one-thirty, there was no call for him anywhere, and so he was accounted for, so it seemed the time itself had actually ceased as they lay there, stopped ticking and dropped them into depthless, sumptuous pause. And so he went on telling her, her naked body beside his.

He told how Jem had gone into town to see a medicine show and had taken up a challenge, "someone from the audience" to compete with their "Wild West gunman." How Jem couldn't outdraw the man, but how he not only put the man to shame with his marksmanship, but won over the crowd as well, not alone for his gunplay but for his winning smile, his genial easiness. And had been offered a job on the spot by the owner of the show. And so had gone on the road. And, a year and a half later, all the trouble had started, somewhere down south, in Mississippi.

vii.

Jem had told Burlton all about it. He said he could never forget it, couldn't stop remembering it long enough to forget any part of it.

It had been in Jem's second year with the show, and they had done the circuit as usual, staying in regional centers— Spartanburg, South Carolina; Meridian, Mississippi; and so on—playing the smaller "rimshot towns," then returning to the larger city to restock the wagons, rest the teams, figure the profits, and make the payroll. They called these slack days in the bigger towns "dead eyes."

The wagons had pulled into Meridian that second year on a close July night and tied up on a flat next to the big railyards. Brownie had begun unloading unsold stock from their wagon while Jem tended his horse, took the mule team off the tongue, broke and chocked the wheels, while lightning flashed like a strobe off to the west, harbinger of a storm that would break later in the night. From their straw pallets in the hot, damp wagon bed, Brownie and Jem had thrown open the shutters, and the two men had sat in silence, watching the pounding rain smatter across the bare flats toward the rail yard.

"Why do you figure a rainstorm makes a feller so god damn homesick?" Jem had said.

* * *

Jem first met Sheriff James Conable the next day, which had dawned fresh and clear. As usual, Brownie had gone down to the "boss wagon" to collect their pay, while Jem unwrapped a dark canvas tarp and drew a heavily padlocked steel container off the side rail of their wagon. Unlocking and opening the box, he pulled out a pistol and a cleaning kit, then closed the lid and used it as a seat, while he took the blue-black gun from its holster and began to break it down. The Mauser nine-millimeter Zig-Zag revolver was old and rare, and Jem used it in the show because it was both a curiosity and an excellent, balanced shooter. After each show, a group of men would gather to look at his weapons and to talk about guns, and Jem was popular for his willingness to spend time talking to folks as well as for his ability as a crack shot.

This revolver was one of two Mausers that Jem carried in the show, both of which he had bought last year from an Irishman in Milledgeville. The second gun was a Broomhandle automatic pistol—the Irishman had called it "Peter the Painter"—carried by German soldiers in the war. In the show, Jem would shoot multiple targets from horseback using the automatic, its wooden shoulder stock attached, like a carbine. He fired from the hip, the stock braced against his flank, sweeping right to left with the curve of the horse's motion. It was the highlight of his act: the country folks were awed by the rapidity of fire, the smoothness of both shooter and horse, as nine clay targets exploded in the matter of a few seconds, while the shells flew out behind Jem's sweeping gun "like spit off a griddle."

Absorbed as he was in cleaning his revolver that morning, Jem hadn't at first noticed an obese, sweating man laboring across the yard toward him.

"Don't shoot, I gives up," the man shouted. He guffawed and waved a fat, pink hand. "How you, young feller?" he said.

"What's the word?" Jem said, pleasantly, shading his eyes to look up at the man.

"Oh, I joust come on up here to say how do. I likes to say how do to the shows come into my town," the man said. The voice had a round, full-mouthed delta accent, accentuated, it seemed, by the man's broad, wet lips and fat cheeks.

"Your town?" Jem said. He shook the sweated hand jabbed toward him.

"Pleased as pie," the man said. "I'm Sheriff Conable, High Sheriff Conable, joust comin' about to say how-do to you boys. Nice mornin', ain't it? You wait a hour or two, it'll be hotter'n Aunt Babe's big black butt, though."

"I reckon," Jem said. "High sheriff, eh?"

"Yisser," the man said. "Yisseree. Been sheriff of this here county goin' on sax year now. Joust come by to say how do, joust lat y'all know who's who. Lat you know this here is my town, so you know you need anything, y'all joust call on me, hear?"

"Pleased," Jem said.

"Lat me know, y'all need any damn thing," Conable said. "That's a hell of a piece," he said, nodding at Jem's revolver. "What in the whorl is it?"

"Mauser," Jem said. "Mauser Zig-Zag. They's a lever turns the cylinder here where the grooves is. That's why it's kindly called a Zig-Zag, you know? It's a old'un. It's been bore out, and I checkered the backstrap myself. Mauser Zig-Zag. You won't see too many of them."

"Mouser? Hell, I reckon that thing could take care of a whole damn pack of mouses." The man guffawed and shuffled away, waving his arm. "I'll see y'all on about tawn. Y'all make yourselves welcome, hear?"

Jem waved.

Conable had kept watch on Jem during the dead-eye days. While other showmen were out whoring and gambling, Jem stayed clear of trouble, worked days near his wagon, and didn't appear to be spending his pay. The sheriff began to come around regularly, talking to Jem, sounding him.

"Never seen a young feller joust set around on his ass most nights. This here's a right busy town, boy. Y'all want a woman or a good jar of whiskey? I can show you how, and I ain't goin' to lat it cost you a whole week's pay, now. I done tole you, you want anything."

"It's all right," said Jem. The fat man eyed him closely.

"What in hell y'all workin' for, you ain't goin' to spand y'all's goddamn pay?" the man asked. "Work for a dollar, y'all crazy to use it joust to pad y'all's goddamn ass. Hey?"

"I reckon," Jem said. "I ain't much the drinkin' sort. Never learnt how to play them card games, neither."

"Shit, you don't say, now," the sheriff said. "Where y'all from, boy?" He watched Jem, sizing him.

"Up in East Tennessee," Jem said. He smiled. "Nobody ain't never heard of it. It's pert far up in the hills. Place called Chimbley Top. My people is got a little farm up thataway. Ain't much. A little t'baccy."

"Well, shit," said Conable. "No wonder y'all ain't out tearin' up hell. Y'all likely don't know how. You hill boys. You talks funny and you all plays funny." He guffawed. "I'd say you send all your pay money home to your folks, hey?"

"Most," said Jem. "Got a big old fambly back home could use it. My daddy's been dead these ten year, so they needs a little help. Besides, I never saw no use in thowin' it down my throat, nor onto a card table, nother."

The sheriff guffawed again.

"That's all right, hill boy." He laughed and waved himself away.

A few days later, he was back.

"Looky here, hill boy," he said. "I wonder how you'd like to pick up a little more jack, send home to them farm folks of y'all's."

Jem looked up. "Doin' what?" The fat man pressed his nostril with a fat thumb and blew his nose onto the ground.

"I got a job needs a clean feller like you that can keep his mouth shut and do joust what he's told," the man said.

Jem looked into the distance. "That don't sound like my kind of a job," he said. "I ain't interested in doin' nothin' troublesome."

Conable shrugged. "Listen," he said. "It ain't nothin' y'all would call exactly wrong. You a hill boy, you probably seen your share of white liquor. Shit. Ain't nobody minds a little white liquor now and again. This here job is just a transport job. It ain't nothin' you need to worry about gettin' your skirts dirty or nothin'. I ain't askin' y'all to kill nobody."

Conable outlined the operation. He knew who the whiskey makers were throughout the county and, being the sheriff, he was in a position both to enjoy immunity for himself and to put leverage on the still operators to sell their whiskey to him, at his price. He had set up a a depot of sorts in an old barn outside of town where he collected whiskey from the area, treated it with creosote to make "scotch," bottled it, and sold it to bootleggers in Vicksburg and Memphis. All he wanted, he told Jem, was someone to transfer the finished scotch from the barn out in the hills to the rail yard in Meridian.

"They ain't a hell of a lot to it," he'd told Jem. "I needs a feller ain't from town, won't shoot his goddamn mouth off to Sister Sue and her cousin. And who don't go out and get his head busted on whiskey his own self. Feller like you, straight and steady, joust pick up a wagonload of the juice when y'all's in town with the show, run it back down here to the yard. City boy on the train takes it from there. Ain't a god damn thing to it. It'll make y'all a damn good wad to send home to that hillfolks farm of y'all's, that's sure."

Jem said nothing.

"And don't get your back up about no law," the fat man said. He guffawed wetly. "Hell, boy," he snorted. "I am the god damn law, these parts. You all can tell your folks up the mountain they'll have them a big old Christmas on the farm. What say?"

Jem sat still, looking at the rail cars that shuttled back and forth in the yards. He made the decision, in fact, as much to have something purposeful to do as to have the extra money to send home.

Jem turned back to the fat man.

"All right," he said.

So Jem began hauling illegal alcohol to the rail yards from a ramshackle barn on an abandoned farm up in what the locals called "mud hill country." He told Brownie he was doing some side work for somebody, and Brownie accepted as much with the incurious laissez-faire attitude of an old show-hand.

Except for Conable, Jem never saw anyone else involved in the operation. Afternoons, during the dead-eyes, he would pick up a small flatbed wagon in the scrub near the railyard. It would be filled with empty bottles, each bearing a green label announcing Blended Scotch Whiskey and covered with a heavy canvas tarpaulin. Thence, he would drive up into the dark, scrub-covered hills to the rambling, vine-choked barn, where he would exchange the empty bottles for a wagonload of full ones. At times, the sheriff would still be adulterating the raw moonshine with creosote and capping the last bottles when Jem drove up.

"Jesus God, who in the hell would drank this here shit, much less pay for the privilege?" Conable said. "Well, here you go, boy. Here's nother load of poison, for nother twenty dollars to send up to them hill folks of you all's, hey? We keep this up long enough, hill boy, you'll make them farm folks rich, hey?"

When the wagon was loaded and the tarpaulin thrown back

on top, Jem would ease the team down the hills and back into town—it would be nighttime, by now—where he would leave the full wagon at the spot where he had first picked it up. That was all. He made twenty dollars for every load—more than he could earn in a week on the show.

He often wondered why Conable had chosen him for the job, and it wasn't until later—after Conable had dry-gulched him and everything had gone wrong—that he realized he had been chosen for his insignificance and expendability.

Because two months into the operation, the federal tax agents had gotten wind of a major bootlegging operation running the rails out of Meridian. As usual, the agents had gone straight to the local sheriff seeking leads. In this case, though, the lawman was the chief criminal and had run his venture secure in the knowledge that he'd be the first to know of potential trouble from the revenue boys, in plenty of time to shut down the entire production.

Going out of business without compromising himself was easy enough. Conable could trust the local whiskey makers. They were as reluctant to meet up with federal officers as was he; they were, in fact, obliged to him for warning them about an ensuing investigation. They simply tore down and moved, putting their worms and thumper kegs out of sight for the time being.

Meanwhile, the man at the rail yard—who actually shipped the whiskey from Jem's wagon to the major bootleggers in Memphis—never knew who made, bottled, or transported the alcohol before he took charge of it. He worked for the bosses in the city, so, as far as he was concerned, the whiskey didn't exist at all until he found it in the wagon by the siding and loaded it into a "skimmed" boxcar.

So that left Jem as the only danger point, the only person who might link Sheriff Conable to the Meridian bootlegging operation. And so Conable had selected Jem with a particular eye toward finding a man who could easily be eliminated, should the need arise. Jem was a stranger, he was only in town sporadically, and he didn't hang around the local drinking spots, talking. If he were to disappear, his absence would not even be noted by his own employers, who expected a handful of light hands to walk away from their jobs each time the show refitted in Meridian.

So Conable went to the barn and waited for Jem to make a last, fatal run.

Jem remembered it distinctly, he told Burl, even the parts he hadn't really seen: the man's shaggy, bearlike form moving out from behind the haycart, near the rackety sliding door of the barn from which he, Jem, had just emerged. "I reckon he'd been there all the while and waited on me to go on into that cowshed and load up," he'd told Burl, much later. "I reckon he figured then he'd catch me a'comin' out before my eyes could get used to the light, you know? But that's what saved me, I reckon. Because I didn't try to take time to aim. Not with my eyes. Because he just must've stepped outen there behind me, after I'd done walked on by. And he called out, 'Hey,' or 'Jem,' somethin' another. And I didn't know what was a'goin' on. Until I heard that gun snap. Then I jest turned and shot him. Once that feller's pistol misfired that once, seemed like I didn't have no choice. And I never wanted to be no killer. But I shot him. Shot him headstone dead."

Jem recalled the way the man's obese body spun to the left, his arms flinging the other way, as the bullet punched him into the barn wall. And he told Burlton how Conable slid slowly down the unpainted planks, leaving a broad smear of glistening blood.

Jem told how he'd gotten back onto the wagon and driven into the next county, where he'd found the sheriff—a woman—and turned himself in. He'd been convicted of manslaughter and sentenced to a chain gang. "I thought they was a'goin' to hang me like a pole bean, but the judge, he half believed that it really was self-defense, and I got off pert light. They knowed I never wanted to be no murderer. Never would've done nothin' like that. It just kindly happened, you know?"

After six months, he had simply walked away from a work detail. "They sent me up the roadbed to fetch some gravel in a wheelbarrow," he told Burl. "Had to unchain me from the crew and sent me up around the bend in the road. Soon as I was out of sight, I shied on over the berm and slid down the hill into the trees. Melted away like lard on a hoecake. And worked my way, over the months, back home."

And as Burl told Rosary, he kept seeing Jem, bent over and shaking with the cold and the fright, after he'd come back, a fugitive, and been set up again. After that last time. And now it wasn't even Burl's remembering, but seemed to be Jem, himself, telling it, as if the image there, inside, at the very back of his brain, were now projecting a voice outward, through him, Burl's own voice telling Rosary *Jem done this* or *Jem done that*. But inside it was the young man in the blue cotton shirt, darkened with the wet and steaming in the iron-dry heat of the big stove and the smell of wet cotton and hot metal and the coffee Burlton had made and poured out for his nephew. It was Jem:

Down in that ole scrub on the nigh end of the island, all amid the swump willers and potweed a'crawlin' hands and knees like a goddamn muskrat, a'tryin' to hunt me a spot where I could just slide in the river amidst the tangles and just take on out of there, so's I wouldn't have to shoot me any more of them boys. Lord, Lord, Uncle Burl. Lord, Lord. Them sonsabitches. I never been so scared in all my life. They opened right up on us while we was just a'standin' there in the twilight. They give me no choice, Uncle Burl. Lord, Lord, what am I a'goin' to do? I done shot 'em. I don't know about all three of 'em, but I killed two of 'em, sure as I'm a'standin' here. Lord God.

And Burlton lay there, letting the Saturday morning ease by, touching Rosary, deciding not to tell her that story.

CHAPTER FOUR

BROAD DAY

On Jordan's stormy banks I stand,
And cast a weary eye,
To Canaan's fair and happy land,
Where my possessions lie.

—Alfred Kargis, 1928

i.

Nole Darlen, he used to make fun of this eye of mine, ever chance he'd get. But he never could say nothin' clever. It was the same old "Sally upstairs with a hogeye man." Hell, if that was a'goin' to bother me, it'd done it a long time before Nole come along. I'd just say, "I reckon Sal knows which one of us to spend her time on." That shut him up.

He went to work at the paper mill about same time as I done. And it's odd to think he's a'workin' in a factory that's settin' right there on his own land. Or his daddy's, anyways. I wonder what he thought about that.

But there he was. I reckon Carl, Nole's daddy, had made him to get a job, told him he wasn't a'goin' to sit around and help count the money, but would have to get out there and see could he maybe turn out a day's work his own self. Which seems about fair until you get to thinkin' about it. Because daddy'd not done a durn thing to get all that money, hisself. So why he was tellin' Nole he'd got to earn his own keep, when Carl had done quit workin' at all, except to watch somebody else build that big old house away out there in Blair's Creek.

Now that ain't quite fair, neither. Because Carl, he'd worked hard in his life, a'farmin' and runnin' that teamsterin' company. Worked hard like the rest of us. But, just like we'uns, he didn't never make nothin' outen it. All that money didn't come from no work anybody'd done. It just came outen the air, so to speak. Or I reckon you could say we fellers down at the mill is a'makin' that money for Carl Darlen kindly after the fact. Workin' here at the dawn of progress. Ain't it?

Still, Carl Darlen, he was a mite of a tightwad, manner of speakin'. Well, most farmin' folks, they're tight with money. Ain't got enough most times to make a jingle in they pockets, so they'll try like hell to keep whatever they get. But Carl, he kept on, even with all that money he'd got handed to him, kindly.

Trouble was, Carl never taught Nole how to work around the farm, and then kindly made him to go work down to the mill so Carl wouldn't have to spend none of all that money he had. Way I figure it.

Well for whatever why, Nole was down there stirrin' pulp like the rest of us. Though if that paper company had depended on him to keep things a'goin', they would've turned belly-up in about fifty seconds. You'd think a feller'd have a hard time findin' ways to do a bad job stirrin' a vat of pulp, but Nole done figured out every one of them. I believe he would have been more use if they'd just hired him as one of them spools to roll the paper onto. For all the work he actually done.

Nole bragged on his daddy buildin' that big old house, at least at first. He'd swagger around and tell us how much it cost and how they was a hand-carved staircase and all that kind of thing. But somehow you never believed he meant it. That is, you never thought he really liked the thing all that much. I guess he went out there now and again, whilst they was a'buildin' it, when he could spare some time from killin' hisself leanin' on a paddle at the mill. Went out there long enough to snatch up that Janey Gill, anyways. Then he'd go out there now and again after the thing was built. Likely just to give that gal a tumble, save her the trouble of gettin' to town, I suppose.

I learned anything, it's too much money ain't nothin' but trouble. Nole, he's likely not a bad feller on the inside. You can look at him and see he ain't a bit happy about bein' just who he *is. Poor feller's stuck spendin' ever minute of the day with his own self. I wouldn't want it. And it's got somethin' to do with that money, I reckon. Because he never got any of it, but it's clabbered him somehow.*

And that's what happened with Carl Darlen: He got enough money he can't squeeze it dry. He was still tight as a swole window, but they's plenty of money to make problems. You understand, it's all kindly like my daddy's sausage-makin'.

My daddy, he'd make sausage outen the scraps left after he'd done salted down all the hams and side meat, and got up the liver and loin for eatin' that week. He'd gather them scraps and the trim-off and all, everything he could get a little meat from, and he'd put it in with a good piece of shoulder, run it through the press—same thing he'd make his cider in. Only this time he'd throw out the squeezin' and keep the meat that got left. My daddy was a smart feller. You couldn't have snuck up on him if you was a angel.

Anyways, he'd take all that meat he'd done squeezed as much grease outen as he could and he'd crank it through the grinder, work in a mess of sage and pepper and roll it into a big fat snake—used a gradin' board and rolled it out, how ever much he'd got—and wrop it all up tight in tobacco canvas, like a tube. Then he'd put it out by the fire for a mite, 'til the fat got to oozing out through that canvas. Wouldn't take too long but that fat'd just souse the canvas. Daddy'd say, "She'll turn from white to dark to white again, and then she's ready for spargin'."

So then he'd take that big long tube all globbered up with the fat into the springhouse and he'd pour a little of the cool water onto her. Then he'd take her and hang her up in the smokehouse. Didn't cure it, nor salt it, nor nothin'. Just hung it raw, all cased-up in its own fat, over to the side of the smokehouse. And all year, you wanted some sausage, Daddy'd go on down there and gawdge off a slice from the bottom of that roll, canvas and all, and bring her in, unwrop her and throw her in the skillet. And you never eat nothin' so good in your life.

I've told folks down here about that sausage and half of 'em says, "Good Lord, Hogeye. It's a wonder it didn't kill you all," and the other half thinks it ought to have been so dry—from havin' the fat squeezed and heated out of it—that you wouldn't want to eat it anyways. And I tells 'em I eat enough of that sausage I oughtn't to be alive to tell about it. And besides— and here's my point—you can squeeze as hard as you damn well want on most any pork you can find, and they's still a'goin' to be plenty fat for your biscuit.

That Darlen money got to be about like that sausage, didn't it? They was plenty fat, even if he did try to squeeze every durn penny. And I reckon Nole knew it.

Nole's mommy never did move into that house, though they say she was out there by herself a right smart while they was a'buildin' the thing. But I reckon she didn't feel too much like livin' in a big mansion and still go watchin' that family livin' on nothin' so Carl can be somethin' big. I reckon she got kindly tired of nothin' but lookin' at the Big Man. So she went huntin' a man the right size to look him in the eye. Way I figure it.

ii.

"Dem dirty bastards," Nole Darlen said, snuffling, drawing his blue sleeve across nose and eyes. "Dem dirty bastards."

"Shush, honey," Janey said, still shocked from his weeping but prepared to try and bring him around to the Nole she knew and loved. She lay back, propped on her elbows, legs splayed, in what she took to be an alluring pose, rolling her weight back and forth on her buttocks. "C'm'ere," she cooed.

He stood, wiping his face again, and walked rapidly to the middle of the room, turned and looked at her. But he didn't see her: He was seeing those men at Donna's, hearing their gibing laughter. His face felt numb and tender at once, like the puffed rawness he'd felt other times, after taking a hard punch. He dabbed at himself with his fingers, as though checking for blood.

"No," he said, harsh, short. "No. You git. I got somethin' I got to do." He realized he'd been hearing the men at Donna's ever since he'd left, calling him *the lady killer* and the *outlaw catcher*, laughing at him, not even taking the deed itself—not even Jem and Merv Craishot—for anything but a joke. He turned in the direction of the bureau, then stopped for a beat. Turned back, looking down at her again. Her eyes were wide, surprised, a little wary, though she still rolled her hips, as if her hearing had not yet caught up with her body. He pointed at

123

her, not at her face, but at the juncture of her splayed legs. "You git on out, now." He pushed his finger, as if he were mashing a button. "Dem dirty bastards."

Janey made a sound, half whine, half sneer, and rocked up onto her feet, already flouncing. "I don't have to come here, you know," she said. "And I sure as hell don't never have to come back." She was still uncertain whether she wanted to appear wounded or wounding. She put her hands on her hips and rocked her shoulders. "I come all the way up here this mornin', and you don't want to do nothin' with me but set and squall like somebody..."

"I said git. Now git," he said. "I got me some business, and I ain't got time to listen to none of your'n." He raised his arm obliquely, showing her the back of his hand. She shrank back, then straightened and huffed from the room, telling herself to move deliberately, just as he had tried at Donna's this morning, but, like him, impelled to haste, her legs moving ahead of her intention. She did manage to slam the door behind her. She would have been pleased to see him give a nervous start.

"Shit." He let the sound of the door empty out of his body. Then he turned to the bureau and yanked the sticky drawer. Hefted out the pistol—it looked blue in the midday light—and tucked it into his pants.

It was a big gun. The barrel reached halfway down his thigh, and he felt the soury tang of the cold metal against his skin, like a taste of iron. The heavy heel of the handle nudged his belly. It was too big. Anybody could see it as he walked along Broad Street.

"Shit," he said again, drawing the pistol and holding it breast-high, like the handle of a shield. With his free hand he yanked his shirttails from his pants, holding the fluffed material while he snugged the pistol into his waistband again. He wafted the loose shirt over the gun butt, sliding the pistol laterally toward his flank and turning the handle in against his side. He fluffed the loose shirt again and stood straight, arms down, as if posing for a picture or waiting in a line. *Not so bad.*

He left the room, still feeling raw from the bout of weeping. His hangover had slackened, but his stomach and eyeballs still felt attached as if by thin elastic lines: When one turned, everything began to slew and shamble. But he was better, and he could already anticipate the wave of sheer pleasure that would flood over him when the pain and nausea would suddenly scud off, as if the breeze had come about—a clearing, a freshening. It was a feeling he had come to look forward to, one of the genuine pleasures of alcohol: the sensation of pure lapse between cessation and onslaught, the end of yesterday's cycle and not quite yet the beginning of tonight's new round. This moment, this pause, perhaps the very best part of life.

But today, the rising pulse of shame and rage began to threaten even this expectation, and so he felt angrier yet, cheated of the few cool, clean breaths, the lull filled by this pressure that had already driven him to tears, that had been building since this morning at Donna's. Or had been building for as long as he could remember; he would have accepted either time frame as true. *Today or every day.* As though a hundred small, blunt arms were projecting from his skull, flailing wildly in perpetual, frantic, meaninglessness, driving him to frenzy in the old shed, where he waited out his father's punishment, or in the classroom, where he stood under the raining jeers of schoolmates, or across a stained splintered bar, where he loudly demanded another drink. Or running, abject and furious, through the scrubby muck along the river, the bullets snapping, with his father's carefully constructed plan—*this time, at last, this time*—gone all twisted. *I know what kind of man I am. But I didn't ask to be this way. Didn't want to be the feller I am.* He had felt it all his life; he had felt it since this morning. Either way. Something was going to happen.

And so he had decided, or at least had found himself acting decisively, fetching the gun and dismissing Janey Gill, because he was going to pay them back for the shame, the taunting *lady killer and outlaw catcher*, and they didn't even know what they were talking about, didn't have any right to know, *it was Daddy, it was my goddamn daddy who put me on to it, made me to do it.* He thought of the pistol again. And so he would pay them back and get this all put away, over and done. He would go back to Donna's and put an end to their sneering for good.

On the street, the day had turned warm and full, and he walked steadily toward Twelve Corners, tapping his inner wrist furtively against the bulge of the gun handle, checking himself the way someone might finger a sore, a pimple, secretly, while talking to other people, a surreptitious security. He felt the long tube of the barrel, stiff against his moving leg, warm now, and heavy, shaping his walk.

A qualm rose within him as he drew in sight of Donna's, and he stopped. He pictured the café, imagined the men leaping up and falling as he shot them, one by one. Across the street, an old man in a shirt the color of diseased gums was squatting under an awning, spitting. Their eyes locked and Darlen's belly quailed, shifted. He touched the gun again and said, "Dem dirty bastards. Dem dirty bastards," trying to goad himself.

He wanted a drink. That was it. He would have a drink and that would steady him to his purpose.

He turned toward the alley across the street, near the old man, who was chewing laconically, watching. Then he stopped again, remembering that he couldn't go to Ketterling's, and he flopped his hand against the pistol again.

"Little Jake," he said lightly, almost playfully. *Little Jake put the edge on, won't hurt nothin'.* He turned back the way he had originally been heading, toward Donna's. Walking quickly now, he passed her door without looking in and continued, fast, a half-block to where a low sign showed mortar and pestle in crude handpainting, and the pasted letters, __POTHECARY, the missing letter showing itself in reverse, a teepeed clean spot on the sign, where the black A had fallen off. Beneath the square lettering, in crude hand again, Lincoln Spencer. He turned through the metal-latticed screen door into a dim storefront, redolent of hot dust, unlit tobacco, and the sicksweet smell of medications. Behind the counter stood Spencer, a fattish short man in wire spectacles, wearing a shirt of startlingly raw whiteness, set off by dirty ochre braces. A perpetual musing smile organized his otherwise eccentric face. His small eyes glittered with an expression not of wit, or even interest, but of dull cunning mixed with veiled absence. He gnawed on his teeth constantly so that his temples bulged and receded, as though his brain were powered by some sort of interior bellows system. He gazed at Nole without seeing for a moment, then snapped into recognition and negativity, holding up a pudgy hand, a gesture of refusal.

"Go own," he said. "Go own, git out of here. I ain't got a thang for yer. Not a thang. Ain't nothin' here, and I ain't got the time to trouble with yer, not now, not tonight, not tomarra. Go own, now."

"Hold on, now, Uncle Spence," Nole said. "I ain't wantin' more'n one. Just one four-ouncer. That's all. And I done paid you some just last week. What in hell you in business for, anyway? Listen. You know I'm good for it. Just one little ginger. It won't hurt none."

"Whut you pay me last week?" Spencer said. "Hell." He opened a drawer slowly, playing it like he was landing a fish, and fumbled inside.

"Never mind, Uncle Spence. I done paid, and I'll be gettin' me some money tonight..."

"Where you goin' to find money tonight?" Spencer sneered, watching Nole carefully, like he was timing him. "Feller like you?"

"My daddy. I'm a'goin' to see my daddy," Nole decided. "He owes me a hell of a lot. So you know I'm good for a little old fifty-cent snip of ginger. Won't hurt nothin' at all."

"Shit," Spencer spat. He turned and picked up a pad of official-looking forms and reached a gnawed fountain pen from his shirt pocket. "I reckon your daddy'll pay me, you don't." He scribbled rapidly at the prescription blank, then tossed the completed form into the drawer. He lifted a tiny ring with two keys from his pants pocket, selected one with exaggerated care, and moved down the counter to a glass case near the back wall. "Four ounces of Jake," he said to the lock, wrenching the key into it. "I'm fixin' to be a rich man yet." He laughed, high and thin. "Ain't that so? Hmm? Nole? I'll be a rich sonofabitch yet, ain't I?"

Nole said nothing as Spencer pulled a small, amber bottle from the case, looked at it quizzically and brought it back along, tapping it against the veneered top of the counter.

"I reckon," he said, sliding the bottle across the counter at Nole. "Don't drank it here. Ain't legal." He laughed again, high and thin, a sound like night insects.

Nole grasped the tiny bottle, screwing it open. He tipped it up and swallowed the sour, syrupy fluid, shuddering coldly as the alcohol struck the back of his throat. He pushed the bottle back across the counter at Spencer and walked out, without a word.

"Yeah. Well," Spencer said as Nole's form disappeared out the screen, a little loose in the knees, the Jake taking hold. "Nice talkin' with you. You tell Daddy I says hey, haar?"

Back in the street, Nole felt the swell and pulse of the toxins bounding to his brain and dropping suddenly to the soles of his feet, to bounce high into his mind again, and he stopped for a moment, waiting for the rebounding ball to settle, each springing recoil a little shallower, a little closer to stillness, letting the Jake seek its resolution, the hot, centered sphere.

He headed now for Donna's, just a few steps down, and he felt himself readied, charged, prepared to let transpire what he felt now to be irrevocably scripted. *It's a'goin' to happen. I'm a'goin' to do it*, he thought. *Dem dirty bastards.*

So this was it. This was the single point of the day, the narrow outlet, where the thing he'd been building toward would suddenly release, and he would know what it was and how well he'd done, and it would explode and settle, completed. And perhaps even the old things, all the reasons they'd thought they could talk and laugh this morning—maybe that, too, could be expunged, one jarring detonation and then the slow, peaceful coming to rest, the sand and pebbles shifting down with a low, shuttled sliding, the soft murble of breeze wafted through emptiness, nothingness.

Facing the smudged and hand-stained door to Donna's now, he recalled his father's voice. Not the sneering insistence on the Jem Craishot thing, but earlier, much earlier, his father carefully and emotionlessly explaining the reasons for his—Nole's— having to shoot his own horse, the paint colt they had given him in the spring of his eighth year, that he had named, wrongly enough, "Happy." Seeing himself, the boy, crying, thinking of the terrible loss, the young horse that had sickened beyond cure, and now the decision or pronouncement that it was Nole's job to "take care of" the animal. So his father had come in and begun trying to explain, in that cold, controlled voice, how important it was to "do your job" and the satisfaction of not letting it touch your feelings. Something like that. And how the more his father talked, about sickness, suffering, responsibility—the more Nole listened to that steady, impassive voice full of *duty* and strength—the more horrific it all seemed, and the more he felt that pounding pressure, the thudding dread.

So that he found himself flailing again: the hundred stubbed fingers furiously waving from his temples, his cranium, and shouting, huffing, like pummeling the air with a punch of sheer inflection, SHUT UP SHUT UP SHUT UP. And it was no longer Happy, the sick colt, lying flat out in the stall with that listless bewilderment in his huge brown eyes, where now the big flies, winged clots of black flesh, landed, laying their eggs in the glistened, unblinking pupils, then rising, to hover horribly around and watch, with a loud, *flubbing* buzz, a disgusting vul-turous tumult. It wasn't the colt anymore. Not even the act, the necessity, of shooting him. It had become just one more version of the old thing, the pressing and the flailing and the rage and regret and *SHUT UP SHUT UP*, all of it falling, pointlessly, against his father's proud duty and not-feeling. And so Happy didn't matter. No. Not the four-months colt he had helped foal and brought to suck and raised and tended and so now this was supposed to mean Nole was the one mandated to wield the rifle. All of that was gone. Because his father had put it all down into explanation and cause and consequence, the thin vaporous words only. And so there was no colt, no history of nudge and nuzzle and the touch and smell, the nervous joy. Only the thin words, the explaining, and so only grief and then this rage and regret, mixed together into the *SHUT UP SHUT UP SHUT UP*. And so he hated the voice that was laying out the words, hated what he even knew was the father's attempt to ameliorate the grief and regret, to spare pain, or at least to make pain understood. Hated the man himself. And had finally said it aloud, "Shut up! Just shut up!" and stormed away, forsaking not only the explanations but the suffering colt as well.

Until his mother found him in the bedroom where he'd gone to cover, seething at the voice, the place, the exigency of sickness, suffering. She had come to him with the loaded .22 rifle in her hands. And she had nudged the weapon forward into the circle of his own grasping. And had said only this, that "it's a heap easier to be doin' than to be fixin' to do." Especially this, she had said, this shooting. "Just to be shed of it," she said. And she had turned and walked out and left him clutching the rifle. And he had loved her. A swollen effusion of love that he had walked through, trembling, terrified, to the stall.

And so he had lowered the barrel of the .22 until it bumped against the colt's skull with the dreadful, dull resonance of metal on bone. And pulled the trigger, hearing the shocking sound and seeing the animal's body jerk reflexively as the bullet thudded through its brain. He had leaned over, then, and looked, wondering, at the dark hole in the colt's temple, the darker bubble of blood, blooming slowly outward welling up into a glistening sphere, then breaking and running heavily, like syrup, through the horse's thick hairs. He reached out slowly and touched the wetness, then drew his hand upward and to his own temple, feeling the cold dab of the blood on this thin, sensitive flesh.

And so, loving his mother, he had administered death and release to the colt. And discovered at least a kind of resolution, himself: an end, for both of them, himself and the colt, an end to the waiting, the appalling, bewildered pain and the moiling of the fat, black flies. And he loved his mother, still, as he walked back into the quiet house and reached up the rifle to the notched rack. Shed of it.

Donna's door swung out, startling him, and hand went again to pistol butt as an elderly farmer in patched and faded overalls limped out the door past him. The grizzled face muttered a vacant *Haddy*, a toothpick working in the tobacco-stained mouth. Nole caught the door before it could swing to and stood on the threshold. He felt a mild tremor run through his thighs. *Oh Lord, don't let that Jake get to shakin' me now.*

With an effort of will, he propelled himself into the room, walking five jerked, brisk paces to the second table. He looked as though he was about to say something, and he made a sweeping motion with his palm, like a speaker's perorative gesture. This was it. He would kill them all. Get shed of it. *Dem dirty bastards.* He saw the men as they leapt up and tumbled, one by one, Nole's bullets answering their jibes, dealing out death and death again.

He blinked. The room was empty. He stood in a kind of fool's wonder, then let fall his gesticulant arm and turned toward the counter. Donna stood silently, her beauty still only a benchmark for incongruity, slowly wiping a plate with a yellow rag. They stared at each other, the small hand running methodically round the plate. Then Darlen broke the gaze and looked back jerkily around the room. No one was there. He turned back to Donna, who was still gazing at him, wiping the plate.

"You fergit somepin?" she said. "Come back fer somepin?" Her eyes swept his figure, expressionlessly, seeming to bounce for a moment at the bulge of the pistol. She returned her gaze to his eyes.

"I was..." he said.

The plate *plackled*, too loudly, when she set it down on the counter. She reached for another and resumed the methodical circular wiping. Her eyes remained on his, but for all the meaning they held, she might have been looking at the huge, empty soup kettle that rounded gleamily from a hook behind her.

"You fixin'..." she said.

He turned and walked heavily out the door. Her eyes followed him, her small hand wiping, slowly, steadily.

iii.

Burlton had once gone by the library office where Rosary worked, late on a Wednesday morning. He had never seen her in this context, and he wanted to. He didn't consider his motivation, the cause for a desire of this sort. He had nothing by way of intimation that this was the clearest sign yet of his falling deeply in love. Because this was love of a sort he hadn't experienced before—the sort that transforms everything associated with that being who is the object of passion. So the sheer pleasure of merely seeing her repeat a characteristic gesture, a smile or a glance of the eye, turns itself into a compulsion to act in such a way as to *produce* that gesture. And here, for Burlton, was the irrepressible longing simply to see her in all her diverse places, the varying contexts that composed her everyday life.

Had he remarked it at all, he might have recognized the strange, inverse irony of the inclination itself: how familiarity—the accumulation of smiles and glances that gradually lost their freshness for him and became "characteristic" of her—how this bred neither contempt nor even a slow mundanity in the relationship, but a redoubled fascination, an increased will to encounter more, more of the places and practices that sorted and shaped her life. He wanted to explore all of her worlds, and when he found himself standing on a new shore, that accomplishment itself drove him further inland in search of another landmark, another defining edge he could claim and mark out, like inking in a feature on a map—one of those distinctive spots we inscribe into the untracked chaos so we can pretend for the present to have defined the principal point that organizes our sense of *region* within this larger place: a shoreline, knoll, ridge, peak, valley, river, lake, knoll, shoreline.

And so this mapping drew the quadrants of his perception, and he noticed an entirely different set of details in the world, things that had never existed before, at all. In church one Sunday, watching a guest preacher—a smooth-browed man with a small curving mustache—he suddenly caught a suggestion of her. There was some fleeting hint in the man's gestures or expression, the raising of an eyebrow or a flexure in the upper body, that was unmistakably hers. And Burlton was rapt, watching hungrily for the thing to appear again in this absurdly unlikely place, the way, sometimes, you will go to a town you've never entered before and some wafting echo will come to you, and you will say *This looks like home.* So he watched the man—an itinerant preacher in a worn frock coat, a little seedy, the eyes clouded unmistakeably from drink—and waited for the moment when Rosary would appear. And she did, again and again, a fleeting glimpse through the veiled self of the shouting, gesticulant preacher, the bright, beautiful, cool woman.

So he went to find her, in this workplace, this new region, inventing an excuse for riding into town on a weekday morning. The pretext, the concocted explanation, was constructed not so much for his wife, who would neither have wanted nor expected explanations—who likely wouldn't have cared anyway—as for himself. Because he was unwilling to confess a desire so abstracted, so disengaged from practical purpose and systematic attainment as this. This compulsion merely to penetrate an unseen portion of her life for the single purpose of being there, watching her. It was as though he had to trick himself, even as he saw himself contriving the excuse, the sleight-of-hand, with only himself as audience. Conceiving an elaborate feint in order to prove he could persuade himself to believe in what he already knew was mere illusion.

He pondered this, and he thought about Jem, who had told Burlton about Brownie, the card sharp he worked with in the traveling show. This, the show business, was Jem's chosen life, and it had led him straight to the one he hadn't willed: the life of the fugitive, outlaw, and killer. But the card sharp became a pal of his, the two of them sharing one of a chain of roughly constructed, gaudily painted box-wagons across Alabama, Mississippi, Louisiana, stopping in an indistinguishable series of what Jem called *penny-plug* mill towns, to gather a crowd with string music, magic acts (the card sharp's job), and trick shooting (Jem's job) for the ultimate purpose of selling them two-ounce bottles of Doctor Clifford's Bitter Crodo Water at fifty cents a *nut*, as they called it.

Brownie had learned his trade, Jem said, in Pershing's cavalry, in endless bivouacs along the Mexican border, guarding against an incursion that never came—*Zimmerman's Zouaves*, they called themselves, in harsh scorn of their own pointless lives—prodding their horses through that unforgiving and unimaginable terrain along the Big Bend stretch of the Rio Grande, seeing no one, doing absolutely nothing.

Their pay followed them sporadically, so when it came it was a relative bonanza. And, as there was nothing whatever to spend it on and nothing else to do anyway, they'd taken to playing high-stakes poker, sitting around a table made of cracker-boxes in a huge Sibley tent that smelled of mildewed canvas, smoke, and sweat. When they could, some of them mixed the gambling with bouts of hard drinking—a fiery mescal, distilled by locals whom the troopers called, quite randomly, *Comanches*—and the combination of cards and liquor often led to sharp, slashing fights, which would erupt suddenly and end just as quickly, one or two troopers lying unconscious and bleeding into the lantern-lit earthen floor. But the real players didn't drink—they gave over all the pent energy and thought to the game itself, where the pot could hold as much as a half-year's pay. And it was here the future card sharp learned his trade.

It began one night when another trooper was caught cheating, and Brownie, being known as a reasonable man with powerful fists, was delegated to administer punishment in the form of a severe, methodical beating, outside in the deep midnight shadows between the rows of Sibleys.

Brownie was frankly astonished. He had seen no indication whatever that the man had been cheating, beyond the winning hands that seemed to fall the man's way on the occasions of his own deal. In his inexperience, Brownie initially saw as evidence of innocence the fact that others had held some very good cards on these same deals. But as he pulled the accused man out of the tent, dragging him along by the rough wool flannel of his tunic—these troops had been given standard-issue uniforms and been ordered to wear them in temperatures approaching 120 degrees—Brownie realized the betting had been brisk and heavy precisely because of all the good cards, and the trooper had accumulated a large amount of cash by merely folding up early for three hands and then winning these big pots on his own high-pocket deals. Still, Brownie had seen nothing at all unusual, or even slick, in the way the man had handled his cards. Brownie, anyway, had been no direct witness to the man's cheating.

So he dragged the man out of the big tent and hustled him around back.

"I didn't see nothin' of no cheatin'," he said, jerking the man's tunic sharply downward to trap the arms.

"I weren't cheatin'," the man said. "I swear it on my dear mother's grave. I weren't cheatin'. On the memory of my sweet mother, I swear to you."

"Well, that's kindly a shame," Brownie said. "Because I was fixin' to offer to not bust you up if you'd teach me how to do that."

"Whut?" the man said, his eyes flicking upward, catching a

faint gleam in the profound dark between the tents. "Teach whut?"

"Teach me how to handle them cards like you done. Because I didn't see nothin', not a thing, no more'n a cricket in the cathouse. So it's a shame you weren't. Because, as Jack said to Jenny, you show me that, and we'll just walk on by the rest of 'em. I won't have to whip you, no how."

"Oh. Well now," the man said. "I can teach you that. I surely can."

So they arranged a meeting, and Brownie scrubbed up his own knuckles on a telegraph pole to make it look like he'd hurt the man, and that was that. Because Brownie could see already the only reason the man had been caught was that he had been too greedy, or too impatient, and had set himself up once too often in too short a time. And Brownie could *bide*, he told Jem. And he had seen a way to break the tedium of the border patrol and make a fair living doing it.

And so they met, and Brownie learned: how to set up hands out of the spent cards from the game before, and how to shuffle these cards into position on top and bottom of the deck, *countin' cards* the man called it. How to effect a *whorehouse cut*. It was actually all very simple in concept, he realized, *because nobody never fools a feller by makin' up complications. Feller gets fooled when he thinks everthing is just as usual.*

The difficulty, of course, lay in the execution. All of the finding and counting and arranging had to take place within a split second. The shuffling and the cut had to be masterfully slick without looking anything but perhaps a little clumsy. And the deal had to look consistent—and, he discovered, had to *sound* right, *because that's where they'll catch you most times. They'll hear them cards click when you pull from the bottom*—regardless of where each card was actually coming from. And the entire process had to be perfect every time. There was no leeway for even the slightest mistake, anywhere in a five- or six-hour poker game. The margin of error was exactly zero.

So he practiced. At first, he practiced the individual movements, the dissected elements of the operation, shuffle-cut-deal. Then he put them together, practicing the movements, the process, but now adding another level entirely. Because this was as crucial as the raw manual skill: the personality of the player, the gestures and talk, the image of bored dispassion, of a trooper more interested in passing the tedious hours than in the details of the game itself.

And he reached the point where he knew he was good. He had mastered it all, and he could do it while talking, chatting, and smoking—even drinking a bit. *But*, he thought, *How'm I to know when I'm good enough?* Good enough to risk life and limb, not to mention banishment from the only form of pastime to be found anywhere within these hundreds of miles of tough, scrub red-rock desert.

So he set up a mirror, and he practiced in front of it. And he told himself, *I won't be good enough until I can fool myself. Really fool myself. Not just once in awhile that I cain't quite see what I'm a'doin', but ever time. Ever time, already knowing what it is I'm a'doin', I got to fool myself into thinkin' I'm a'doin' somepin else. Ever time. When I can do that, I'm ready to take her out into a game.*

Brownie told Jem about all of this during a driving spring rainstorm that had already eliminated the possibility of a show later that day. It was just mid-morning, and the two men were crouched inside one of the box wagons, listening to the steady monotony of rainfall drumming on the wood of the roof. Jem had said, "Onliest thing duller'n puttin' on these here shows ever day is not puttin' on one of 'em." And this had loosed Brownie's memories of the dry desert tedium, and he had begun by saying, "You know, when I was your age, I spent nine months in the middle of nowhere doin' just exactly nothin'."

And he told Jem the story, the two of them hunched inside the close, warm wagon, listening to the rain. And as Brownie talked, he absently flipped a deck of cards into fans and falls, waves and windrows. One moment, the cards would lie in a cold, stiff block. Then he would touch them and they became elastic and alive, in flow and counterflow, as he told the impossible tale of learning a skill so well you could watch yourself with a calculating scrutiny, looking for the precise movements you knew you must be making, and fail to see them, blind to your own skill, the blindness the perfect reflection of the skill itself. And sometime during that long day, during the slow telling, Jem had interrupted him, irritably, saying, "Would you stop twirlin' them damn cards around? Jesus Christ, how can you do all that while you're tryin' to talk?"

"Do whut?" Brownie asked, tipping the thin squares into retrograde ripples.

Folks likes to be fooled, Burlton thought. *I reckon they only get het up iffen they's money involved. But folks takes real pleasure in bein' fooled. You take the littlest bit of a kid and you can show that kid a coin maybe, make it disappear, and watch that child just start in to gigglin' and wrigglin' around just tickled pink. I don't know. Folks'll pay money, go to the show to watch a feller, and they'll laugh and clap they hands, just from the pure pleasure of havin' some feller trick 'em. They like it. They surely don't like it too damn much when that feller fools 'em in a poker game, though. Do they?*

And now Burlton was engaged in something very like Brownie, diligently watching himself practice the misdirection and feinting, the pretext of simplicity—*I just better run in and see about them loan papers*—all designed to create an illusion of normalcy so complete that he wouldn't be able to see himself waving the wand. So that, perhaps, like Brownie, he could make a lifetime's work out of it. Perhaps that was the goal, after all, and the truest indication that he was, in fact, being driven by love itself. Because perhaps he was demonstrating—to no one at all, unless it was Rosary, the way only the queen knows how and why she has slipped into that precise location in the deck, where she can fool even the knave who dropped her there— perhaps he was demonstrating the fundamental truths of this sort of love, love grounded in a passion so mysterious and so dangerous that its subject must diligently rehearse the gestures and diversions necessary to hide its true face from himself, to cover it, palm it, confuse and distort its identity, lest it spring forth, fully defined, and overwhelm him.

So he told himself he must get to town; he had business— nothing urgent, nothing critical—but he *mayt just as well get it done*. He might be already in the middle of the morning's work, might even have begun harnessing mule to plow, or uncovering a strip of tobacco seedlings for setting out. And he would stop suddenly, the canvas half thrown back, the hame strap fed through but not buckled. And he would muse a moment— setting up the mirror or picking up the deck, perhaps—and would tell himself *it's fixin' to rain b'fore I even get to the field*, so this may as well be the morning to head into town and talk about that loan, or that hail insurance, or put in that order for arsenic of lead. And he would let the dew-wet canvas fall back or slide the oiled leather strap out. And then turn slowly and walk toward the house, to dress for town, to tell his wife it was going to rain, and maybe she could gather the kids inside and seed a few shoes full of that cotton.

This time he rummaged through the house until he found some loan papers, hollering out the window to Janey Gill to *tap up* his little mare, Harding. By eleven, he was riding up School Street and feeling the contrary impulse—an anxious search for reasons to flee—as he saw the bright brick severity of the new library bulking into view. *You reckon you oughter head on over to the bank first? Besides, she mayt be too busy for a visit. What if she don't like it, you bein' there? I ain't sure they'll let you in without a badge or somepin. I don't believe I'd better just burge on in there, do you?* By the time Harding stood in the circle fronting the new building, Burlton was thoroughly frightened. Still, love has a powerful inertia of its own, and this entire enterprise had, after all, been an exercise in the peculiar motivations of love. So it—the terror, the instinct to flee—couldn't compete with the impulsion of that need to see her, to discover a new stage upon which to watch her perform, this graceful woman, whose every gesture called upon him to stand and bear testimony, just as he had on that first morning when he had gazed down upon her impossible presence: *My sweet Lord.*

So he dismounted and went in, stood at a sign called IN-FORMATION walking his fingers along his hat brim, inwardly rehearsing the inquiry, *Is Miz Raferty Darlen around?* When there she was, standing at his shoulder, as though she'd come to see him, and he had turned, surprised, to find her appearing at his side.

"Well good morning, Mr. Hobbes," she said. He had never heard this tone, these inflections. "You're just a bit early." She turned to the thin woman behind the INFORMATION desk and said, "Mr. Hobbes has a luncheon appointment with me. Perhaps he'd be interested in a tour of our new library while he's waiting. Would you like Miss Taylor to show you around, Burlton? This is quite a modern facility." Her eyes glimmered at him.

He stammered and fed his hat brim through twitchy fingers. "I don't reckon..." he said. He wasn't even aware of her amusement, so astonished was he at her voice, her diction, the clipped, bouncing intonation, so unlike the liquid mildness he knew, the voice he understood so well because its timbre matched the accents of his own. This was as though she suddenly had pulled forth a strange reeded instrument and had begun playing a series of complex arpeggios in quarter-tone scales. He didn't much care for the music, but he was overwhelmed with admiration at the proficiency and ease with which she could play it. He looked at her wonderingly. *My sweet Lord.*

"I don't reckon..." he said again. She took his elbow very softly, caressingly, and said. "No, I suppose one library pretty much looks like another. You can just come on into my office and wait until I finish up a few things." He walked in a state of complex bemusement, more in love than he'd ever imagined possible, alongside this woman, this Rosary, who could speak in such tongues.

As soon as the door closed on the small cubicle entitled CIRCULATION, she turned him into her arms, kissed him, and said, "You clombered all the way into town on a Wednesday just to see me?" Then, "Whyn't you go on down to Pineola and wait on me? I got a whole hour to eat some dinner at noon, and I ain't the least bit hungry."

iv.

Nole Darlen left Donna's, his body twitching and shaking, half in frustration, half in reaction to the Jamaican Ginger that had worked its way through him and was now tingling his hands and feet. His revenge, the moment he had sought as release, discharge of all the rage and shame and regret, had been suddenly closed off to him with the astonishing emptiness of Donna's, so that the echoing interior itself seemed to be laughing at him as he left. He felt at once entirely deflated and full to bursting, and this strange sensation so disoriented him he walked for several blocks west—toward the center of town—before he had given any thought to destination or even to the action of walking itself. Like a mortally wounded animal will often leap back to its feet and run powerfully for several steps before the final fall, Darlen's movement paradoxically demonstrated his complete lack of physical will. His jerking pace resembled the terrible flight reflex that causes a trapped bird to beat itself to death, responding to each new shock of pain and injury with a redoubled impulse toward flying, beyond thinking or control, the reflexive stimulus and response itself not even reaching the brain, but firing back and forth within the minuscule, fibred, gray horns of its spinal cord. So he walked, automatically, coming to the first groups of Saturday strollers, the country people. They saw a ravaged young face, mottled from the effects of this morning's hangover and this afternoon's new intoxication. It walked with the shambling, loose-ankled sprawl that signified a future bout with full-blown Jake leg. In his carelessness, the pistol had bulged outward from his hip so that its presence might have been unmistakable were this not a bright Saturday afternoon, dedicated to a routine leisureliness, in which the existence of a pistol was literally inconceivable. And so, although the groups of people shied a bit at his approach, allowing him plenty of room, no one recoiled in fear, alarm. He was a sight, but no more. Just a scrabbled man.

And, in fact, he was at this point quite beside himself. He had no more presence—as a self, or as that multiplicity of selves that constitutes real sentience, active personality—than a dead man. Only the loose-jointed walk, and those invisible, bud-like fingers writhing even more wildly from temples and forehead, and an incessant voice, crying inside: *I didn't ask to be this way. Didn't want to be the feller I am.*

He turned onto a small side street, just short of Broad. He was heading south, now, and this narrow street was void of people. For some reason, the combination of empty street and the sun on his face caused him to cease his automatic walking. He stood a moment, and then he heard the small ticks inside, his brain reconnecting, the *chirr* as his thoughts began to turn, as he came back into life.

He needed drink. The Jamaican Ginger was worn out now, except for the after effects, the incipient Jake leg that could be deferred only by something of a relatively higher quality. Corn liquor would be best: good, double-run moonshine, made here by men who knew their customers and cared whether or not their product was worthily crafted, or at least whether or not they were likely to poison a neighbor or a cousin. The alternative solution would be to find something even worse than the Jake. Canned heat, Sterno, strained through a piece of bagging, would produce the kind of intoxication that could run roughshod over the lingering effects of the ginger. But this was a malevolent cure—the worst kind of stopgap—because canned heat would produce a brand of horrific aftershock that could be stilled or at least held at arm's length only by more canned heat. And so it was the bane of the poorest of the drinkers. It was cheap, exceptionally powerful, and commandingly addictive. Nole had always been able to afford something better, and he considered canned heat "nigger slop." He felt himself immensely superior to the addicts who had been able to manage nothing better and who now would, could, settle for nothing less. In truth, he would not have hesitated, himself, to drink the stuff, were it his only choice.

And today money was an issue. There had been cash in his pocket last night. Not a lot of cash, but it had disappeared somewhere. Of course, he had spent some of it on liquor—he remembered having bought two quarts of good moonshine early on—but the remainder was a mystery. Someone had taken it from him, he decided. And he recalled that he had left his new Washburn guitar somewhere. And all of this was somehow scrambled up with his treatment at the hands of Hutch Cantwell and his pals this morning—the jeering and the laughter—and he found himself saying "Dem dirty bastards" again.

But that didn't matter right this minute, and he shook off the bitter regret. Money was what mattered. Two dollars, anyway, for a quart of something. Five to be certain. At least five.

He could draw pay at the mill today, but he hadn't gone to work, and he wasn't prepared to show himself there now. He was going to lose that job sooner or later, no matter who his daddy was, and an appearance today—two hours or more after quitting time and fully six hours after he was supposed to have been there in the first place—would be likely to rile someone up enough to toss him out on the spot. So the cash draw at the factory would not provide the answer.

He was walking again. He had turned east, a block or so back, and now he was struck with the desire to know where he was. He crossed diagonally at the corner and read the street signs.

He was at the corner of Hand and Pineola, and as soon as he saw the sign he knew the answer to his problem, just as when a dog first strikes a scent, it knows instantly which way to follow the line, which way is forward and which backward, unerringly, as though the single act of smelling has carried with it the entire process of map and compass and even clock, so there need be no hesitation about any of it: The trail is already known, the outcome assured, and it is now just a question of relative speed. And the hound has the advantage here, too, since the hound already knows precisely where he is going.

"Mamma," Nole said aloud, turning quickly onto Pineola and moving straighter, with more alacrity, than he had gone anywhere, all day. *Mamma'll give me money, almost without my havin' to ask for it. Sure now. Mamma.* And he felt a full swelling of confidence, because he would not only obtain what he was after, but he would get it from her. From her.

He hadn't been here in quite some time, he realized, as he opened the door and entered the big brick building. He didn't like his mother to see him drunk or even hungover, and he had been one or the other pretty much constantly for a matter of months. So, at first, he was timid about being here. But he felt her presence immediately in the very air of the place—the dark, dim, close hallway—and he responded at once to the sense of her proximity. It calmed him, somewhere deep inside, and he knew he felt better just being surrounded by this aura, better than he had felt all day. Better than since he could remember. He leaned momentarily against the thick, nubbled wallpaper and breathed in the fulsome feeling. *Mamma.*

He worked his way, as decorously as possible, up the stairway, helping himself along with the handrail, pulling against the inertial drop of the Jake. He was self-possessed now, and the combined anticipation of seeing her and receiving the money that would satisfy his physical craving, that would buy a few quarts of pure, colorless relief, all of this combined to make him feel almost happy. It was not going to be so terrible after all.

He reached the landing at her level and, in a flush of embarrassment, remembered the pistol. He wouldn't want her to see that, and he suddenly felt abashed and childlike. Once, when he was a little boy, he had dropped and broken one of her precious possessions: a pretty porcelain dog. He had been in her room, alone, had crept in, as he had done many times before. Of course it was not only her room, it was his father's, too—*their room, their* room—but it never felt like the man, only the cast-off leather shoes, or the banded hat, smelling of cigarettes. Everything else—the very shape of the room, the cedar smell, the fluffed frocks in the closet, everything—made it hers alone. Her room.

And Nole liked to come into the room when they were away, and to stand at her dresser, watching himself in the mirror. Watching himself to see what she might see if she came in upon him, caught him. And he would lift the porcelain figure. It was a setter, with flopped ears, but that wasn't what he cared about. It was the long, smooth turn of the body, the curve of the flank into the haunches, so sleek and cool, so amazingly cool. And he watched himself feel the thing, sliding his hands along its arched length, until it was no longer silky and chill, but warm and frictive. And he would lay it down, still watching himself with her eyes, and wait for it to cool again, for the flush to ease from his hands. And then he would lift it again, again the cool, smooth play of hands over back and flank.

And one day he dropped it. One moment he was holding it, stroking it, as usual, and the next—some convulsive twitch of his hand, perhaps—and he heard it shatter against the chestnut dresser.

He was shocked and terrified and filled with remorse. And he picked up the pieces and dropped them carefully into his pockets, quickly, furtively, but with infinite concern. Because he didn't want to leave a trace, as though she was less likely to miss the thing if it had disappeared entirely than if there had been some remainder, some tiny sliver, to glint against her eye and cause her the pain of loss.

But it wasn't really that—her grief over the lost object—nor was it his own fear of punishment that drove him running out the back door with the broken shards of porcelain tucked into his pocket and pushing sharply against his thigh. It was the horror of having her discover that he, he had broken the thing. It would be as though he had been vouchsafed some intimacy and had treated it with disregard. And he couldn't bear to have her believe this of him. Not this. So he took himself into the woods and down into a damp ravine, where he emptied his pocket and buried the broken thing in the wet, sticking loam. And he wept as he hid the thing, remembering its sleek feel, the gleam of the haunches, and his mother's eyes in the mirror.

So now he must get rid of the pistol. He couldn't have her know he had carried this heavy weapon around with him, had brought it into this building, so soft and full from her presence. He was ashamed and regretful, and he searched for a hiding place.

There was an alcove just off the stairhead, with a small, high window cut into its curved surface, and he determined to lay the heavy Colt onto the ledge. He turned and moved aside, into the recess, reaching upward to feel for the window ledge, looking over his shoulder to assure himself he wasn't seen. He tucked the pistol onto the sill: It made a low *thumpling* sound, and he looked backward again, furtively.

At that moment, Burlton Hobbes emerged from Rosary's apartment. He saw Nole in the alcove but didn't recognize him. Only barely registered the young man's presence, because he, Burlton, was more worried about being recognized himself, and he hurried to the stairway and pirdled rapidly down the shallow steps and out of sight.

Nole saw Burlton, though, and knew him instantly. He

thought immediately of Janey Gill and assumed Hobbes had come to register some sort of complaint with his mother. But it didn't ring true, and Nole knew on the instant that he was trying to avoid recognizing the obvious explanation. Hobbes had moved with a guilty air, not at all like a man who had just finished complaining, demanding, or threatening. No. It was entirely the look of somebody...

"That ain't it neither," Nole said, loudly. "No it ain't. It ain't." And he felt the frantic hands, the nubbed fingers again, as he lurched to her door.

He knocked once, very quietly. Then, shifting his shoulders, he lifted his other hand and rapped loudly. He felt his head swelling, reeling.

"It's unlocked, Burl," her voice called, singsong, lively. "You forget somepin?"

V.

"Burl? Burlton? You forget somethin'?"

Nole didn't want to believe what he already knew—that his mother's lilting response had been meant for the man who had just left the apartment, who had just gone down the stairs, too furtively to be there for any other reason. So when he heard her confirming tone of voice, beckoning to this man, *It's unlocked, Burl,* he acted at first as though he hadn't heard, as though she hadn't answered the knock. And so he stood, silent. He didn't want to touch the doorknob. This was all too hard. He had felt so much better. And this was unbearable.

"You out there?" his mother's voice called. "Burlton? Come on in."

So Nole turned the knob and swung the door in. She was not in sight, so he walked quickly, through the door into the bedroom. It was suddenly as though he needed to see, needed to find out.

She was walking toward the bedroom door, belting a thin cotton gown around her body and tossing her head to clear her hair away as the gown settled over her bare shoulders. He felt a hot flood rising within him, a familiar pooling and swelling, but suddenly there seemed nothing to staunch the flow, nothing to contain any of this. Her hands drew the narrow sash to a bow while she walked, closing the gown's front, just as she realized this was not Burlton, but Nole. She stopped, staring, and he saw her take in a deep breath. Through the thin pale cotton, he saw the push of her nipples.

She noticed the direction of his gaze, and she automatically crossed her arms.

"Nole," she said. "I was just..."

"Just what?" he said, his voice rising. "Just what?" He looked at her, the careless hair, the thin veil of fabric over the flesh. Something was pushing up inside him, swelling, too fast and too large. He laughed, a cough of bitter regret and anger. "You ain't sleepin' in the middle of a day. Ain't you?" He laughed again, without the least hint of recognizable feeling. "Or was that the doctor, come to do a check-up? Huh? Was that it? That the doctor?"

He was beginning to shake visibly now, and she felt the first real wire of fear.

"Nole," she said, trying to sound deliberate, explanatory. "He's a friend of mine. And we...he..."

The tears burst forth from him, like a mad shout, and he was holding his head in both hands, weeping. He rocked back and forth, and he began to wail, "Mamma, Mamma."

"Nole," she said. She was anxious, worried, now. "Nole, it's not..."

"You're just a damn whore!" he shouted, through the wet, heaving sobs. "You're a goddamn whore!"

She reached out and touched him, at the elbow, and he yanked, flung his arm out of her reach. Then, in one motion, he turned and slammed his forehead against the pale wall, so hard she thought he must lose consciousness, or at least fall, stunned. But then he raised up and swung his arm back toward her. He grasped her gown at the neck, hard, and wrenched it, pulling wide the thin fabric, then, grabbing the flimsy sashed opening with both hands, drew the halves away, wrenching the gown wide, exposing her naked body.

"Nole," she said, her tone a mixture of her outrage and the need to calm him, the mother's voice. She tried to cover herself with her hands. "Don't you..."

He hit her, hard, with his fist, and her body snapped back onto the bed, where she lay still. Wracked with sobs, he leaned over her, reaching out both arms and, taking her hands, he drew her body upward until he held her standing, his arm swung around her hips, as her weight tried to crumple her to the floor. Then, with his free hand, he stroked the length of her naked torso, first upward, then down, his palm pressed firmly against her flesh. Feeling her.

"Mamma," he sobbed, sniveling wetly. He caressed again, up then down. "O Mamma."

Then he hit her again, driving her back onto the bed, her slack arms flying out over her head, leaving her spread back in a posture at once shamelessly wanton and childlike.

He turned and ran from the room, rubbing his sleeve across his face and choking out sobs.

In the hallway, he gradually composed himself, scrubbing his face on his sleeve, then, in a sudden shift of attitude, smoothing his shirt, running hands assessingly through his hair. He moved, then, swiftly, skipping down the stairs and into the vestibule, where he stopped and looked around, seeking Hobbes, or just checking to see that he was alone—he couldn't have said which. Then he moved through the door, into the street. He stopped, turned halfway back, and snuffed. His eyes glinted and his whole body twitched. Then he sprang through the door, back into the building, and bounded up the stairway, flinging a nervous glance over his shoulder.

He ran into the apartment again, into her bedroom, where she was stirring, trying to turn over, to push herself upward with her hands. He ignored her, the flagrant female body, the naked wriggling, and he went straight to her dresser. In a shallow tray, among a few scattered hairpins, he found a thin fold of bills.

He grabbed these and stuffed them into his shirt pocket, then ran out of the room, not looking at her again.

He began the tumbling run down the stairs for the second time. Halfway down the first flight, he stopped, jerking to a halt so suddenly he nearly fell headlong. Then he turned and floundered upward again. At the landing, he bolted to the right, to the alcove, where he retrieved the pistol. He stood quite still for a moment, breathing hard, and tucked the Colt into his pants, turning it to his flank, with the over-scrupulous care of an insane man, or a drunk. He fluffed the shirt and straightened himself for a moment, posing. Then he threw himself at the stairway again.

By the time Nole left the building, the deliberation had turned back into agitation. He was losing control, frenzied, and he sprang into motion as though trying to outrun the day, as though he thought he might be able to erase the hours, the years even, not by turning the clock back, but by drawing out in front of all of it, all elapsed time, ahead of even the present, so that the ticks of the hours could never catch him again. He began to weep again, long tearing sobs that seemed to trail off behind him, streaming tattered shreds of grief, so that now he wanted to outrun these, too, and, like a paranoiac trying to rend himself from his own shadow, he desperately tried to find some clear space between himself and these rags of sobbed tears pouring continually in straggling strands from his eyes, his mouth.

He turned onto his own street and made for his building. He was running pell-mell now, and he all but crashed into the entrance way. He took the stairway in a headlong, stumbling scramble, nearly tripping at every riser but just catching himself, so that the motion of falling down was indistinguishable from his wild upward momentum. At the top, he flung himself into his apartment. At the center of the room, he came to a sudden, frightful standstill, as though some being had thrown a switch, severing whatever power source had driven him on this clashing careen home, and left him stock and disconnected. Except for the glisten of tears on his cheeks, and the small, constant tremor of his hands, he might have been some object, inanimate and fleshless.

He was not thinking at all. Along with his physical motion, the course of his thoughts had come to a complete standstill. His mind was not blank—it was more as though the continually shifting back-projection of mental images, thrown out from the wall of his mind like images from a mirror, had gotten stuck, suddenly, and he stood looking inward upon that static picture of his mother just tying the sash of her gown, her hands, the attitude of her body, the toss of her hair, everything speaking the same sentence: *I was naked just a moment ago, in the sight and the feeling of that man, that Burlton Hobbes*, whom Nole had watched leaving the apartment, like a sneak, a thief, who had touched his mother, who had been offered the complete freedom of that nakedness. Burlton Hobbes, upon whom she had spread herself, ravished herself, buttered herself. Nole closed his eyes, but the image only burned brighter. And he became aware of the memory on his own hands, the way the receptors in the skin hold the resonance of what they've touched, so he felt her curved, moist flesh in a dying echo on his hands. But he watched only her image as she sashed her gown, and this carried with it the reflected afterimage of her nakedness, not for him to see, but imprinted on the eyes, the hands, and the body of Burlton Hobbes.

Nole sprang frantically into action again. Now it was the money that held sway over his thoughts. The money had been, after all, the reason for his visit to her in the first place, and he became suddenly concerned lest he be caught with the puny fold of bills before he had time to exchange it for the alcohol he needed even more desperately now. He moved jerkily about the room, snatching up one thing or another, holding it in his palm—a bowl of shaving soap, a bedside lamp—as though the heft and swing of the object would tell him something about hiding the money. He made a complete circuit of the room this way, lifting every movable object that lay within reach—a box of matches, a bandanna—none of which would afford anything like a hiding place. He was mumbling something now, as he moved around the room, but the words were inaudible, and even he couldn't understand what he was saying. It was just sound, two syllables mumbled again and again, just a meaningless, rambled accompaniment to this meaningless, frenzied search.

When he completed his sweep of the room, he stood again at its center, still stuttering the syllables that meant nothing, even to himself. His eye fell on the rumpled corduroy jacket snarled into the corner, where he had flung it this morning. He went quickly to it and picked it up, holding it out by the collar, letting it unroll and hang free. He reached into his shirt pocket with his free hand and removed the fold of bills. It wasn't going to be much money, he decided. But it will go into the jacket and the jacket will go with him to Nosey Ned's to pick up some liquor. It was enough. Enough.

He felt a small glimmer of pride at this accomplishment, marrying coat and money so rationally in the midst of this storm of sorrow and indignation. He fluffed open the jacket and reached the bills inside, to the interior breast pocket. But there was something already there, so he set the bills carefully onto his bed and reached in again with his open hand. It came out holding a massed wad of crumpled money, greasy and damp. He stared at it in wonder. Then he dropped this money to the floor and reached into the coat again, pulling out a few more crunched bills—then a few more—and, as he looked at these, he felt a sharp pain coursing along his brow, temple to temple, and he remembered last night, Ketterling's and the stolen gun, and this stack of money, snatched up from the card table as he staggered out the door.

Nole looked now at the neatly folded dollars lying on the bed, the money he had grabbed with his hand still warm from his mother's bare flesh, the stroking and the smashing assault. He looked at the crumpled bills lying like dead birds around his feet, the fives and tens from Ketterling's, and he began to laugh in a low moaning tone, *huh huh huh huuunh huhuh*, which grew gradually louder and higher pitched until it had transformed into a penetrating pulse of chuffed cackling.

"I be God damned," he gasped. And now it was the chuffing laughter rhythmically interspersed with the breathless, dense voice. *Huh huh I be God damned huuunh huh.* He thought of the day, the sneering jokes this morning, the reminder of his lost girl, Merv, of the betrayal that had changed everything. And then the emptiness at Donna's room when he had returned to exact revenge, at last. And now, his mother and that man. And here was the money that had driven Nole toward all of this, here, all along, in the pocket of his discarded jacket.

He sat on the bed, still holding the jacket out by the collar, and laughed, until the cackle had risen and thinned to a wail, the words lowering and thickening into wet sobs.

CHAPTER FIVE

TWILIGHT

Oh he taught me to love him and promised to love,
To cherish me over all others above,
Now my poor heart is wonering, no misery can tell,
He left me no warning, no words of farewell.

Oh he taught me to love him and called me his flower,
That was blooming to cheer him through life's weary hour,
Hw I long to see him and regret the dark hour,
He's gone and neglected his frail wildwood flower.

—Carter Family, 1927

i.

Nole Darlen had first met Merv Craishot—and her brother, Jem, as well—at a dance, one of the few paying jobs he'd really been hired to play and had, in fact, been able to stay with the string band long enough to actually do the night's work. The place was a dusty, barn-sided, hollow shed of a dancehall sitting awkwardly on the edge of a small knob just beyond the south slope of Chimney Top. Nole was playing guitar with Cham Bowman's family, a large dance band with two fiddles, a mandolin, a five-string banjo, the guitar, and an enormous doghouse bass. Bowman himself played the front fiddle, and he was probably the finest musician in the region. In tandem with his banjo player, James Keen, Bowman created music that was driving and lively and evinced the free-wheeling, loose-jointed spirit most sought after for dances, without losing the tight, triplicate-perfect timing essential to any mountain string music having any claims to quality. Like other musicians who worked behind Bowman and Keen, Nole was energized and inspired by their playing, and so, though he was a rather indifferent rhythm guitar player at other times, he transcended his own limitations when he worked with this band, and his playing was true and steady—unnoticeable, the way precise guitar rhythm should be. And so this dance marked the absolute apex of his musical life, for it provided not only the opportunity to pick with great musicians, it also allowed him to taste the sweet grace of playing really well himself.

He had never reached the level of ability he had seen in these truly gifted players: that point where the very act of playing well generates its own improvisations, grounded in the facility of the playing itself. He knew that playing at such a level was itself a distinct species of thought—a state of mind, framing the possibilities, determining the relationships of notes, the spaces between notes, the essential material of the music. So that tonight's renditions wouldn't be improvisational versions of individual tunes. Instead, it would be the other way around: Any tune Bowman and Keen played would redefine itself, tonight, in the individual performance, so the absolute act of playing the tune would determine the tune, fundamentally. Now.

So this was one of the rare, joyous nights of Nole's life. Bowman didn't allow drinking on stage, and so Nole was also protected from the hazard of rejecting the grace as it was being offered. He remained sober and played consistently well. For this one evening, he stepped off the downward trail of self-destruction, letting bow, banjo, and flat pick ride him along upward through the night. And the dark, hazy decrepitude of the dance hall, along with his own dissipated, despairing self, were transformed utterly, and became bright melody, mountain music, the deep, driving time, and the bright tang of rosin and reel.

Dances like this one were the most popular secular activity in the entire area, and when a band of this quality was playing, people came from all across the foothills region. The parking area, a graded plain on the east shoulder of the knob, was filled with wagons, saddle mares, Model-T cars, and cut-down flatbeds. All through the night, the field would be visited by men in overalls or in cheap serge suits, many wearing flat-topped, narrow-brimmed straw hats, known locally as *cheese wheels*, and women in loose, homemade gray or blue dresses, or in flower-print frocks from downtown. They would wander from the dance, in twos and fours, to draw fruit jars of clear white liquor from under car seats or wagon boards. The women would hold out tin cups already half-filled with coke or molasses-water, which would be *livelied-up* by a man pouring stiff doses of the corn whiskey. Then the men would tip and drink directly from the jars, passing them around. Occasionally, someone would tip the jar, obliquely, and shake it, checking the bead, while everyone discussed the quality of the run: *Now, that's some pert good corn, there,* or *Waterboy don't make a bad jar of corn squeeze,* or *That run won't hurt nobody.*

Inside, the band would be playing "Forked Deer" or "Closer to the Mill" while crowds of dancers beat suffocating swirls of dust into the air, flat-footing or clogging or doing a thing they called the Bristol Backstep. Some were with partners while others danced alone, and it would be difficult at any given time to determine which pairs were actually couples and which were merely single dancers juxtaposed. Meanwhile, along the interior sides of the shed, people talked and lingered, in small groups or in twos. Young girls stood in bunches of three or four and giggled or shrank as angular young men strode determinedly back and forth in front of them.

He had seen her the moment he walked through the door, guitar case in hand, into the nearly empty shed, a half-hour before the actual dance began. At least this is the memory he chose later to call forth when he wished to reconstruct that night: She stood by the bandstand, talking with Keen as he tuned his banjo. With her was an assured-looking, pleasant-faced young man and an older fellow with a weathered face and pale, mild eyes. This latter was Burlton Hobbes, although neither he nor Nole would later realize they had met that evening. The younger man was Merv's older brother, Jem, who would kill his first man within six months and be sentenced to a Mississippi chain gang, expected to spend some fifteen years. On the night of the dance, though, to the people of these foothills, he was just a nice young kid, brother to this graceful, blooming young woman, who turned a pair of blue-gray eyes Nole's way, when she touched his arm and said, "Oh. Do you play in the band, too?" and she had asked him if he knew Carter Family songs, "from up in Mace's?" And could he play "Wildwood Flower," she asked, half joking, and she sang a snatch of tune, in a self-deprecating way, looking at him with eyes at once bashful and inviting.

That had been the beginning, and he remembered the remainder of the night as a kind of golden glow, the music thrumming through a turning tableau with, now and then, Merv's dancing body, the bending grace of hip and flank, or her broadly smiling face sliding into the tune, her eyes on him, the night's duration no longer measured by the clockface but by these appearances, her laughing eyes, the flow of limbs, the jounce of her slight breasts, and the dance. He was in love.

He drank himself into the usual post-dance stupor, but he awoke around noon the next day with no thought but to find this girl. And he had set off immediately to track down Keen, who had first introduced them.

"I don't mind tellin' you, Nole," Keen had said as they sat on his back steps in the early evening. "She's a nice gal, sure enough, and she lives on up beyond Blair's Crick. Little place tucked on up under Chimbly Top. Chaw?" He pulled a twist from his overalls and waved it at Nole.

"I reckon not," Nole said. "It don't suit me. You wouldn't have a mite to sup on, would you?"

Keen looked him over. "I got a little smidger of Waterboy's," he said. "I don't mind lettin' you have some, don't mind iffen you drank ever drop. But you need to be kindly careful with your drankin', Nole, I'm tellin' you as a friend. It ain't doin' you no good the way you gets sprangled up and takes to fightin' and all. You ought..."

"I b'lieve I'll have a sup of that, thank you," said Nole.

"Awright, Nole," Keen sighed, getting up. "It ain't none of my place to tell you how to tuck up yer mules. And you know I don't grudge you nothin' atall, Nole, iffen you're..."

"That's kindly," said Nole, his eyes ushering Keen off the porch and back to the shed, where he kept the jar wrapped in burlap bags. Keen returned a moment later, still talking.

"...feller over toward Bowmantown used ter keep himself a grat big ole bar'l of corn stetched up in his boxwood hedge. He'd roll it on out and take yer jug and he'd fill it right outen that bar'l. You know, his place was just kindly settin' right there by the high road. You'd come by there see three four wagons braked up along that hedge a'waitin' they turns."

"Let see that jar," Nole said.

So Keen told about Merv and the family, while Nole drank—how Jem Craishot had gone off to work with the medicine shows as a trick shot, but how he liked to come back through the area whenever he could.

"Jem's pa went down with the influenza back ten year or so, and so Jem, he keeps a purty good eye on the old home place. I ain't sayin' you oughtn't to go see that gal iffen you want, but I b'lieve Jem won't likely take too well to a young feller like you a'nosin' around his sister. I don't reckon he's like to care much for you, Nole."

"I don't give a God damn if he likes me or if he don't," Nole said. "I ain't fixin' to court him."

"Well, now, I don't mind tellin' you where to find that gal. It ain't none of my bidnits what you do, iffen you want. Jem, he's a right nice young feller, too. You ever met him before?"

"I reckon not," Nole said.

"Nice kid. All the way down. Nice kid." Keen examined his fingernails for a moment.

"Did I ever tell you about how I seen him throw three silver dollars in the air and shoot a hole through the middle of each one of 'em afore they hit the ground?" Keen reached into his pocket. "No. I don't reckon I did," he said. He drew out his tobacco again and looked at Nole with a face perfectly innocent of expression or irony.

"You right certain I can't give you no chaw?"

* * *

So Nole decided not to approach the Craishot homestead if there was any chance of facing Jem. Instead, he determined to wait for Merv as she was getting out of school. She was pleased to see him and, after a few such meetings, she had no reservations about conspiring to avoid her older brother. Keen had been correct: Jem had no use for the likes of Nole Darlen in any proximity to his sister and made it known to Merv that he did not want her seeing any "low-down city feller that can't hold a snuff of likker 'thout tryin' to fight everbody in a place."

But Jem was on the road most of the time, and so the way was mostly clear. And to Merv, young and inexperienced as she was, Nole Darlen appeared sophisticated, rather than conniving; clever, rather than brash. She resisted Nole's sexual advances for the most of a month, but he was perspicacious and eventually took the girl in a corn lot, greedily and stupidly, the way he did most things. She had regretted the event, but he had soon repeated it, and she had begun to surrender herself with more fatalism than desire.

For his part, Nole was smitten. He wanted Merv to leave home, run off somewhere with him, immediately following her graduation from the high school. But she said she had promised her brother she would stay and help him tend to their mother's farm. This fidelity to her brother's wishes galled Nole, who saw in Jem a rival and an obstacle to his happiness.

What he didn't know—what none of them knew—was that Jem was no longer with the medicine show. Instead, he was on the run—a thousand-dollar price on his head—having walked off the chain gang and headed out, working sporadic shifts as a farm hand.

Eventually, a letter had come to Merv, not from Mississippi, but from Oklahoma, where Jem was hiding out after having eluded a posse in a driving rainstorm. *I reckon they couldn't see good enough to shoot me*, he had written his sister. He was coming home, he said, to settle his mother's property debts and to "square up" things with Merv. She imagined he meant that he was going to give her some money. "Don't tell nobody I'm comin', and don't expect to see me at the house. I'll send word about meetin' with you. I'd sure be proud to be home in time for your graduation from the high school."

All of this presented a problem for Nole, who had been happy to have the brother out of the way and who feared and hated Jem's affection for his sister. Nole knew Jem could, and would, force him away from Merv, and he was as furious at his own inability to face up to the man as he was at the man's obstruction of the affair.

The romance with Merv, in fact, had gone a long way toward changing Nole for the better. Merv loved and admired her brother, and she had taken Jem's warnings straight to Nole.

"He says I could ask anybody about you, they'd say you're a no-good rounder." And, for once in his life, Nole had responded forthrightly.

"I know it, Merv," he said. "I ain't behaved too good. But I swear to you, I'll straighten out and be the kind of feller you want." He turned toward her, reached, and framed her face in his hands. She thought he was about to kiss her. Instead, he looked at her, direct and serious.

"Don't you see, this ain't the usual thing?" he said. "You ain't the usual girl. Not to me. Ain't it likely I been such a rake hell because I never had me nobody?" He shook his head slowly. "Nobody. Merv, I been so goddamn lonesome. Since even I was a little boy. Didn't have nobody, not since I was out of Mamma's arms. They just let me be." His eyes were as earnest as his voice. "When they ain't no one around, you know, it seems you may just as well tear things up, like what the hell difference does it make, you know? But to find somebody like you. It makes me want to do right."

"I wish I could know that," she said. She reached and grasped his wrists. "Wish I could know it."

Merv felt an abiding care for this graceless young man. She could not have explained it, had not even been able to say what it was when her brother had confronted her. Perhaps, like many girls her age, she was drawn to the loneliness of the "bad boy," the hell-raiser who exiles himself by his own behavior. Perhaps she felt her attempt to humanize a boy like Nole would somehow fill her own needs: the desire to lend warmth and comfort, a feeling so consistently stifled by the harsh daily drudgery of the Craishots' tiny mountainside farm. At any rate, she cared deeply enough. And if she could, in fact, believe what Nole was saying right now, she actually might find some escape in the recognition of his own sense of life's new value. Because, after all, she would be the cause.

"You just watch me," Nole said. "You'll see. I ain't the no-good I was."

And, over the next several weeks, it had appeared to be true enough. Nole had stopped drinking, had worked steadily— enough to attract attention at the plant, where his co-workers wondered what he was up to—had taken notice of himself. He began to learn to touch Merv with more of tenderness than demand, to react to her response in a new way that opened up an entire universe of contact and communion. He had felt a longing for such soft, speaking contact, but had never believed in it, as though it would require a return to some world that had disappeared, a place he thought he had left, forever, without even actually remembering he had been there in the first place.

And here it was, revealed in the shy passion of this young country girl, the way she opened herself to him, the intake of her breath, the liquid sigh that transformed all of his demanding desire into an imperative to give her pleasure, to learn how she felt, and to ease himself into accompanying her wise warmth.

And then it had all gone smash. He had offered her marriage, and she had urged him to wait. Wait until she finished school, wait until Jem approved, wait until they had some money to live on. And he had waited. Until, now, the first hurdle was crossed: She was graduating. And so there were the other two issues, and he felt powerless in the face of the brother's implacable resistance. And money?

Well, his father had more money than he knew what to do with. Enough that he had gone out and built himself an impossible estate in the middle of foothill country, where the man never could—never wanted to—belong. But the father had coldly refused to give Nole anything. At the same time, he had continually reminded his son that the abundance was there, saying, again and again, "They's plenty of jack a'comin' your way. But you ain't a'goin' to see a penny of it whilst I have to be around to watch you spend it." So Nole could expect nothing from his father.

Still, in despair over the thought of losing Merv, he had approached his father and asked, only to hear the terrible mocking laughter. *Whut's a'matter with you? I believe even you could figure out how to handle such a little thing as that, don't you? Even you?*

ii.

So Nole had arranged it all and had Nole had tipped off the chief deputy, Cal Boarder. He had known better than to go directly to Sheriff Simmons with his plan, in part because he'd had a few run-ins with Simmons, himself, in the past few years, and in part because he knew Simmons was not the sort to relish a setup.

Sheriff Rick Simmons was quite well-liked and was respected for his fairness and honesty. He had allowed numerous small farmers to escape federal prison time through the simple tactic of talking too much about where he was headed tomorrow to bust up a still. On occasion, the still would be found standing in place, and he could indeed break it up. But, more usually, the moonshiner and the whiskey would have cleared out overnight. Area people—even the majority of "drys"—appreciated Simmons's sense of balance about such things. *He'll enforce the law,* they'd say, *but he don't get scrabbled about it like some do.*

In short, Simmons was an uncommonly reasonable lawman for these times and these foothills, and the county's population was divided between those who admired the man and those who feared him. He was a tall, big-boned man, with a shock of long, wavy red hair that made him appear even larger (as it was, he stood six feet, five inches, in his socks), and he had that certain geniality of spirit that only big men seem to have.

Notwithstanding, when riled, he knew perfectly how to arrange voice, gesture, eyes, and height into an imposingly commanding unity of expression. It was a rare man who could confront an angry Sheriff Simmons without quailing. And Nole Darlen knew he was not such a man.

Simmons had been born and raised in Roalton, so the new magic city had, in effect, grown up with him. His mother, who owned and ran a sprawling rooming house, had been widowed six months before he was born, the result (the widowing) of violent disagreement during a dice game. Almost immediately, Mrs. Simmons—formerly a reticent wife dominated by her large, brawling, hard-drinking husband—appeared to have transformed herself into an intense bundle of grit and determination. Perhaps it was the shock of loss, or the opposite: the sense of responsibility that was coming, along with a new baby, in a few short months. At any rate, she had become a new woman: strong, savvy, and unassailable.

She was tiny, and her hair went gray well before her thirtieth birthday. She had inherited the house from her parents, both of whom had died of scarlet fever within a week of each other. The craps game that had killed her husband had taken place in the basement of that very house, and Mrs. Simmons's response gave a fair indication of the sudden change in her character.

She went below, that first Friday night, and cleared the whiskey and the whiskey-drinkers out of her basement, herding them up the stairs and out the door, all of them cowed by the authority of her assured voice and her assuredly swollen belly. "It'd been easier if she'd pointed a loaded gun at us," one of the men told Hogeye later. "Leastways, you could take and grab a gun away from her, point it back at her, and tell her how it was a'goin' to be. You can't do that with no belly in a shape like that. Ain't nothin' to do but obey the woman, I'd say."

But she kept the dice and, the following week, the game recommenced. The whiskey was replaced by scuppernong wine, and the players were now elderly men and women, who spoke in low, drawling tones, saying, "Pass the dice thisaway, if you please, ma'am," or, "I believe I'd bet a nickel on this here next throw, if that's all right with you, ma'am," speaking to a woman less than half their age.

And so it went, every Friday night, without incident, sleight-of-hand, or argument, all under the watchful gaze of the little woman with the flashing eyes and the iron will, so that, even now, with her son the high sheriff of all Washington County, the dice still crickled and rolled in the basement of Mrs. Simmons's boarding house every Friday night while, upstairs, she maintained a strict—some would say "severe"—control over her household, her kitchen, and her self.

Rick Simmons grew up in this house, working as something of a maintenance man and caretaker almost from the time he could walk. He knew everything about the place, excepting Friday nights, when he wasn't allowed in the basement, and he learned enough about the gas lines and plumbing to fix any basic problems. Meanwhile, he somehow found out about electricity before there was any to study in the house itself, because, at age twelve, he begged and borrowed what he needed and installed electric lighting throughout the house.

Meanwhile, he grew. And grew. So by the time he was wiring the house, he looked like an eighteen-year-old, with a hard, muscled body that seemed to repudiate any connection to childhood.

On a Saturday morning, about that time, he had answered the front door to find a silver-haired woman weeping, wringing a hanky, and asking for his mother. When Mrs. Simmons appeared, the woman told a story about having been waylaid last Friday night by a group of young toughs who had taken her dice winnings from her.

"These was town boys?" Mrs. Simmons asked.

"I reckon so," the woman said. "They was kindly hanging around down to that new culvert. I'd seen 'em by day, before, but I'd not thought nothing of it." She blew her nose. "Then last week they come out and stopped me. They said some of the terriblest things to me I ever heard, and then they took away my money."

"How much?"

"Five dollars. Oh, Miz Simmons, I don't see how I can ever play the game again."

"Well, now, Miz Thompson," Mrs. Simmons said. "I'll go on over to the police this afternoon, and I'll say to clear them boys out of there, make sure you can get on home without a slew of hooligans a'bothering you." She took Mrs. Thompson's hand. "Ricky, run upstairs and get my bag."

When Rick returned, Mrs. Simmons fished around in the big straw handbag and produced five one-dollar bills.

"You take this, Mrs. Thompson, and I'm sorry you had so much trouble. Dry your eyes, now. And Ricky, you can take my bag back upstairs."

But Rick was nowhere to be seen.

Years later, folks in town would still tell the story of the twelve-year-old boy marching into a pack of eighteen-year-olds and taking them all on until they'd given up five dollars for him to take back to his mother. And how he threatened to return and do it again if he ever heard of them troubling Miz Thompson, or anybody else, for that matter.

And folks said that was when Rick Simmons decided he wanted to be the high sheriff.

So Nole had gone to Cal Boarder, the chief deputy, a man who wouldn't balk at taking on Jem Craishot, as long as the odds were good. Boarder was a good shot, a big bluff man, with a streak of the adventurer in him. So he was the man for Nole's plan.

Nole had believed the whole scheme would show Merv that he was a man, unafraid of Jem, able to handle himself. Meanwhile, it would solve the difficulties over money. With the reward, they would be able to go off and be married, as they both had dreamed. And Jem would be out of the way. Besides, he now felt he had something more to prove. Because his father had pushed him: refusing money that Nole knew the man had and, instead, laughing at him, saying he ought to be able to figure this one out himself. He thought of his father's voice: *Man runnin' from the law ain't got no friends. Ain't got nothin'. Only thing this one's got is a price on his head, ain't that right? Whut's a'matter with you?* That was it. His father had made him feel that it was easy and logical. Just get Jem—who objected to the romance anyway—out of the way, and pick up a pocketful of money, and the problems were all over.

iii.

Hogeye listened to his own legs splashing in the shallow water. He was getting chilled, his fingers stiffening and beginning to burn in the frosted air, and the water felt warm, now, when he submerged his hands again. *It's cold as hell yet on my feet, and it's warmer'n a hog's blood on my durn fingers*, he thought. He was having some difficulty getting the clumsy trap to lie right, in the water, *so's the rat ain't a'goin' draw it up on the bank, leave me nothin' but luck*. He had caught more than a few three-footed muskrats in his life, creatures that had escaped once, dragging traps up onto the land. There they could gain a purchase and slash through their own flesh, snapping off the trapped bones at the joint and severing the paw with one or two harsh, clenched closings of those powerful jaws. *And that's a'goin' to be nothin' but bad luck, seein' as how a rat's foot ain't no rabbit's foot. Not by a heck of a sight.*

At last he had found the right set, and he prodded the trap into the still water, his hands feeling nubbed and clumsy but not really needing anything of dexterity now, because he knew the balance and heft of the trap, knew its slow, foundering way of seeking its own spot in the water, the way he knew how to keep a huge double-blade axe weightless—by swinging it down first, letting the movement itself draw the heavy steel blade upward, never stopping to let it catch up to its own ponderous heft. *Onliest time you ought ever to feel a axe is heavy is before you get to commencin' and after you've done finished*, his daddy would say to him. *Iffen you're a'workin' it, it oughtn't to weigh no more'n a warble.*

And so he had found a slanted rock, four inches below the surface, where the trap would settle and remain until the muskrat would spring it, and animal and trap would collaborate to pull themselves off the rock and into deeper water. He wouldn't have admitted it, but he took a certain comfort in knowing that a good set meant the animal would pull the trap over on top of itself, and this would hasten the drowning. *Do it right, she don't suffer much.*

He notched the trap jaws, having to spring back suddenly when his hand slipped and the teeth *statched* shut, throwing up a little explosion of silvered water. He cursed but went smoothly and methodically back to work, getting it hung this time, and settling it onto the rock.

It was getting on toward dark when he dragged his sploshing feet from the water, stepping tentatively on the nubbins of cold flesh and bone, blowing on his fiery hands. He could smell his own cotton-wet dampness rising up from below to mix with the leaf-sharp twilight.

"I don't reckon I'd do this for fun," he said aloud. But a muskrat pelt would fetch a dollar, and he had set five good traps tonight. A muskrat is a nasty animal, *all stank and oozin's*, but it skins easily, and with its thick ridge of loose fat against the skin side, it scrapes down fast and clean. *Slicker'n a rat skin*, they'd say, as in *I'd not trust that feller; he looks slicker'n a rat skin.*

Hogeye thought, *Nole Darlen*, thinking, *that feller, it just wrangles me to think what all he's done got way with, kindly slicked it over onto the other feller's plate. That Craishot ambush, everybody knows he set that up, him and his poppy.* It appeared clear enough to Hogeye that Nole wouldn't have—couldn't have—executed any such thing on his own hook, sidestepping the sheriff by going to the on-duty deputy, luring Jem into a supposed meeting with Merv—Jem's sister. *Too complicated. Besides, Nole was stuck on her at least enough so he wouldn't set her up unless he was in trouble hisself,* thinking, *and then he wouldn't care who in hell he set up.* So, Hogeye figured, it must have been Carl Darlen who had conceived the scheme and had made—shamed—his son into carrying it forth.

You figure here's Jem Craishot, a big ole outlaw who'd got hisself out of jail, and everbody 'round here knew he'd come back thisaway, where he'd got so much family. And family or no, everybody up there liked him and would hide him from the law. And then here's Carl Darlen finds out the government has done put a big reward on Jem about the same time as he finds out Nole is makin' hay with Jem's sister. Well, Carl Darlen, he knows a money-maker when he sees one, ain't he proved that before? So I bet you fifty million dollars he cooked it up and kindly made Nole do it. And Hogeye figured Nole for enough of a coward not to say no to his father, and enough of a fool actually to waltz into a gunfight with Jem Craishot, arm-in-arm with Jem's sister.

"I don't reckon I'd do this for fun," he said again, stomping his wet feet, trying for warmth.

Hogeye had actually eaten muskrat only once, when he drove Pastor Durden up the mountain to officiate at a wedding and had been served up a hefty slab of the stuff for the celebratory dinner. The meat was deep brown, redolent, and glistening— *shipperin'*, he called it later—with grease.

We'd got into that new A-Model flatbed of mine to go on up there. I remember b'cause Preacher said he reckoned now we mayt could drive the straight 'n narrow like God intended and weren't a'goin' to have to go back'ards all the way up the mountain, takin' turns kindly standin' on the reverse pedal while the other'un rubbernecks to see where we's a'goin'.

Well I was a mite discomfirted when Preacher Durden first clombed in, because I had kindly left a two-quart jar of corn a'settin' right out there on the seat to his side. I'd plumb forgot to tuck her away, and there she was, right out in the open for Preacher to look at.

Well he didn't seem to take no matterin' about it. I kindly says, "I'm dreadful sorry, Pastor. I know I oughtn't to of had this likker. And I reckon I'd just pour it out iffen I thought it mayt do me any good. But I reckon I can't do nothin' about it now but to beg your forgiveness."

"Well now, Brother Hogeye," he says. That's just what he says: "Brother Hogeye." Can you beat that? "Well, Brother Hogeye," he says. "I don't b'lieve God spends too much of his time a'worryin' about iffen a feller takes a sup of corn now and again. Feller that works hard and goes to church and makes up his tithe and all, it ain't a'goin' to matter none in the eyes of the Lord iffen he sups a mite now and then."

So then I thinks, "Mayt be he mayt be a'wantin' a mite of this here corn hisself." Wouldn't be the first preacher ever did, I'd say that. So I kindly just nudges that fruit jar a half a inch in his direction like, show him he can snup a mite iffen he wants.

But he says, "No. No thank you, Brother Hogeye." Don't that just kill you, that Brother Hogeye? "No," he says. "It wouldn't do for me to compermise my callin' as a man of the cloth, not right before the weddin', kindly just on up the mountain. But I thank you. And don't you worry none about that corn and the Lord, you want to take a sup once 'n again after hard day." Well he was a right nice old feller, never the kind of preacher that mayt get real hard on a feller for any old thing. He always was pert sensible, for a man of the cloth.

So I tucked that jar away under the seat and stopped worryin' about it and got that A-model crunk and off we went to the weddin' away yonder across Johnson City and up them big mountains off Erwin, way up in the laurel thickets and all, up to Owen's Cove. I mean we was plumb out from town, I'll tell you.

Well now I come from mountain folks, just over to Shelton's, so I weren't too surprised at anything. And these was mountain folks, I'd say. The groom was a big ole boy, rawbone, with a snatch of hair a'standin' right up on end like it was kindly a'pointin' the way home, and the gal was about twelve year old with a hair-lip looks like they done stitched it up in the shed sometime between cuttin' and gradin'. The both of 'em was likely wearin' somethin' on their feet besides mud for the first time in their lifes.

But it don't matter. Them is good folks, I'll tell you. Treated us like we was Abraham and Isaac and the Hebrew children all rolled into one. Them cove folks'll give you ever damn thing they got iffen they think you even possibly mayt like to have it. They ain't got nothin', but they'll be tickled pink iffen they can get to watch you eat their last chicken and feed you that little slab of ham they was a'savin' for their Sund'y.

So you can bet, this bein' the big weddin' and all that, well they was kindly a'fixin' to set out the best thing they had on the whole damn ranch.

So Preacher done the weddin' and everbody said how happy they all was and then we all set down for the big weddin' dinner. And here comes Mawmaw a'totin' a big old platter full up with roasted muskrats. There weren't no doubt at all about what they was because they still kindly looked like muskrats, you know. And ain't nothin' looks like a skun muskrat but a skun muskrat. You know.

Well it smelt so bad I like to huckle right on the spot. Now I don't reckon all muskrat cooks up a'smellin' that bad. I reckon these folks had done nailed these out on a board in the sun and forgot about 'em until it was next month or so. Whatever it was, it kindly done the trick, I tell you. Phew-wee, it done the trick. Weren't much doubt but that was rankled meat.

I kindly snuck a look at the rev'rend kindly tryin' to talk to him with my eyes you know. Like tryin' to say, "You reckon this here meat'll kill us in a hour or two or is we goin' to have to suffer overnight?"

Well there weren't no question, we had to eat it. Them poor folks would of been purely shamed iffen we'd not eat their best meat. Here they had done fixed up their big weddin' supper and had made us to set right at the head of the plank, right next to the bride and groom. And they'd done put out salt risin' bread and a big bowl of soup beans and all. And that big ole platter of meat. They must of been six or seven muskrat corpses lyin' on that trencher, at least from countin' the legs you could see pokin' up here and there, all of it kindly shipperin' around in the grease.

So there weren't nothin' for it but to eat the stuff, what with Gran'maw and Gran'paw and Aunt Whojigger and all a'settin' there lookin' at us like they'd done just give us the prize bull. But I tell you it skeert me to put any of that into my mouth. I seen one or two folks got into bad meat, and it weren't no candy-pullin', I'll tell you.

So they's all a'gazin' up the plank at Pastor Durden with that meat a'steamin' up into the whole room, and Pawpaw asks Pastor would you honor us by givin' the blessin'. So the preacher gets hisself up right slow, kindly eyin' that big ole platter like it was a rattlesnake or somepin. And he says, "Dear God."

"Dear God," he says. "We thank you for bringin' together all this here fambly for to witness to the joyful union of young Whojigger and this dear girl. And we ask you to bless this here food that we are a'fixin' to receive. We ask you to bless this here food real good. For Jesus sake. Watch over them that's about to eat this here bounty with your most tender mercy and care. Keep all us folks safe in thy healin' power, and Lord forgive us anything we mayt of done to pervoke your wrath. Dear God. For Christ's sake. Amen."

And he set right down. And they fotched us each up a grat big ole hunk of that muskrat. And I tell you it had to of been settin' out in the hot sun for a month, or maybe it'd lied in that trap in the swump water for six weeks before anybody'd remembered that it was what we was a'goin' to eat at the big weddin' supper so run down and fotch it back up here this mornin'.

And Preacher, he tucked right into her, shovellin' down grat forkfuls of that stuff, just a'gollopin' it down without hardly chewin' on it, kindly like a hound dog would, like he couldn't eat it fast enough. And about pert near ever four bites, he mumpfuls out, "Dee-licious," or, "That's some fine eatin', ma'am." And right back to the fork he goes. And they was right tickled to see how much he was enjoyin' his muskrat meat. You could see it made 'em all happier'n Billy in the lowground. And so they grabbed another big ole glob of that meat and dropped it on his plate, and he went after it the same way, like he just couldn't get enough of it. Well, I reckon that's what makes him a preacher, ain't it?

Me, I'd gawge me off a little glibber of that meat, and I'd grab two fat pieces of that salt risin' bread and kindly wrop 'em around my piece of muskrat. And I'd dip it in the bean likker. But even then you couldn't taste nothin' but critter, and that grease that kindly stuck to your tongue and all round inside your mouth and your gullet like. It really was the awfullest thing I ever put within a half a mile of my teeth, I'll tell you that.

"He shore likes that salt risin' bread, don't he?" Gran'maw says, happy as hell, and starts to pushin' what's prob'ly their last loaf at me. Which was just fine and dandy with me, under the circumstances. And they're all a'settin' there eatin' down that muskrat like it's a pheasant on the half shell, or what have you, best food anybody'd ever dreamed of. And down to our end, there's Pastor Durden a'shovin' that stuff in his mouth and bobbin' his head up and down and a'mumblin' "Dee-licious" ever twenty-two seconds.

So you ask me iffen I ever have eat muskrat, I got to say I have. Now, tell you the truth, I'm right certain it was bad muskrat. It was kindly clabbered, and that's a surety. So I ain't never eat any good muskrat. Iffen there is any such thing to speak of.

Well now, we finally got outen that place, after we done shook everbody's hand fifteen or twenty times and congrattylated the happy couple and all that. And we made it out into the truck, and I didn't give a damn about ceremony nor preacher nor *nothin': I just kindly slid that fruit jar out from under the seat and wrasted her open and poured a batch down, kindly slooshin' it around to scowge that grease outen my mouth if it was at all possible. And I handed the jar to the preacher. I weren't rightly sure I should, but I figured we was most likely both a'goin' to be dead in a few minutes so it weren't a'goin' to matter much one way or the t'other. And anyways, he done snatched it from me like it was the Book of Revelation.*

After a minute, I kindly looked over at him. "Tell me, Preacher," I says. "Flat out. Did you really like that meat yonder that you was shovellin' down your throat like lye down the sump hole? And tell them how dee-licious it was? Was you atchually tellin' them the truth about how you liked it?"

"Oh yessir," he says. "I couldn't lie to them kind folks. I liked it. I did." Then he turned up that jar of white likker and took three grat big ole swallers, one-two-three, just like that. "Oh," he says. "I couldn't lie to them." And he lets out a enormous gurglin' baalch. Like a heifer with the glanders. "I liked it, sure enough." And he starts to hand me back the jar. Then he stops and kindly looks down into it.

"But I tell you one thing, Brother Hogeye," he says. And he takes another purty fair pull on that moonshine. "I didn't like it very God damn much."

iv.

Hogeye had no interest in anything but working fast, on this chilling evening. *Just let's get 'em set, get on outen here.* He was a good trapper, so there was none of the despaired hope, the drop of doubt that dogged most trappers waiting through a night of complete inaction, because the hunt was going on without the hunter—was, instead, a struggle taking place entirely within the mind of the animal itself. It was a battle between the muskrat's wary, intelligent individuality and its automatic, inherent regulating drives: the profundities of instinct operating beyond individuality, the deep resolves of repetition and routine. This is where the struggle would take place, and so the trapper would wait through the night, hoping always for the victory of the routine—the deterministic, instinctual drives that said *follow this path, go into the river here, feed thus, behave as a muskrat—* that would carry the animal into the teeth of the trap, set to accord with the habits of the species.

Even so, the trapper who set his lines based entirely on this reading of the animal's indefinite instinct would not be a successful trapper. Because the very best trappers, who certainly would have to know what muskrats could be invariably relied upon to do, night after night, must also know what some particular muskrat might choose to do when, tonight, it is confronted with the scent of doubt. And more. The best trapper had to know how to counter the one animal—not *they*, but *he*—who could escape the trap only by denying the predelicted instinct and by improvising, willing, acting as only an individual, a self, can act, choosing, for the sake of his own solitary life, to break the intricate mechanics of instinct, ticking away, as synchronous as clockwork, and to choose. *Tonight, I smell doubt. Tonight, I must not act as he knows I will; tonight, I will choose to step here and not there.* This is the battle the expert trapper will fight, internally himself, too, since hunter and animal will not meet. Each will play this game in the complete absence of his opponent, the one thinking, wondering about what could happen later tonight, selecting, setting, laying, and covering entirely within the realm of hope, anticipation. The other, shifting and investigating, suspecting, wondering *what has happened earlier tonight*, responding, improvising, reordering entirely within the realm of regret, consequence.

And Hogeye could win these struggles, these absentee battles fought out between instinct and improvisation. He knew how to listen to his prey, how to build on the basic knowledge, the behavior he could count on from the muskrat *because it's what makes him a muskrat, just like me, settin' here fixin' to kill him without ever bein' here to see the killin' done, I reckon that's what makes me a man. So I know already what he's a'goin' to do because he's a muskrat. Now I got to kindly figure out what he'll do because he's this muskrat, the one feller out there that I'm a'fixin' to trap. Just like he'll smell a man and he'll know how a man'll try to kill him, bein' as how that's what he can count on a man doin'. But now it's right here and it's now, to-night, and so he needs to start figurin' on this man, the one fell-er out there that's done set this here trap, tonight.*

And so they are like two good musicians, fiddle and banjo, both knowing the tune and both knowing what a fiddle and a five-string can be counted on to sound like. But now it's listen and learn who this banjo picker is, and what does he do that no one else has done on this tune, in this place, and how will you draw a little harder on this bow stroke or slide off this note a bit, because you can feel what he is going to do you've never heard done before. And so you work up this version of the tune, one of you playing to the improvisations of the other. So by now, Hogeye and the muskrat are both focused on the one thing, the single six inches of water and rock that holds this trap, and both working up the tune together, so there are no muskrats or men, either, anymore, just these two, unique, individual, weaving a fine mental maze of turn and counterturn around this trap, this water, this night, these two.

As he bent to straighten his sodden pant leg around his brogans, Hogeye's eyes snapped into focus upon an oblong, creased, and stained package of brown oilcloth, about hand-sized. It was lying on the damp, dark earth beneath a small bramble bush, about three feet off the trail where Hogeye was bent down. He never would have spotted the thing if it hadn't been for the single diamond-shaped glint of light that had drawn his brain to focus prior to his own knowing, seeking, anything. So it was some profound instinctive response to the presence of even this minuscule spark of light glanced from a brown booklet lying in darkened solitude, in the dimming twilight, suddenly composing the entire scene, centered on this singled object, reorganizing bramble and wet earth, pebble and sodden bits of decayed vegetation set autonomically into relationship with this booklet now taking dominion everywhere through the primitive ticking somewhere in the stem of his brain. *Look.*

Because it was a book, wrapped in cold brown oilcloth, because someone had wanted to keep it enough that he—or more likely she—had measured and cut and folded this protective cover, a measure itself against the very fondness that would carry it into danger. She had known that the book, being of such importance to her, would consequently find itself carried about and used in the broad, dangerous world, so inimical to tender paper and watery ink. She knew that the very affection she felt for the little thing—this rectangle of delicate pages stitched in cob linen—would subject it to hazard and dissolution. And so she had formed this hopeful shield against her own passionate handling. So it was no longer just a booklet; it was *this* booklet.

And so this oilskin, which announced the endangered condition of its contents in the first place, saying *I am this book that will be carried and used, subject to damage* had, in fact, been harbinger of its incongruous presence here, on an island, beneath a bramble.

"Looky here," said Hogeye, dropping to his knees and fetching the thing, drawing it carefully along under the overhanging thorns until it was clear and he could raise it along with himself back up into the dusky sky light along the path. "Looky here."

It was a hymn book. He recognized it instantly, having seen untold numbers of the same volume, printed somewhere by the tens of thousands in the huge northern city on the enormous lake, two day's travel from anyone who might actually put it to use— the songbook, with its gospel melodies laid out in triangles and squares, circles and diamonds, and even Hogeye had learned, been trained, the *fasola*, so that, right now, in these sodden overalls on this river bank, in the fading light of day, he could have opened the book to any page and sung whatever song came up: "Camping in Canaan," or "Where the Soul Never Dies," or "The Royal Telephone," not even aware of whether or not he was reading the shaped notes or simply remembering the tune and its *fasola* text, singing, *mi mi mi re do re mi re,* because he had heard it, sung it himself, as often as he had heard, sung *out of Egypt I have traveled...*

But, he reminded himself, running his thumb over the slicksticky oilcloth, it was not a hymn book, but *this* hymn book. And so in order to confirm the fact, that out of a positive ubiquity of copies—he could assuredly have gone into any country church for a hundred miles around and put his hands on fifty or sixty copies in each place, so if he wanted one he could simply have walked off with it, even taken a spare, and the owners themselves would have wished him joy and good use of his new books—out of this plenitude of hymnals, here was one.

He opened the cover and peered down at the flyleaf, where he read the faint, waterbled inscription, and said, "Well I'll be God damned."

Merv Craishot. MY BOOK. 1926.

"I'll be God damned," he said again, staring at the flyleaf, blank except for these four words and the date in orbic, schoolgirl's hand. And, in a flash, he saw it again, the thing he'd been seeing over and over for these past three or four years, though he hadn't been there to see it when it actually happened, hadn't even known she was there until later, when he had heard that part of the story and had begun seeing it: the pretty, scant girl, probably dressed still in her school clothes *although I reckon she'd had 'em off at least once that week*, and he hushed himself, not wanting to hear himself think that way about her—*or else fixin' to later*—and shushed himself again. *Or at least he was*, he thought, and that was all right, because he, Nole Darlen, was the one to blame for it, the ambush, all of it, and thinking about him this way was about the only way there was to think, and this way he, Hogeye, wasn't disparaging the dead, *that poor little gal*. The girl must have been excited and a little anxious: her brother was, after all, an outlaw and a fugitive, even if he was just Jemmy, and she was here with Nole Darlen and she knew Jem wouldn't like that, didn't like him. But Jem had agreed to meet with her, to say hello and to be a part—albeit hidden and too brief—of this event, this graduation that he was so proud of: *My little sis, who'd of thought I'd be seein' her to be graduatin' high school?*

All of this, Hogeye had learned from the papers, like everyone else: that Jem had come back into the area, running from the law in Mississippi, and the folks out his way had hidden him out. That he had wanted to see his sister, to help her celebrate, and they had arranged to meet on Long Island, in the evening, where he wouldn't be seen. But someone had tipped the law off—not going to Sheriff Simmons, but to his chief deputy, a loud, brawling man named Cal Boarder. And Boarder had rounded up four others, rowed out to the island and waited in the brush, been laying for Jem. And Hogeye could imagine it, her bright eyes, young, eager, and Nole Darlen standing there with her, on the island. And Jem appearing, maybe a little furtive, but glad, happy to see Merv. Maybe narrowing his eyes in Nole's direction, maybe thinking *I got a few things to say to him, too.*

And then the sudden noises—and Hogeye had actually heard these, the actual gunshots, too, because he'd been that close, laying traps right over here that day, too, just a piece further down the island; so the memory of the gunfire was real enough: one, two, three separate shots, then a pause, then a fusillade, too many to count, all going off together. Then another pause and two more separate concussions. He had heard all of this as he stood knee-deep in the water, a trap hanging from his hand. And maybe that's why he kept seeing her, because he had been so close and had not seen her, hadn't even known she was there.

So his memory saw things he'd never actually witnessed: the men, shooting and cursing; Jem instinctively returning fire, turning and shooting in one motion, and hitting three men with three shots.

But what Hogeye saw clearest, and had seen again and again, was the girl, Merv. And it may seem impossible to remember what you have not seen. But Hogeye knew it was impossible to forget at the same time: Merv Craishot. The startled shock and the instinctive glance toward her older brother, Jem, who would know what the gunfire meant, what to do. And then perhaps the rough hand pushing her, shoving her aside. *Why is Jem shoving me so hard?* The hurt and resistance to this sudden assault from the brother she had looked to for aid, and there was no way to know that he was pushing her out of danger's way, since she hadn't yet come to any consciousness of hazard. So it was still only surprise and then anger, perhaps, at her brother's sudden brutishness. And so perhaps Merv turned to Nole Darlen now for support, explanation of the terrible noise, and retaliation for Jem's rough rudeness. And he was not there. He had disappeared entirely, as though these loud detonations had been the accompaniment to some sort of conjuring act. Or perhaps she caught a glimpse of his fleeing form, the swift shape already blending into the scrubbed sedge and thorns of the island's edge, already running.

And then Jem, again, Merv's gaze jerking back to him, and now he had the pistol in his hand, and he pushed her again and hollered, "Git!" and then, "Git, Merv, goddammit," and then she could only see his mouth moving as he fired the shot that killed Cal Boarder, and the blast wiped out everything, everything but the fear, and she turned and ran, shrieking. She was crying out, but she couldn't hear herself over the gunshots swelling and thrusting across her sense, across the island and the sky, pushing her, shoving her along just as Jem's brute hand had. Only this time it wasn't outrage, it was sheer, shrieking terror.

And so Hogeye stood here, now, in the insect-gnawed twilight of the island bank, holding the carefully wrapped hymnal with her girl's writing, proudly, assertively, MY BOOK, and he now saw the rest of it, in close flashes. The young, terrified girl, scratched and frantic, throwing herself under these brambles beside the river, curling into the slight space, caught here and there on the tearing thorns. *And she was likely cryin'*, he thought with a terrible pang.

And he already knew the rest, how she had somehow gotten herself back home, entirely on her own, and how they had bundled her off—or perhaps she had done this herself, too, sent herself away—beyond Chimney Top, out of reach *of the law, or of Nole Darlen, both*. And how, later that year, she had died in childbirth, at the age of seventeen, crying out in her suffering not for the father, Nole Darlen, who had turned and run from her on this island—*the last she'd ever seed of him, leavin' that poor gal out here alone*—crying out not for him but for the brother, Jem, who had gone into hiding because he had killed the chief deputy and another man in the shootout, and a third he had wounded, crippled for life.

V.

Hogeye had told the story about a week after the shootout. Jem Craishot had gone to cover, and the whole town was abuzz with the news. So it was something to have been on the scene, or close to it. And, besides, Hogeye had information that hadn't been in the press.

Well I was down on the river, and I done heard all the gunshots. It was a regular bust-up, I'd say. And I says, "You just stay right here, Hogeye, and read it in the papers. You ain't improvin' nothin' by goin' on up there and gettin' shot by the bad guys. Or the good guys, one." So I just stayed put and let 'em shoot each other. And after them gunshots kindly quieted down, they was all sorts of hollerin' and cussin', and you could kindly imagine five or six fellers a'runnin' around half outen they heads and wavin' them guns around, gettin' ready to shoot each other because everbody who ain't this'un must be the one this'un is scared is fixin' to gun him down. So I stayed put some more. I come up outen the water—I'd been settin' me some traps—and I thought, "Maybe I'd be a purty good target for a stray bullet standin' out here in the river." So I clumb on up the bank onto the path. Right down the far end of the island. Just gettin' on real dusk.

They was up there around the railroad pass. I reckon you

read the same papers I done: Jem, he was fixin' to see his sister
once b'fore he took on outen here, on the run, and she somehow
told him to meet her down on the island. And they was a'waitin'
on him when he showed up. Chief depitty—Cal Boarder, you
know—four more.

I reckon them law was purty scared, even if they was the
fellers that had done set up the ambuscade in the first place. I
reckon they didn't want to give him no chance to give up, for
fear he'd just commence to usin' that pistol he could use the
way other folks'll handle a knife and fork maybe.

Jem, he weren't a bad kid at all. Nice young feller, everbody
said so. Always happy to see folks, always jokin' around like. I
liked him what little I knowed of him. It just seems like he
couldn't keep hisself out of a scrape where he'd kindly have to
start killin' folks. He'd done already killed a feller out west
before this here, so this'un'll make three. Three-and-a-half, you
mayt say, what with poor old Luke skumpled up for the rest of
his life. So you can't dezactly call him "a nice young man"
who's done happened to kill three, three-and-a-half men by the
time he's got to be twenty year old. Can you?

But still, iffen what they're a'sayin' is true, ever last one of
them fellers was a'layin' for Jem, fixin' to get the jump on him.
And this time, somebody set it up, and I ain't a goin' to say
who. And the feller set it up knew goddamn well not to go to
Sheriff Simmons with the idea, because he wouldn't cotton to
none such a thing, but to work kindly around behint his back, go
to the depitty when sheriff weren't around, set it up thataway.
Set up or not, I reckon them law didn't know, or didn't figure
anyhow, about how Jem could shoot the eyeballs outen a jay
bird whilst he was peelin' up taters to fry for dinner. Because he
weren't only a crack shot. You take the crackedest shot you
ever seen and put him on the back of a half-broke mustang and
maybe give him a bowl of grits to hold on to and make sure it
don't get spilt. And ast him could he please knock them eyes
outen that jay bird whenever he got a free second. That was
Jem Craishot, I'll tell you.

So they either didn't know or they was damn fools. Tryin' to set up and gun down a feller like that. No. Jem never went huntin' no trouble. It just seemed to kindly keep on a'comin' back and a'huntin' him. So I reckon he just naturally shot them fellers down without ever stoppin' to think too much about it, you know? The way you and me would kindly swat us a fly or two?

Well, anyways, they was a'settin' for him right out by that railroad pass. Merv—that's his sister—and Nole Darlen had fixed up to meet Jem there, so he could see his sis. Now once you find out Nole's involved in somepin, even if it's just to stand around holdin' the hats, which is about what he done told everbody was all he was doin' up there. Like I said, once you knowed Nole Darlen has got within a mile of it, you figure it's too damn close for anybody else. And I reckon by now everbody has done figured out how them deppities knowed just where to set in the particular spot with they guns all drawed right when Jem shows up to give his sis a little peck on the cheek and say congraddylations. She had done finished high school, which is about like gettin' elected president to them folks out toward Chimney Top. It don't happen to one of 'em ever day, you know. So Jem, he was tickled and he was a'goin' to make sure to see Merv, fugitive or no fugitive. And I reckon if he knowed Darlen'd be there with her, well, that'd give him the opportunity to kindly bust Nole's skull a mite for runnin' with his little sister, wouldn't it?

So there Jem was. He had a thousand-dollar reward out on him, too, so I reckon that sounded all right to them deppities, not to mention to that rat that set him up in the first place. But I found out about that, all about that, on that very day, after all them fellers got tired of shootin'.

Because like I said, I was a'standin' on the bank, there, just had clumb up outen the water where I'd made me a set. And I could hear them boys a'shoutin' and cursin' on up the island. And I weren't thinkin' about nothin' but keepin' myself from gettin' shot by whoever it was mayt think I was whoever the

*other feller was. And here come Nole Darlen just a'tearin' down
that path toward me. And I mean he was on the hop.*

*Now like I say, I was wary about gettin' myself gunned
down, so I weren't too happy to see him. But he catches eye onto
me and gives out a yalp like he done saw the Final Cast and he
dives in the bushes off the path there, gets hisself all snarled up in
briars and he's a whinin' and a'whimperin' like he done just read
his name in the Book, what have you. So I weren't too worried
about him. I decided he mustn't have a gun hisself or he would
of already shot me by accident. Or hisself, one. So I weren't
none too excited by then. But, buddy, he sure was.*

*"What in hell's goin' on up there, Nole?" I says. "Git up
outen them bushes. You crazy, somepin? What in hell's all the
shootin'?"*

*And he kindly screenches hisself outen them bushes. And he
didn't look good, I'll tell you. Big-eyed. And scared. Scareder'n a
guinea hen in a hailstorm. And it was crazy-scared. You know?
Like a feller that keeps askin' you what time is it, and you can
tell he ain't listenin' to the answer, so he's still askin' you what
time is it when the train has done already rolled out. You know?*

*And he starts in jabbering right along, so fast you couldn't
much tell what he was sayin'. More like he had somethin'
crawlin' around in his mouth, the way he was workin' it. And
after a while, I come to realize he was talkin' about the fracas he
just done got out of and how it weren't right to take his information and use his plan for the whole setup and then just up
and shoot him without givin' him a chance to get outen the
way, like.*

*So I says, "You been shot?" But he don't even stop talkin'.
He gets goin' on somepin about "Daddy said this," and he just
better get his thousant or they'd see who they was a'dealin' with,
and more of that sort of talk. So I says again, a mite louder,
"You shot?"*

*"You're goddamn right I'm shot," he says and goes right
back into it about how Daddy said, "Call Cal Boarder and you'll
have that reward in your pocket," somepin like. And about how*

*he done set the whole thing up and them dirty bastards shot him.
That's just what he said, "them dirty bastards."*

*Well he was right scared and like I says, kindly wild-eyed, so
I reckon he mayt of thought they'd done shot him somewheres.
But I tell you, I didn't see nothin' looked like he'd been shot.
Oh, he was kindly tore up from jumpin' into them thrashers
and thorn bushes ever time he decided they was fixin' to shoot
him again. He didn't look none too pert, I'd say. But shot? I
reckon not.*

*So he went on about how them dirty bastards was fixin' to
get him and get theyselves outen havin' to give him that thousant
dollars. And he says, "Whyn't they just get a bead on Jem and
shoot him down when he first come in there, like I told 'em to?"
And then he stops and looks at me like am I goin' to answer him
or not? Kindly peeved, like why in hell doesn't I tell him?*

*And I says, "Jem?" And he's still lookin' at me like that. So
I says, "Jem?" again.*

*And he hollers out real loud, "Jem Craishot, you dern son of
a bitch." And right after, from on up the island, you could hear
somebody yell, you know, like a hound that done caught scent.
"Arr he is," or some such. I reckon they heard Nole Darlen
a'hollerin' at me. And next I knowed, he was in the dern crick
and paddlin' across like a burr mill on the fly. And that was that.*

*You know, he never once said a word about that poor gal.
None of 'em did, 'til later, after they found out they own skins
was safe and sound. Not a single word—*

bramble and nobody And today, Hogeye looks at the small
hymnal, its sad little oilskin cover, and he thinks, *That little girl
all skownched down under that to give a good damn what's
become of her or is she all right. The one blastin' his way
through that pile of deppities, and the other runnin' off like a
busted flywheel, scared to death about his own hide. Who set it
all up, Nole and his daddy, I reckon, in the first place. And
didn't never think too much about what mayt happen to her*

even away back in the settin' up. So I reckon she was just on her own.

Didn't do a bad job of it, did she? I reckon she lay there and cried, frightened outen her wits. Just as scared as any of them rounders who think they was so tough. And here she is. 'Til it got good dark, I reckon. Then picked herself up and got herself home somehow. Made her own way fifteen, twenty mile out to Chimney Top. And Hogeye saw it again—this new part—the young girl, huddled and afraid, tucked under the arch of brambles.

Well, and then they weren't none of them there eight month later when she was a'tryin' to have the feller's baby was they? Poor girl a'layin' out there dyin', with a baby that rat give her. I reckon she done took care of that, too, all on her own. And he said aloud, "Well, damn all."

He drew a handkerchief and wiped the oilskin cover, then tucked the booklet carefully into his dry shirt pocket and turned along the path, thinking, *I'll get this out to her folks. Maybe they'll be wantin' to keep hold of it.* He stopped. For a moment, he didn't move at all, didn't appear even to breathe. Then he reached the book back out of his pocket and flapped it open with one hand. In the still twilight, he could only just see the words.

Merv Craishot. MY BOOK. 1926.

He closed the book and stood again. Then he stepped back along the trail, back toward the river.

When he found the spot, he dropped to his knees and carefully pushed the hymn book back into place, in the darkness below the curve of bramble. He rose, wiped both hands along the thighs of his overalls, and turned for home in the gathering dark.

CHAPTER SIX

SUNSET

High sheriff told his deputy,
Go fetch down Lazarus.
High Sheriff told his deputy,
Go fetch down Lazarus.
Fetch him down dead or alive, boys,
Bring him down dead or alive.

Deputy said to the sheriff,
Where in the world will I find him?
Deputy said to the sheriff,
Where in the world will I find him?
Sheriff said, I don't know, boys,
Lord, I just don't know.

Today they found old Lazarus
Found him between two mountains.
Today they found old Lazarus
Found him between two mountains.
Blowed poor Lazarus down, boys,
Shot poor Lazarus down.

Everyone's a' cryin' for Lazarus,
Laid on the coolin' counter.
Everyone's a' cryin' for Lazarus,
Laid on the coolin' counter.
Shot with a forty-four gun, boys,
Killed with a forty-four gun.

—Grayson's Magic City String Band, 1929

i.

Nole had played no part whatever in the events following what came to be called the "Long Island shootout." The papers carried the story of Cal Boarder's and Sam Tompkins's deaths, and of Jem's "desperate escape," though there was little about the details of the actual ambush. Meanwhile, Nole had made several efforts to find Merv the following week, but each time had been turned away by armed men in brogans and overalls before he even began the climb up the slope of Chimney Top. "You stay in hell away from her," they had said. "And that don't mean just for today."

He had been heartsick and spent the following week going over and over the overwhelming fact of his own betrayal of the young woman he loved. *Whywhywhy?* He continually asked himself. He was incapable of understanding how he had come to believe capturing Jem, by the "strategy" of exploiting Merv's confidence in himself, would lead to the blissful end he had envisaged. And with the realization that all had gone wrong—two deaths, and Jem on the run, and Merv as removed from him as if she'd been on another planet—Nole was inconsolable, stunned, and bewildered. He stayed at home, reclusive, for most of the next few months. Then, Merv was gone for good and, gradually, Nole began turning up at Ketterling's and at local dances, usually already drunk. In short, he began to resume the life he'd led before Merv came along. And the very pain of separation helped drive him to forget about the young woman who had died, alone, up there, somewhere on the west slope of Chimney Top Mountain.

Jem had swum the river that day, his gunbelt wrapped around one arm, held high above the skirling water. He left Cal Boarder and Sam Tomkins dead, and the third deputy critically wounded, and he had forgotten Nole and Merv, both, in the need to get away. He had spent that first night at his uncle's house, on Blair's Creek, then had merged into the woods and coves of Chimney Top Mountain.

Thus began the largest manhunt in the region's history, in part because of the scores of local and county police officers sent out with the distinctly unhappy task of "scouring" hill, homestead, and hollow, searching for a desperate young man who was well-armed and easily able to outshoot any of them. Meanwhile, the residents of the area—many of them openly sympathetic to the fugitive—were not at all likely to take easily to having their barns and outbuildings "scoured."

As a result, more than one lawman was faced with the sort of situation confronted by Deputy Lon Palmer in the mountains above the Nolichucky River. Palmer had spent a hot day searching the area for Jem; in fact, Lon himself had been lost most of the time, stumbling up trails and traces in the thick, steep country. Finally, he found himself working up a declivitous, rutted lane that doubled and switched every twenty yards—so much that he'd become convinced he was simply walking round and round one gigantic, deeply jungled mountain. As the tones of late afternoon filtered through the leaves, he rounded another sharp cut and stopped, startled.

Standing about fifteen yards up the new offing, a shoeless

man in dirty tan overalls peered down at Palmer through deep, hollow eyes, shaded by an outlandishly broad-brimmed hat. He might have looked like a clown of some sort were it not for the wide-bore double barrel of a sawed-off eight-gauge shotgun he pointed, from his hip, directly at the deputy.

Palmer immediately dropped his own carbine onto the trail and raised his hands. "Iffen you'd think I'd try and outshoot that big old scattergun," he said later, "you can think somethin' else. If he'd let go with even one of them barrels, he'd of turned me into a damn pie safe. That and kill six or seven birds and rabbit or two, and the same time. And maybe git him a bear over yonder hillside."

The man glared down the slope, still holding the shotgun aimed from his hip. He said nothing. Palmer opened his hands and tried to assume a friendly expression.

"Howdy, friend," he said.

"Git," the man said.

The two stood in silence for a moment. Palmer said the sweat had broken and run off his brows. "But I was afeared to wipe my eyes. They was a'waterin' up right smart, but I figured iffen I'd tried to wipe 'em with my bandanner, I mayt get it to my face and find nothin' to wipe but the hole that feller had just blowed in it, kindly. So I jest stood there and blinked at him, a'lookin' up with this feller kindly swimmin' and blearin' around through the sweat and the tears. It weren't no barn dance, I'll tell you."

Palmer said he tried to do his job.

"We're jest up around these parts a'huntin' a feller that killed a couple deputies down to Roalton," he told the man. "You ain't seen nobody up this way, has you?"

"Git," the man said.

Palmer said the man seemed to work very hard dragging back the hammers on the two barrels, "like as if they was stuck in a boar waller." For the first time, he said, he was genuinely afraid. "I reckon them hammers was pert old, and I was jest as sure one of 'em was a'fixin' to slip and go off whilst he was a fightin' it back. When I heard them lock, boys, I was a happy man. I figures, 'Well, at least he ain't a'goin' to shoot me on accident.' That ain't too much to feel good about, is it?"

Palmer raised his hands high over his head and said, "Now listen, neighbor. I ain't a'goin' to bother you no longer. I done asked my question, and I'm right sure you would of told me iffen they was anything I oughter know, kindly." He began to back gradually down the trail, feeling his way with his feet. "So I reckon I done my job and I'll jest kindly stroll on outen here. I ain't come to bother none of your'n. I'm jest a poor old boy tryin' to carry out my duties."

"Git," said the man.

At this, Palmer turned and fled, leaving his weapon, and careening crazily down the slope, racing for the switchback. Later, he said, "When I come round the bend, outen line of that shotgun, I reckon that next stretch of trail was about the purtiest view I ever seen."

ii.

In addition to all the police from differing jurisdictions looking for the fugitive, a numberless legion of vigilantes, thrill-seekers, and reward-hunters joined in the search for Jem. This unsupervised, untrained, and often highly intoxicated group caused major headaches for Sheriff Simmons, who found himself spending as much time disarming drunks as hunting outlaws. Three days after the Long Island Ambush, two of these soi-disant bounty hunters lay dead, killed—in separate incidents—by overeager members of their own hunting parties. The following day, a third man was seriously wounded by a farmer near Chimney Top and, two days later, a fourth kicked into a liquor still and was killed by a frightened moonshiner.

"Jesus," Simmons said. "We're fixin' to have us fifty million shootin' matches if we can't straighten all these boys out." The entire project was already such a headache, he declared, "I'd just as lief go hide out somewhere with Jem my own self, wait for all these boys to shoot each other, and then maybe the two of us could come back down here and have us a little peace and quiet, kindly."

Along with the lawmen and reward-hunters, there was a third group seeking revenge. These were the brothers of Cal Boarder, the man who had led the Long Island Ambush, had fired its first shot, and had been killed within seconds by Jem's immediate, almost instinctive, response.

Like Cal, the surviving Boarder brothers were yard-men with a reputation around Roalton for toughness—or at least belligerence—and when they vowed they'd kill "that Craishot bastard," nobody doubted they'd go after Jem as soon as Cal's funeral ended. Nor did anyone doubt they'd bring as much firepower as they could carry.

On the afternoon following Cal's burial, Sheriff Simmons rode over to what he called "Boarder Country," though it was actually a sprawling upstairs apartment over a feed store north of Twelve Corners. He expected to find the four Boarder brothers together, loading their weapons and handing around a jar or two of white liquor, and he wanted at least to make an attempt at stopping them from exacerbating an already impossible situation by going out after Jem.

The sheriff climbed an open gray wooden stair in the building's rear and rattled at the screen door, saying, "Sheriff Simmons. Want to talk with you boys," to a group of shadowy figures he could see sitting around a table.

"Come on," one responded, and Simmons swung into the room. He stopped a moment, drawing air. The room was breathlessly hot.

He had been right: the four brothers were gathered on crude chairs around an oak table, shoving a jar of liquor back and forth. The room was bare, except for the table and chairs and occasional black scrawls—mostly obscene—drawn on the wainscot with charcoal. Someone had nailed a cat's skin to the back wall, and two rifles leaned into the near corner. A third lay askew on the table itself, next to a large box of cartridges, while Elliot, the youngest brother, cradled a carbine in the crook of an elbow and tipped up the jar with his left hand.

"You got bidnits with us?" he said to Simmons, who made note that the brothers had done nothing to hide the illegal alcohol from his gaze. He realized at that moment, he said later, that he was wasting his time.

"I just come here to have a little talk about this here Jem Craishot problem," Simmons said. "And to pay my respects, your brother's memory."

He stayed a few minutes longer and tried to warn the brothers not to "get carried away," saying, "I got enough problems with ever Harry and Dick out there a huntin' that Craishot boy. I don't need to worry about you fellers a'gunnin' for him."

Lennox, the eldest of the brothers, pointed a finger at Simmons. "Sheriff," he said, "He killed my brother Cal, and I'll find him and kill him. That's that. You jest see iffen I don't."

"Don't forget," said Simmons. "Your brother laid for that boy and shot at him outen a ambush. Iffen Cal had come to me with all this in the first place, like he was supposed to, he'd be a'settin' right there with you boys, a'tippin' that jar. They's a heap would say Jem shot him in self-defense."

There was a long moment of silence.

"Besides, boys," the sheriff said. "You know I could just take and run you all in for drinkin' that moonshine, if I'd a mind."

Lennox reached for the jug.

"I reckon you'd best get along, Sheriff," he said, tipping the jar as he talked, the clear liquid running down and dropping off his chin. "Before we has us some trouble."

So it had been a hard, nerve-wracking week for Simmons. He had "half the state out a'huntin' Jem," he said, "while the other half is a'hidin' him out." Because he knew, too, that Jem was probably right up on Chimney Top, "tucked into some bear holler," and being fed and protected by friends and family. "He ain't kin to more'n four-thirds of the folks up thataway," the sheriff said. Meanwhile, there were lawmen, and everyone else, spread out across three counties, looking for a man they had extremely little chance of finding. "Or of catchin', neither, without gettin' they heads blowed off."

Thursday afternoon, Simmons was on the narrow canvas cot in his office when he was awakened by a phone call. He had been out all of Wednesday night, trying to unsnarl a series of rumored leads, and at noon he'd had his first chance for a rest since the shootout. "I'm a'goin' to grab a nap of sleep, and I don't give a hoot iffen the whole county shoots each other dead."

But he'd been interrupted after a few hours by a thick, obviously drunk voice on the phone, saying, "We got the sonofabitch for you."

"What's that?" Simmons said.

"Got that Craishot sonofabitch," came the voice. Simmons sat up, wide awake.

"Who's this? Where you at?" he said, reaching for his boots.

"We got the bastard. He's out to Spivy. He's right there in the church, you want to come get him. We fixed him up so he won't never shoot nothin' nor nobody, nevermore."

"He's dead?" the sheriff said.

"He ain't dealin' no cards," the voice said, laughing thickly. "You go on out and pick him up. And we'll be on in for the reward, presently. Don't you worry none about that."

"Who is this, goddammit?" Simmons shouted to the dead line.

Hogeye told it later:

Reason I got involved was Sheriff; he picked up the phone and called Montroll, the undertaker, says, "Get somebody with a wagon to meet me out to Spivy. I got Jem Craishot's body for you all to pick up." And Montroll, he calls me and says, "Hog, get that truck of your'n out to Spivy and meet the Sheriff there. He's got the Craishot boy dead."

So Sheriff, he runs out and gets his Henry crunk and heads on out to Spivy. And I does the same thing with my truck.

The county had got Sheriff Simmons a Model-A in 1928, about the day they come out, while everbody else was still a'crankin' away at their old T models. The big boys at the factories had said the sheriff better have him a automobile to run his rounds on, they said. I weren't far behind, a'buyin' my truck.

It was about required that you'd buy you a Henry if you worked in town. That was kindly the sign that you wasn't livin' up the cove no more but was a city boy, workin' man. Everbody just had to have one. Me too. I got me a T model in 1924, soon as I got my four hundred eighteen dollars put aside. Wasn't nothin' much to spend my money on anyways, so I didn't have me a problem savin' up. Some of these boys could run through money like hell among the yearlin's. But they'd get them a Ford, just the same. Get a promissarry note from the bank at four percent, get them their Lizabeth to ride around in. Nole Darlen, he got him a A model even quicker'n the sheriff done. But he got drunk and tore it all up before the paint'd dried on the goddamn thing. So he was back to ridin' that poor devil of a horse of his'n.

Me, I had to have one, too, but I paid cash on it. And I never liked it much, once I got it. It seems like people wouldn't be linin' up to spend money on a thing that's as much trouble as one of them damn T models, don't it? Good Lord, you'd have to mess around with that box of coils, rammin' little wood pegs in betwixt them just so's they'd fire off once in a blue moon, iffen you hadn't busted your arm a'crankin' the thing. And get far enough down the road that you can't walk back, you'll get a rim cut and lose a tire.

Billy Adams, he had it all figured that he'd fix them rim cuts with some leather and a handful of rivets. Said he could work it so he never had to buy him a tire, just patch the tube and keep on. He was sure he'd invented the next thing and was fixin' to be rich. But it took him nigh onto two days to rivet-up one of them rims, so it weren't worth the trouble you'd take to cut the damn leather. I don't know. Folks gets crazy when they get into messin' with a car, I reckon. I told Billy, "You're workin' too damn hard on them things to be rich."

Well, it don't nevermind, I fooled around enough with the damn things that I kindly got so I could fix whatever happened *pert near all the time, and I was a good hand, you know, with them flats and all. I was a right good driver. I don't know, I reckon I just had a knack for it. And once the A model come out, I could see it weren't a'goin' to be half the trouble, and folk was needing things hauled and this and that, so I got me a A model truck. So folks that had to have one on hand, had to get somewheres for bidnits, you know…the undertaker, sometime, or someone got to pick up a load, or take a mess of folks to the station, or just wanted a driver to take 'em somewheres, what have you. Well, they'd kindly call on old Hogeye to drive his truck. And it's funny, I kindly liked to do that, drive folks around, pick up a little pocket money. Who'd of thought a feller from away up the mountain like me would wind up drivin' folks around town in my own puckmeup truck? Not in a million years. But there you have it. Stranger things have happened, I reckon.*

But it took me a while all the same. I never did like that T model, and that's the one started everbody into bein' car crazy. It was too damn much trouble, and half the time it didn't go, anyways. And if I wanted to go home, up the mountain, it didn't climb them big slopes at all, unless you done it backwards. And then the fuel wouldn't run, you get it too slanted, you know. So I says, "This is a lot like ownin' a work shed that moves around once in a while." So I got rid of mine, by and by. But I didn't mind that A model truck, with the shifter and all. Not one bit.

Anyway, this time, Sheriff thought he'd have to bring in Jem, so he called the undertaker, who called me, and Sheriff and me we both of us fired up the Henrys and off we go up to Spivy's Church. I got to say they was a voice kindly naggin' at the back of my head, a'sayin', "What in hell is Jem Craishot doin' up to Spivy's nohow?" But Sheriff, I reckon he was so fired up a'thinkin' he was a'goin' to get Jem and finish the whole thing off, kindly get the county settled down. I reckon he'd had all the manhunt he wanted for a coon's age. So off we go. And we met up at Spivy's Church, pulled in the same time.

He didn't know me too much. I reckon the sheriff don't get too familiar with folks that ain't a'gunnin' each other down half the time. We got to be pert good friends, though, after that trip. Well, that's the sort of thing'll bind folks together, a'havin' to handle a awful thing like that.

So I kindly introduced myself, said Montroll had sent me out there to do a job with my truck, and Sheriff, he says, "Let's go get 'im," and waves me on into the church.

It was late afternoon, and the sun a'shinin,' so when we first went in, we couldn't rightly see what it was up to the front. A'hangin' there.

And the view, it kindly cleared up slow, you know? Your eyes got to seein' it clear, and you wished maybe you hadn't of got used to the dark to see somethin' like that. Well, I tell you, it was a plain terrible thing, that poor young feller a'swayin' from a rope they'd throwed over the beam, his neck broke.

Sheriff, he moved pert quick, almost runnin' up that center aisle toward that poor boy. And he gets about five feet away and stops all of a sudden. Says, "O my Jesus." And jumps back quick. Because he'd seen he was a'standin' in a big puddle of blood had come off that boy, where they'd cut off both his hands and layed 'em both up on the altar.

Well we just kindly stood there for a mite, a'feelin' about as bad as a feller could. Presently, I says, "Good Lord, Sheriff, who in hell'd do somethin' like that to anybody? I don't care if he is Jem Craishot, he don't deserve somethin' like this." And Sheriff, he looks about as wan as that poor feller a'hangin' up there without his hands. And he says, "I know damn well who done it." And then he says, "Jesus." And he looks at me and says, "Who done it, that ain't the problem."

And I says, "Hmm," or somethin' like.

And he says, "Problem is, this boy a'hangin' here ain't Jem Craishot. Not by a long shot."

So they had done hunted down and killed some poor boy hadn't done nothin' to nobody. And cut off them hands. It'll make you sick to think of.

So we got that poor sonofabitch down and loaded in, and

then Sheriff had to go back into the church and get them hands. Now I don't rightly understand it, but you can bundle up a dead body without it bein' too much of a trouble to you. But to go and pick up a pair of hands that've been cut off and set somewheres, that's the worst thing you could imagine. I jest don't know how the man could go back in there and pick one of them things up.

Though he didn't have hard evidence, Sheriff Simpson arrested the Boarder brothers for the murder of George Staple of Spivy. "I ain't got much to go on, except you know they done it, I know they done it, and they know they done it," he told the county prosecutor. But, of course, that wasn't enough and, besides, the prosecutor was a distant relation to Cal Boarder himself, and the grand jury turned back a no-bill. Immediately upon their release, the brothers vowed publicly to get and kill Jem.

Sheriff Simmons went to see them in "Boarder Country" again, only this time he went at five in the morning, bringing four heavily armed men with him, and entered the apartment while the brothers were sleeping. He found and confiscated three half-gallon fruit jars of white liquor, arrested the boys for possession and, this time, turned them over to the federal tax agents. "They'll get three years in Kansas, iffen he wants to give it to 'em. So I reckon they'll spend their time a'raisin' a crop belongs to the president, kindly, and ain't nothin' the county boys can do to stop it. It won't pay for killin' that boy, but it'll at least make 'em wish that hadn't of done it."

iii.

The hunt for Craishot continued, spurred by a raise in the reward money, and on Saturday morning of the following week, Sheriff Simmons gathered his deputies into his office.

"Now listen up," he said. "They's plenty folks up thataway that'll hide Jem out, and there's one or two might shoot you to keep you from gettin' to him. And if you do find him, be damn sure he can drill a hole through your forehead quicker'n you can kick a dog. So let's just stop tryin' so goddamn hard to get someone killed. Let's all just ease back a mite and let it all slow down a bit. You all get on home and have you a rest and a good Sundy dinner tomorrow. I'll go on up to Chimbly Top and see can't I get a word with Jem's folks, see iffen I might get to talk to him direct, or leastways, get a message to him, let him know it's a'goin' to be a whole site happier for all his folks up there iffen he just comes down and gives hisself up. He'll see they ain't no profit in stayin' up there hid out, a'makin' his own folks break the law, puttin' them into trouble and danger. He'll see that and, iffen we can be a bit patient, I reckon he'll come on in."

So Simmons rode along up Chimney Top the next day, headed to Jem's home place, a dogrun plank house tucked into a deep cove on the western slope of the mountain. The summer undergrowth had beaten off any attempts at clearing a yardway for the house, which was so nearly swallowed in vines and creepers that, from fifteen yards away, the place was virtually invisible. At the same time, starting up the trail from the broad meadow at the mouth of the hollow, Simmons knew he could be seen by dozens of hidden men up in that brush, knew he would present a clear and constant target every step of the way.

"I reckon that's why they pays me to be sheriff," he said aloud.

He hesitated, thinking, then swung himself off his mount. He tied the horse to a rangey locust tree, then slowly unbuckled his gun belt, doing everything with exaggerated deliberation, so each movement could be read by whoever might be watching from up at the house. He hung the belt over the horse's saddle and slowly drew the revolver from its black leather holster. Holding the gun nearly at arm's length, he broke the cylinder and shook all six cartridges out onto the ground, then replaced the revolver in the holster and left it hanging off the saddle, in line of sight from the house.

Simmons stepped back and turned up the trail, walking easily, almost strolling his way up the thickening green incline. When the undergrowth began closing in—about halfway up the hollow—he raised his hands, showing his open palms to the scrub and trees ahead, and repeating in a loud, calm, even voice, "It's Sheriff Simmons, come to have a talk. Sheriff Simmons here to pass a word with you all. Just come to talk."

The trail rose and curved lightly to the right and, suddenly, here was the house, its unpainted vertical planking peering through bush and sticker, looking as though no one could have lived here in years. The suffusion of growth made the scene appear so paradoxically barren that Simmons gave a start when he realized there was an old woman standing barefoot in the open door of the house, not twenty feet away. She wore a pale blue bonnet, its shade obliterating her features, except for a long, hawkish nose above the pale clay pipe clenched in her broadly downturned mouth. She had a crooked straw broom held level at her hips, like a ropewalker's balancing pole. The skin over her knuckles was translucent amber, like a paper lampshade. Standing beside her was a naked, round-faced little girl about three years old. Her wide gray eyes stared at Simmons.

The woman said nothing as the sheriff stopped and slowly lowered his hands.

"Haddy, Miz Craishot," he said. "Sheriff Simmons come to have a talk with Jem."

"Ain't here," she said. She wrung her hands tightly around the broom staff. "Ain't nobody here. Nobody but just me."

"Well, now, I reckon not," Simmons said. "I reckon your menfolk is all out to the fields yonder, a'suckerin' the patch?" He turned his face toward where he knew the cleared fields would be, though all that was visible from here was a tangle of briar.

"Ain't nobody up to the fields neither," the woman said. "Ain't nobody here nowheres." She cocked her head. "Have you eat?"

The sheriff turned his eyes back upon her. "You reckon I mayt could get a message through to Jem, iffen I was to leave one with you?"

The woman loosened her hold on the broom and carefully leaned it against the doorframe. "Come on in," she seemed to sigh. "Have you a bite of beans and cornbread." She turned and walked into the house, the toddler following, their bare feet sounding like brushes on the worn poplar floor. "You'd like a mite of coffee, I expect," the woman said over her shoulder.

So the message was sent, and Sheriff Simmons finished his bite of food and returned down the trail where, as he had expected, he found his revolver and cartridges gone. He rode the twenty miles to Roalton and sat back to wait.

iv.

The heat of summer seemed to coalesce on that Friday, when Sheriff Simmons saddled up for the ride down to Lick Branch to pick up Jem Craishot. Word had come the evening before, by way of a rattling at the screen door of Simmons's office.

"What's up?" shouted Simmons. After an interval with no response, he shouted again, "Come on in."

He looked up to see a skinny, barefoot boy of about thirteen, wearing a pair of cut-down Bic Mac overalls that were so large on the boy's narrow frame they looked, Simmons said later, "like he could do somersaults inside 'em." A sagged straw hat hid the boy's eyes, but Simmons could see a humped nose, sugar-bowl ears, and a punkled chin. Two lines of dark amber stained downward from the corners of the wide, soft mouth.

"Lord, boy," Simmons said. "How long you been chawin' tobacca?" He watched a moment and said, "Oh. You from up Chimbly Top?"

"Yessir," the boy said, and then, in answer to the first question, "Own't know." His voice was plain, inflectionless. He shuffled his bare feet on the board floor. "Jem says he's a'comin' in. Says you pick him up down to the Lick Branch tomorrow midday."

The boy yanked his hat off, showing bright, colorless hair.

He bowed slightly, swung the hat back onto his head, and turned, already running out the door.

The sheriff sat still a moment, then slapped his thigh. "Praise the Lord," he shouted. "Praise the damn Lord."

Simmons gathered his men the next morning and explained that he would go up to Lick Branch alone and on horseback, so as not to draw attention with the new Ford. He wanted his men to follow later, wait on the high road two miles up from the falls, and form a guard posse for bringing the outlaw into town.

"I'll bring him up from the branch, and you boys fall in around us. And keep both eyes peeled right smart, ever beat of the way. I got Cal's brothers in custody, but I ain't got ever first cousin nor second cousin nor back-porch cousin locked up, and it ain't outen the question but what ten or fifteen of them boys'll try and take a shot at Jem whilst we're a'bringin' him in. And I'll tell you what: one of them fires a gunshot from behind the hedge, kindly, I'll shoot whichever one of you'uns was supposed to be a'watchin' that stretch of road before I go after the sonofabitch a'hidin' there. I promise you that. You understand?"

The men nodded in tandem.

So the sheriff rode out at ten, a half hour before his men. The morning was already hazy with heat, and he rode surrounded by the sharp smell of sweated horseflesh, his thighs and buttocks sticking wetly to saddle leather.

So it was a sweet relief to turn off the high road, two hours later, and drop down into the valley. Sweeter yet to turn along the creek bend and drop into the ravine, then further down to the narrow flats at the base of the broad, sheeted waterfall. The air felt at least ten degrees cooler here, in the roaring gloom of damp moss, rock, and fern. Simmons dismounted, pulling his sweat-glued clothing away from his skin and turning his face upward to gather the cool waft of misted breeze that seemed to float on the booming noise of the plunging falls. He sighed, pulled a red bandanna, and swabbed his face. Looping his horse's rein around a thin swamp willow, he sat on a curved block of glistening, salt-and-pepper granite and waited in the steady, slapping rush of sound from the tumbling water. The heavy sound seemed to throb and pulse, swell and recede, like dozens of intermingled, shouting voices.

Simmons drew out his bandanna again and wiped the dewy spray from his brow. He stood and tucked the bandanna back down into his pocket, then sat again onto the cold, grainy rock. He didn't have long to wait.

With a start, he realized he'd been looking at Jem Craishot, silhouetted on the bright yellow-green rim of the ravine. Jem appeared to have been waiting for the sheriff's twitch of recognition because, now, he began walking slowly down the trail toward the narrow flat.

"Well, now," Simmons said, standing. He began to walk very slowly toward Jem.

The two men stopped about fifteen feet apart, in the middle of the flats, which seemed composed as much of mist and sound as of solid earth, stone, and sedge. In the wet gloom and the rumble, the men looked like figures in a watercolor, recognizable and real enough, but faded and edgeless.

Simmons tucked his hands into his pockets, gazing at Jem. "I reckon I'd ought to thank you for comin' on down, Jem," he said.

Craishot cupped a hand around his ear and cocked his head. Simmons shouted over the voices of the falls: "I'm right glad you decided to come on in, son. I think you done the right thing, not alone for your own self, but for all them folks of your'un."

Jem nodded, then stood still. His gaze seemed unfocused, or directed toward something beyond the sheriff, perhaps at the falls itself. At last he spoke.

"It's a nice cool spot here," he shouted. "Ain't it?"

"Pert nice," Simmons yelled back. Both men dropped their heads back to throw their voices over the throb of the cascade, so that their heads bobbed as though they were arguing, rather than passing pleasantries.

They stood in silence. Presently the sheriff spoke.

"Well, son, I reckon we'd best get this over with."

"Over with, you say?" Jem shouted. "What's that you say?"

Simmons pulled out his red bandanna, bringing it up to mop his face.

Instantly, Jem leapt backward and drew his pistol.

Simmons saw the gun and threw himself sideways and downward onto the pebbled ground, rolling away and grabbing at his service revolver. He didn't know if Jem had already shot him or if he'd even heard the gun go off. His own pistol in hand, now, the sheriff rolled onto his belly and propped an elbow, seeing Jem, still standing, his gun pointed.

Simmons clutched his left hand to his right wrist, steadying the revolver and firing, once, twice, three times.

V.

So when it was finished, Burl remembered, and knew it had all come about because, though Jem had killed three men, he had never actually shot at anyone. Never would have done so, never so much as pointed his gun at a fellow human. No. In every case of "murder," Jem had fired at a gun blast, a muzzle flash or, in that first case, at the snapping sound of a misfire: at any rate, he had reacted instinctively, unerringly, returning fire without ever seeing who or where he was shooting. He had never faced an assailant. Burlton realized it was probably a lucky thing, in an odd way, that Jem had been ambushed every time. Because he would have refused to shoot a man in a face-to-face confrontation. *Likely they would've been able to walk right up to him, take aim, and shoot him dead, because he wouldn't never have been able to kill them. Not once he looked 'em in the eyes. Saw a man.*

And so, at the last, he had indeed failed to protect himself, face-to-face with Sheriff Simmons, who had to fire three times before he could even hit Jem, who stood there, meanwhile, pointing his own weapon and never firing, until the sheriff's third bullet struck him down.

But this—the eye-to-eye confrontation—wasn't everything, either. Hogeye told it later.

Three shots? Three shots and the first two of 'em missed? Now you got to think about this. Here's Sheriff, a pert fair shot his own self, and he fires three times against a feller that could close both eyes and shoot you in the belly button whilst you're a'clog dancin' in the next room? That don't figure to me.

Look: here's Jem, a'comin' down the mountain to give hisself up, and the whole goddamn country a'layin' in the bushes a'waitin' to shoot him down, just so's they can put a thousand dollars in their straw tick. And what do you reckon is the odds if maybe ten fellers starts to shootin' at him all at the same time? Even if they was to get him? What you figure is the odds they's a'goin' to be enough fellers left over to carry the goddamn coffins? I wouldn't give you a mouse's chance in a owl's nest.

And what happens? Well, now I wasn't there and nobody else, nother, but here's how I reckon it was, and I'm pert damn sure it was somethin' of the sort. Here Jem comes, down to Lick Branch to give hisself up, just like he'd sent down and said he was kindly fixin' to do. And so he comes down to the falls and here's Sheriff Simmons a'standin' there with his hands in his pockets. And Sheriff says, "I'm right glad you seen to reason, Jem, and come in peaceful like. And I'll see to it you get the best break the law can give you under the circumstances, kindly." What have you.

Is there a way to picture all this? The water a'rumblin' down over them falls, and Sheriff and Jem a'standin' there, the one of 'em thinkin' mayt be we can get this over with and get this boy into jail without him or no one else has to get killed no more. Not this week, anyways.

And Jem, it seems like he looks right into Sheriff's eyes for a mite. Then all of a sudden like, he yanks a gun outen his shirt and levels it down a'pointin' at Sheriff and says, "I reckon you're wrong about that."

Now seems to me, that'd scare Sheriff as much as he's ever been scairt since he was just a little feller and they was boogermen under the bed. Jem Craishot pulls a gun on you? You kiddin' me?

So I reckon that's how come Sheriff missed with them first two shots before he hit the boy. And scared enough not to even realize Jem's just a'standin' there a'pointin' that gun and kindly waitin' on the sheriff to shoot one in the right direction. Just stood there a'waitin' on him.

Which, I'll tell you, was the whole goddamn problem with the whole damn situation. Folks just couldn't wait. They had to go a'stormin' out into them woods, all loaded up with weapons and whiskey, a'roustin' all over the patch, tryin' to catch Jem. When if Sheriff Simmons had his way, he'd of sat there in town and waited for Jem to see it weren't a'goin' to do no good to hide out. Wouldn't do nothin' but cause all sorts of trouble for his folks and his sis that was a'fixin' to try and have a baby by that slick feller, Nole, whether Jem knowed that or not. I don't know.

Anyway's, that's about what the sheriff done, ain't it? Sent Jem a message somehow. That ain't hard to figure, since you just go on up Chimbly Top and talk to the goddamn trees, the chances are one of them sassyfrasses is cousin to Jem. Anyway, Sheriff, he sent the message up there, sayin', "Let's just take her easy and not get nobody else killed and you take your time and think her over, you'll see you mayt just as well come on down and get it all done with." And set back a'waitin' on Jem to work it all out.

And it would've worked, iffen the rest of the goddamn country could've waited on it, too. But they kept on a'crawlin' around in the laurel, just couldn't wait to get they hands on that reward, where Sheriff, he wished they'd all just go home and he could raffle off the reward once he got Jem in, safe. Like I says, folks nowadays, they don't know how to wait on somethin's worth waitin' on. Salt cures your hams because they don't want to wait a year. Or take the trouble to pack 'em down twice. Or to get that sugar and salt down good into the shank, hang that ham upside down for a year's time. It don't matter if sugar-cure is the best ham you ever eat. Ain't got time to wait on it. Salt-cure and you can have it this year, even if it ain't half as good. But you won't see no sugar-cure hams around Roalton. Down here, nobody'd cure a ham for next year, don't matter how good it mayt be. Just can't wait. You see what I'm a'sayin'?

So then the question comes, don't it? Why did Jem pull that gun in the first hook? I mean, here he was, a'comin' down to give hisself up, like the sheriff had said. So why, at the last second, does he yank a gun outen his belt and point it at the man, who didn't have no choice, kindly, but to shoot him? And here's the way I figure. It ain't necessarily the way it happened, but I bet you a new pup it was somethin' like this.

Here's Jem has done decided the sheriff is right: ain't doin' nobody no good to have folks huntin' him all over East Tennessee, and Carolina besides. And he never wanted to kill nobody in the first place. It just seemed somehow they was always somebody a'huntin' him. It just kindly happened to him. Like turnin' up a bad card four, five times in a row, you got to start wonderin', "Am I just one of them fellers that's bound to turn up bad cards ever damn time I play?" And so I reckon he's feelin' perty sick and tired, and ashamed, I suppose. So he figured it's time he turned hisself in. So he sends down to Sheriff and says, "I'll meet you down at the falls of the branch." That's why they calls it "Lick Branch," they's a good size falls up the crick, where the water comes off the ledge like spilt stew offen your table top.

But let's say Jem starts on down the mountain on his way to give hisself up. And he gets to thinkin' about them bad cards and about how ever step of the way down this here mountain they mayt be some crazy sonofabitch behint ever one of these bushes, a'fixin' to have a shot at him. And Jem, he ain't so much scared they'll kill him as he is scared he'll have to kill two or three more folks before he can get hisself down to the falls. He's feelin' that keyed up, you know?

And let's say about halfway down, he's goin' through by a hedgerow and CRAACK! he hears a branch snap, or a footfall, or some kind of a rattlin' sound. And quick as a eyelash—he ain't even thinkin' about it, he's movin' so quick—Jem's got his gun out and he's a spinnin' around to shoot the sonofabitch. And out around the hedge comes a little boy about four year old, a'draggin' a sardine can on a string.

And that's how close Jem come to killin' that little boy.

So he starts in to shakin', thinkin', "O Lord God, am I a'goin' to start killin' everbody makes a noise behind me?" Be-

*cause he knows there ain't nothin' for it but folks'll be a'sneakin'
around a'huntin' him, and him a'findin' hisself havin' to gun
folks down. And he finds he's a'standin' there shakin', saying,
"It ain't my fault. It ain't my fault. None of it. I never asked for
none of it." But that don't seem to help him none.*

*So he stops and gets hold of hisself. And he says to hisself,
"Well. It mayt not be my fault. But I reckon it's my goddamn
responsibility. And ain't nobody can put a stop to it—nobody
but me. So I reckon I know what I got to do."*

*So he marches on down there. And he walks up to Sheriff
Simmons and pulls his gun on him. And stands there until Sheriff
can manage finally to gun him down. Put a end to the whole
damn show.*

vi.

Simmons knelt back into his chair.

"God damn it," he said. "The whole mess wouldn't never happened iffen that Nole Darlen hadn't set up that ambush with Cal Boarder. And what made Cal Boarder go do it, behint my back? Well, Nole must've told him you'll get a piece of that reward, and it must've seemd like the perfect set, with Merv a'meetin' Kinnie, right here at Cal's doorstep, so to speak. God damn it, anyway. And Cal is dead, and what's his name, the other feller at the ambush? Tomkins, Sam Tomkins, the poor sonofabitch. And another deputy crippled up. And now Jem's dead, and that poor boy over to Spivy's, and three or four of them fools that went out huntin' Jem and got theyselves shot. Jesus. All because Nole Darlen decided he had to set Jem Craishot up. Now what in hell was that about? Nole Darlen? You got to be kiddin' me."

And Hogeye said, "Well, Sheriff. You can't charge Cal Boarder for the ambush, because he's dead. And you can't pick up them Boarder boys for the murder up to Spivy, because you ain't got nothin' on 'em. And you can't charge Jem for killin' them fellers at the ambush, 'cause Jem's dead. And you can't take and charge your own self with killin' Jem, because he pulled a gun on you. So maybe you can go out and pick up

Nole Darlen for startin' the whole show."

"What am I a'goin' to charge him with?" Simmons said. "Bein' a hell of a damn fool? Christ God, iffen I could pick up a feller for that, I could arrest the whole goddamn rasher that's been out there a'huntin' that reward. Ain't no different from Nole Darlen, 'ceptin' he started the whole thing. What in hell was he thinkin'?"

"I don't believe thinkin' is dezactly in his line," said Hogeye. "Hell, I reckon you're right, he ain't no worse than any of the rest. He's just one of them poor fellers that's got too much a'goin' for him so he winds up a'goin' nowhere at all. Ain't that it? A rich daddy that don't really give two hoots about Nole, or he wouldn't of raised him to be the way he is, would he?"

"How's that?" said Simmons.

"Well, looky. Here's he is, and his daddy's got a pile of money he won't spend on Nole. But he ain't about to let Nole forget he's got it right in his pocket, nor that he thinks his own son ain't worth two cents. And why? Because Daddy never bothered once to teach that boy how to work or how to just treat folks, or gals. None of it. Never give Nole nothin' to go on, and what do you expect from a kid that never learned how to do somethin' as simple as work?"

"Didn't teach him how to drink, nother," said Simmons. "I do wish to hell he'd taught the boy that much."

"Well, you can't say Nole ain't worked at learnin' that 'un," said Hogeye. "That's one grade he's kept repeatin', I'd say. Maybe he'll get the hang of before somebody whoops him to death."

"I wouldn't bet the farm on it," said Simmons.

"Still and all, it's kindly hard to blame a young feller knows as little as Nole does. A feller like him don't go out and strut around and raise hell because he thinks he's the best bull. He gets into all that mess because he's afeared he might be the scrawniest one on the whole ranch. Don't like the way he is, so he takes and makes everbody agree with him. He ain't a'havin' no fun, tearin' things up, you mark me."

"Hell," said Simmons. "You're a'goin' to have me in tears in two shakes."

"And don't never believe Nole set up that ambush his own self. Feller like that? No sir. I bet you my hat against your bootstraps he was put up to it. And I bet I know who."

"Now, whyn't you just tell me who?" said Simmons.

"I bet you Daddy done. Kindly said somethin' like, 'I ain't never seen such a nobody as you are.' To his own boy. Said, 'You want anything but folks laughin' at you, you'd best do something big around here. Like maybe you grab that Jem Craishot reward. And that way maybe we could both of us feel a mite better about havin' you in the fambly. And we could both of us stop a'worryin' about all that money I got that I ain't a'fixin' to give any of it to you no time soon.'"

"That's a pretty big heap of supposin', seems like to me. Whyn't you figure Nole to just up and make a grab at Jem his own self? He's fool enough to make a try, ain't he?"

"Because he'd never of thought to do it. Not that way. Because that gal, Jem's sis? That Merv Craishot gal? She's the one he had to set up to meet with Jem. And he was sweet on her, I reckon. Damn sweet on her. And even Nole Darlen wouldn't set up his best galfriend like that, without someone who kindly shamed him into a'doin' it."

"So maybe I could go arrest Carl Darlen?" said Simmons. "If it ain't illegal to be a damn fool, maybe it's illegal to raise your boy to be a damn fool."

"I reckon it ought to be," said Hogeye. "I reckon it mayt of been a hell of a lot better for Nole Darlen, or Merv, or Sam Tomkins, or everbody else iffen they'd set up and ambushed Carl Darlen instead of Jem."

CHAPTER SEVEN

DAY'S END

Some moonshiners make pretty good stuff,
Bootleggers use it to mix it up.
He'll take one gallon, well he'll make two,
If you don't mind boys, he'll get the best of you.

One drop will make a rabbit whip a fool dog,
And a taste will make a rabbit whip a wild hog,
It'll make a toad spit in a black snake's face,
Make a hard shell preacher fall from grace.

A lamb will lay down with a lion,
After drinking that old moonshine,
So throw back your head and take a little drink,
And for a week you won't be able to think.

—Tennessee Moonshiners, 1931

i.

Nosey Ned ran a still. This, in itself, was not a particularly remarkable thing. But it was extraordinary, singular in fact, that Nosey Ned's still was nestled into a corner of the big Hancock Paper Mill at the head of Long Island, within the city limits themselves. The factory straddled the Holsten River, whence it diverted the millions of gallons of water necessary to the production of its paper. This water was channeled to the mainland, pumped upward into a huge holding tank and released as needed through an elevated sluiceway that doubled back over the river and emptied into the pulping cookers at the head of the island. Nosey Ned, the "waterman" in charge of monitoring and controlling the flow, actually lived at the mill, in a rickety shed beneath the sluiceway, on the island side. In addition to this spartan dwelling, Ned's holdings consisted of a rowboat he had fashioned into a rider-driven pulley-ferry, and his still, the thumper keg of which stood between his shed and the river, and the water supply of which he also monitored and controlled from the company's holding tank on the main shore.

Since he also maintained the outflow sluices, where the tons of wastewater were drained from the cookers back into the Holsten, Ned was widely reputed to have experimented with various "blends" in the making of his mashes, so that folks around Roalton had come to describe any blistering bout with drink as having *got into some of Nosey Ned's downstream blend.*

Ned neither confirmed nor denied these impressions, though he was quite forthright about his own degree of dedication to his craft. He called his liquor *slooshins,* and he would not identify the water sources or any of the other variables in his recipes. "It don't make no different," he would say. "If it looks good, it is good, I say. And I takes particular pride in the looks of my slooshins, looks as good as anybody's in the valley. You get a bead on it you could count to ten on, and it's always just as clear as granmaw's conscience. So it don't matter none iffen it come from up the crick or down the crick, or from the waters a Babylon or what. You don't like it, you can give it to some other feller to drank, I reckon."

Nobody trusted Nosey Ned. Nobody much liked him, for that matter. Still, everybody bought liquor from him at one time or another, whenever the need for ready alcohol overrode the desire for good alcohol.

For Ned, this meant he stayed busy well into the night filling orders for *slooshins,* and this, in addition to his regular employment at the mill—not to mention brewing and running the whiskey in the first place—made for a remarkably busy life. What he did with the substantial amounts of money generated by all of this labor, no one knew. He lived in absolute squalor in the exiguous shack beneath the sluiceway. For all anyone had ever seen, he subsisted entirely on the roasted corn kernels he munched nervously and constantly from a filthy cotton sack that always lay turned open next to the split-bottom chair in which he sat and transacted his business. He wore, day and night, the stained and greasy Hancock Paper uniform issued him by the company four years ago with, pinned to the breast, and the only clean thing about him, the brightly polished brass lozenge that proclaimed him chief of security.

The demand for Nosey Ned's *slooshins* was such that there was often a line, a queue of sorts, on the pulley-ferry's mainland landing—a few thousand square feet of muddy towhead just outside the company's fence and, like everything else in Ned's domain, beneath the sluiceway, which crossed over the river on a line precisely with the ferry, and which provided the company and Ned with that crucial secondary resource. Because, as Ned was fond of saying, *You can have you a million pounds of wood chips or a million of corn sprouts, and ain't neither goin' to do you no good without you got plenty water—so it's the water kindly makes it all work, kindly.* In addition to the regular customers, a small shanty-town of sorts had grown up on this notch of land, generated by an odd quirk of what might be called generosity in Nosey Ned's nature. Because he was wont to supply green beer and backings free of charge to a handful of older indigents who, as a result, had become semi-permanent residents of the landing. On any evening, the mainland crossing point would contain a few waiting customers and four or five "residents," lonely, half-crazed old men who appeared to stay alive for no reason other than to drink some of Nosey Ned's donations, which, of course, would guarantee Ned a steady supply of regular customers if ever these men found themselves with cash to spend.

Into this place stumbled Nole Darlen, a matter of a few hours prior to murdering his father, desperate for drink and carrying over thirty dollars in cash. He was only half-aware of the other men there, so overwhelmed was his mind with the reeling image of his mother's nakedness, her body flung out unconscious on the bed, where he had landed her with his fist, and where he had left her. This memory, mixed oddly with a searing recognition of his father's absence from the scene, and the accompanying knowledge of his mother's encounter with that man—he had forgotten the name—Janey Gill's uncle, rooted around in Nole's mind, grabbing at the flailing fingers and snapping them off, as he staggered from Twelve Corners east to the river, muttering aloud, continually, *I don't know what to do I don't know what to do I don't* as he drove himself along toward the single thing that he understood he had to have before doing anything.

When he arrived at the landing, there were three men sitting along a felled log, each awaiting his turn at the ferry. They were talking in low tones and passing a twist of tobacco along among themselves. In the background, lying prone or squatting on heels, their expressionless eyes fixed idiotically upon nothing whatever, were five of Ned's charity cases, the residents of the landing.

"Git out," Nole frothed at the men on the log. "Git outen my way." And he lurched toward the crude wooden slip where the pulley-boat would tie up. "I'm a'goin' next, so clear out."

The men laughed. "You'll set and take a turn with the rest of us, or you won't be goin' nowheres at all," said one. "Nowheres but home with a new headache and somethin' broke." The man stood and hoisted his pants, threatening.

Nole was seized with trembling fear. His eyes rolled whitely, and he began to whine, cringing.

"Oh, now fellers, just let me go on. I didn't mean nothin' but that I'm kindly in a rush, you know. Just let me to step on out there ahead of you all. I don't mean nothin'." He brightened. "Here," he said. "I got some jack. I'll pay you for it, the goin' ahead." And he reached out a handful of bills.

The men laughed again, hollow in the twilight. "How much you got there, Nole boy?" a second man asked, standing.

"Got plenty," Nole said. "Here. C'mon and take it. Just let me to get on that boat."

"Sure now," the first man said. He was still standing in the shadowy dusk of the landing. Behind him, one of the residents was fumbling with a scorched coal-oil lamp, trying to light it. The air was beginning to chill quite suddenly, the high, thin cold, dropping and filling over the last warm echoes of the day. The man reached out and snatched the money from Nole's hand just as the boat hove into sight, drawn hand-over-hand by its rider, slowly traversing the river, the upstream water piling and fluffing against its gunwales. "They's your boat," the man said, already beginning to count the bills.

Nole crowded himself toward the slip as a tall, thin figure stepped carefully from the boat, balancing two quart fruit jars, their gold metal bands glowing dully in the last of the light. The lantern suddenly flared brightly, hissing yellow highlights onto the man's long face.

"Gettin' damn colt," the man said as he stepped up the bank. "Goin' to be damn colt tonight, get you a piece of Nosey's downstream blend'll keep you fit fer a colt night."

Nole ignored him, pushing himself by and down to the bank. He grabbed a piling on one end of the slip and half-jumped, half-fell into the dank, shallow boat. He grabbled at the hemp line and began to draw the tubby craft across the stream. Behind him he heard the toneless laughter of the waiting men, bobbing silhouettes against the grainy amber lantern glow.

Midstream, a breath of really chill air overtook him, and he began to chatter, his hands stiffening on the rough twists of the rope. He found himself muttering again, *I don't know what to do I don't know what to do*, but he couldn't hear himself against the *cradle* of the current hitting the broad beam of the boat. He pulled hard on the rope, drew it back and reached ahead, grabbing onto the next stretch of hemp, but the line seemed not to give in the least and so, even though he continued to pass rope through his hands, he felt as though he were cemented, entirely motionless, in the middle of the darkening evening, all alone in this compacted space, as though all time, all motion, had come to a complete halt—not because nothing had ever happened, but because all that had ever transpired had caught up to him with a rush and so now there was nothing else, nothing at all, except himself and this constant cackling water, like a thin stream of cosmic wind in the vast, empty universe.

And then, without seeming to have moved at all, the boat was into the quiet water around the island, and then scumping into the log slip, and he was no longer cold but was burning, sweating, his hands afire, and he was there, on the flat tongue of land in front of Nosey Ned's shack, smelling the sharp soursweet of wood pulp, the enormous paper-cooking vats standing like high purple shadows in the early evening's deep flow.

Ned himself was sitting in his split-bottom chair, next to a small table upon which stood a pint jar of whiskey and a small iron cashbox. Seated by him, on a squat overturned firkin, was a fattish short man in wire spectacles, wearing what appeared to be a phosphorescent shirt. The man's small eyes glittered at Nole, but Nole did not recognize him, so intent was he upon the stacks of fruit jars glinting in a silvery pyramid behind the two seated men. Nole moved quickly toward them, fishing the last of the crumpled bills from his pocket. He had no idea how much he had given the men on shore, but it had been a substantial portion of what he had. Now he waved the remaining bills in Ned's direction.

"Gimme jar," he said.

"Hell you doin' hyar?" the other man said. "Hell you get that cash?" The voice was high, cunning, and Nole now recognized the "_pothecary," Lincoln Spencer, sitting on the firkin, whittling a stick of red cedar with a Barlow. "Hey. That cash ain't your'n, Nole boy," Spencer said. "'S'mine. Ain't it, sonny?" Spencer grinned up at Nole, a tight, humorless grimace. "Little matter few pops of J'maica. Ain't that right?"

Nole stared at Spencer, still holding the bills outstretched. He turned toward Ned again and repeated, "Gimme jar," thrusting the bills further toward the man on the split-bottom chair, whose chest brinkled with the shiny brass lozenge. "Gimme," he said a third time.

"'Zat your money?" Ned said in a flat, nasal voice, inclining his head toward Spencer and waving his left hand toward the bills that had begun to shake in Nole's hand.

"Damn right it's mine," said Spencer. "This boy's run up a right smart line on my cuff, buyin' Jake and swearin' he's good for it soon's he gets him some cash. He done come by my place

today and bought him another four ounces on a promise."
Now Spencer pointed at the bills, so all three of them had
hands extended, reaching toward each other, as though drawn
together by some magnetic force, or preparing to clasp and join
in some ritual dance. "And so, sonny," Spencer said to Nole,
"if that's your jack, I reckon that's my jack."

Nole's eyes snatched back and forth, from Spencer to Nosey
Ned to the pale, silvered stack of fruit jars. "This here ain't that
money," he said, beginning to feel the drop of despair. "This
here is..."

"Like I says," Spencer interrupted. He drew back his hand
and hooked it into his stained braces. "If you got any money at
all, you best just hand it over to where it's owed, is the best
way." He gave a tight little laugh, like squeezing air out of a
balloon. "You cain't spend what you ain't got on none of Ned's
slooshins. Don't know nobody can spend what he ain't got.
Can he, Ned?"

"But this ain't that money," Nole said, speaking directly to
Ned, now. He felt like a little boy who had suddenly lost his way,
looking for his mamma and finding, instead, the unbending,
harsh rejection of the empty and unfamiliar street. He felt as
though he might cry. And, in a quick flash, he saw his mother
again, knocked out by his own hand and lying stretched and
naked on the flat bed, no longer his kin, no longer even an
abstracted concept to whom he might appeal, petition. And
then, worse, saw that same moist nakedness poised and beckoning to the man, Janey Gill's uncle, whose name he could not
recall. "Ain't that money at all. This here's money for a jar of
that corn..."

"Ain't got no corn for none of you'uns," said Ned in a flat,
inflectionless voice, like some sort of large buzzing insect. "Not
iffen you got bidnits with Spence, first. Ain't no liquor here for
none of you'uns."

Nole stood, amazed, his eyes fixed on Nosey Ned, his hand
still extended, the crumpled, damp bills shaking steadily. He

didn't move as Spencer leaned forward, watching Nole's eyes intently, and slowly closed his hand around the cash, drawing it steadily from Nole's grasp, saying, in a low, patronizing tone, "That'll be all right, then Nole boy." He dropped his weight backward, settled onto the firkin, and tucked the money into the luminously white shirt pocket. "That'll be just fine."

"But I got to have..." Nole said.

Spencer squeezed out another high laugh, that shrill, cracking sound, like something peeled from his pharynx, and completely devoid of humor.

"Well, now. Ned ain't a hard man, are you now? He won't let a poor feller have to go 'thout a drank b'fore he can ride out to see his daddy and get more money to pay for it like any a honest white man. Will you, Ned?" Spencer keened another laugh and reached across to lift the pint jar from the table. He unscrewed it slowly, sniffed at the contents and sipped it, luxuriously. The lid made a *wowing* sound as he screwed it closed. He set the jar back onto the table and slowly wiped his white-sleeved forearm across his wet mouth, watching to make certain that Nole had seen. "You got some mashy backin's for this poor feller who ain't got out to see his daddy yet, Ned? He's good for it, I'll vouch for that," he said, tapping his breast pocket. "You got any that good pulp-likker mash for a poor feller?"

"I reckon," Ned said, flat and nasal. "Sumpter!" he shouted.

From behind the stacked jars came a gaunt, bald boy of around ten. He said nothing, standing just across the cash-table from Ned.

"Run on and fetch some squeezin's from outen the hole," Ned sneered. The boy turned and zipped away behind the shed with remarkable speed, reappearing almost instantly with a small, yellow clay jug, stoppered by a stub of vinewood. He brought the jug to Ned, who bumped it lightly and held it to his ear, as though it were a tuning fork.

"These here pulp waters won't hurt you none, you get 'em up b'fore they puts the hydrachloric in 'em. Makes a good brew. Stronger'n a Darb ram on a day rut. You tell me it don't pass the time, young feller." He thumbhandled the jug to Nole. "That's free of charge, now. I don't mind helpin' a poor feller out. Don't mind it a mite. You take'n have some of that beer and get yerself on out to your daddy's like Spence says. Bring us back some money what don't belong to nobody but you, we'll set you up right smart. Don't mind it a mite."

Nole took the jug. He was trembling uncontrollably now, in shame and fury and raw need. He drew the vinewood stopper with his teeth and dropped it onto the table without touching it. He tipped up the jug and took a long draw. It tasted of bleach and pine gum and was so strong he literally fell back a step. He lowered the jug and blinked at the two men. Then he turned it up a second time and drank, full and hard.

"Don't mind helpin' out a poor feller," Nosey Ned said. "Pleasure's mine, young man. You head on out to daddy's and fetch you some cash."

ii.

On the way home in the wagon, Janey Gill and the kids lying asleep in the bed, Burlton discovered finally that he was going to tell Maydie. He had been planning to do so for quite a while now, and yet he knew that planning wouldn't really be the way of it. The moment would simply come when he would find himself speaking to her. And so he did.

"Maydie. I got to tell you. I been keepin' time with somebody. I been kindly carryin' on, I reckon you'd say."

Burl had discussed all of this with Rosary, more than once. Most often the question would arise toward the end of a visit, after the loving and after the good talk, and after the long elapse of silence, the feeling of the other's bodily immanance in the room, the fading echo of voices, even the weather: the smattered rain on windows or the bright, bird-called wind overflowing now and again into the room and wafted over their uncovered, breeze-licked bodies. And then he would say it:

"I got to tell her."

And Rosary would touch him very lightly or would take his hand and give it a small squeeze. These were touches, gestures, with no particular meaning at all, beyond the enormous significance of the touch itself: *I am here, you are here, we are here.* The sheer casualness of the movement, the run of her hand

along the outside of his leg or the toss of her forearm across his
chest, fraught with meaninglessness. Because, had she brushed his
leg like that three years back, he would have started nervously, or
even run off, or shouted something. So now, the motion and its
familiarity, emptying the caress of its power, its passional energy,
meant far more in its meaning so little. *We are lying here, naked,
together, you and I, and I can reach over and take you into my
hands, and it seems as though I have done so unexceptional a
thing. Because we are here, present, in each other's normal
selves, so much.*

And so her touch meant this: *Talk to me, talk to me of anything—your wife or your farm, your rheumatism or the conges-
tion in your chest. Or tell me there is a part of you that I can't
have, that belongs to her, your family, you and her. It doesn't
matter, it makes no difference.* And in this, in this careless
intimacy of routine touch, lay all the distinction.

Because it was a settling, that's what it was, the way you
would tamp down the wet earth into a mound around the
tobacco seedling, a motion at once gentle and firm, saying, *You
stay here. You stay here.*

Burlton realized he never touched Maydie this way, nor she
him. *We never knowed how to*, he thought, with something of
sadness, regret. *We knowed we was supposed to be in love, I
reckon, but we didn't know how to do it.* And he knew if he
reached out and clasped Maydie in this way, she would react,
pull away, say, "What you doin'?" As though all the time of
their lives had been a subtraction rather than an accretion, a
lessening and not an increase, so the careless significance of this
settling touch had never had a chance to develop—so the most
mundane of gestures, intimacies, had become the most shocking.
Maydie would not have been alarmed, probably not resistant,
had he grabbed her bodily and initiated sex with her, though
they hadn't had a sexual encounter in years. But it was this, this
undemanding, offhanded tamping that would startle and repel
her: "What you doin', Burl!" she would say. He knew this. *We*

just never knowed how, he thought again, regretful.

They had married young, like most couples out here in the foothills, and it had seemed a matter of course, just the next thing to do, as though love was like whiskers, or calluses, something you discovered you had. There was never—as far as he could remember—the fulgent glowing aura connecting body and emotion, like he felt with Rosary, so that he couldn't tell flesh from feeling. No. With Maydie, it was like finding a new pair of boots, a little unusual and uncomfortable, but nice enough; and then the waiting for the gradual softening and easing, until the boot felt as though it had always been wrapped around your foot, and you took it on or off without much noticing the difference.

Though, even so, he believed it had been love. He hadn't been indifferent to this young country girl, this Maydie, who he had known as long as he could remember. He had wanted her out of all the girls, wanted her passionately enough, he supposed. *Or at least as much as I knowed how*, he thought, realizing, again, *We didn't know nothin' about it, did we?* And again he felt that salt tang of regret, riding home in the worn wagon.

He remembered the first time he had kissed her, and he tried to identify the feeling, now, as the wagon creaked and rolled. It hadn't been like kissing Rosary. But then he—they—hadn't been more than fifteen or so. It had been at a camp meeting, where so often the young couples would sneak off from the brush arbor to spend some time alone. He remembered hearing the people, off in the distance, singing "We Shall All Be Reunited" as he looked at Maydie's young, pretty face and thought, *This is it. I'm a'goin' to kiss her.*

She had been a lively, laughing girl, with long chestnut hair, and a bright sense of play, and he had always found himself a little abashed in her presence, as though he might be making a fool of himself simply by being there. She seemed somehow older and cleverer than him, and so the decision to kiss her had been a momentous one. It had taken all the nerve he possessed.

They had wandered off from the camp meetings before, certainly, but never in this direction, never without two or three other kids. So he was certain that she knew what was about to transpire, even as he felt he was stepping into a void all by himself. He had never felt such a combination of eagerness and fear.

It had been exciting, because it had felt like they were up to something forbidden. At the same time, he hadn't felt passion so much as pressure. Because he had brought her out under the trees to kiss her, not out of any interior impulse, but because he knew that was what he was supposed to do. The time had come when he was expected (he couldn't have said by whom) to bring his girl away from the hymn-singing, out into the trees, and give her a kiss. So the memory itself was confused: It had been exciting and sweet—her lips had been soft, and both fresh and familiar at once, like cooling bread—but it had also been as though they were both following a command, with no real warmth about it—turning the roll onto a player-piano, rather than improvising a tune.

That was it. *We didn't know how*, he thought. *Never learned how*.

They had married and begun the rhythm of work and child-bearing that would warp their bodies and dull their minds, so that those few sweet first days became a mark of what had passed, not a beginning so much as an end.

And now, somehow, the unimagineable thing had happened, and Rosary had appeared, stirring him, blowing into heat the glimmer of desire and hope and feeling that survived under the hardened, weathered skin, somewhere deep in his heart. *And she taught me how*, he thought. But Maydie never had the chance. *Never anything for her but the work and the suffering*. Oh, he had loved her. Loved her now. But he couldn't have touched her—touched her fully and deeply—even if he had wanted to. It wouldn't mean the same thing, even if it could be the same touch.

He remembered that terrible winter night, the sharp stinging cold and the harsh smell of the coal-oil lantern, when their daughter had died of diphtheria. They had wept together, arms about one another, and he had said, "Maydie. O Maydie."

And she had lifted her hand to his wet cheek, run it along the stubbled, weathered face, and said nothing. And, in spite of the terrible grief, he had felt completely loved, as though this contact, her hand and his tears, knew all there was to know about life and sorrow and caring. She had never touched him like that, before or since, and he realized, now, smelling the night coming on, feeling the air turn thin and frigid, that he had longed to feel that touch again. *But we never knowed how*, he thought. *Never knowed how.*

So Burlton told Maydie he had been keeping time with some-one—he didn't tell her whom—and that he didn't mean to insult her or hurt her. It was something that happened, he said. But he was unable to explain the thing. Because he had been schooled to talk about such feelings in the language of the affair itself. *And she—we—don't talk that way.*

So he said as much as he did and they sat in silence, listening to the *tlock* of the horses, the rasped wood *skeeing* against the cart iron, their bodies lurching and rolling with the wagon, entirely unaware of the motion, they were so used to it. At one time or another, a rut would throw them into physical contact, shoulder-and-shoulder, though they were no more conscious of this touching than of the press and turn of the rough wooden slat against their buttocks. On they went.

"I reckon you're fixin' to leave?" she said, at last. Her voice was flat, uninflected, though he knew she was trying thus to cover the plaintiveness.

Burlton didn't answer. He had never considered leaving. He wouldn't have known how to leave any more than he would know how to touch her. It was not something to be considered, not because it was either painful or desirable; it was simply inconceivable. So he said nothing. And he knew his silence reassured her.

"So what are you goin' to do?"

The wagon wratched and skreeked, tossing their unresponsive bodies into soft collision, the feel of the other's fumped shoulder as familiar as the way itself, that he could drive without thinking or looking. The driving the horses themselves could do, and had done many times, while the people dozed, to be awakened by the feel of the particular bounce and turn that meant *nearing home.*

"Do?" he said. And then he was silent again. He thought of the kitchen at home, where they would eat a supper of biscuits and fried ham, and maybe some field greens, and would listen to the kids talk about the day in town. Or Maydie would tell him about someone who had passed on or who was down sick, someone she'd heard about today. And they would eat slowly, talking slowly in the smell of woodsmoke and stove metal, cedar and earth.

"I reckon I ain't a'goin' to do nothin'," he said. She was riding a little straighter, holding herself a little tighter than usual, against the jolting. And, looking straight ahead, Maydie said, "Well, iffen you ain't a'goin' to do nothin', I believe I ain't neither. I know about your gal in town, Burl. You take me for a fool, to think I wouldn't know? Hey?"

He looked at her, but she didn't turn her head. She held herself stiff, now, to keep from letting their shoulders jostle.

"Well now," he said. "Maydie, I never..."

"Shush," she said. "I know it, Burl. It ain't much, is it? Not much to bear after 247aveled247y247 else. Is it? So I reckon iffen you think you can bear it, so can I. I done bore a hundred things more than that, ain't I?"

And he thought of the lost children, two of them, and he believed he had never ceased hearing her keening grief. Thought of her in the cold kitchen, winters, barefoot, in the worn nightdress, stirring up the stove at the break of day, calling, "Get on up, Burl." Yes. He loved her. He loved her the way he loved the farm itself, he reckoned. Not the way he had learned from Rosary, not the close, breathing love and touch. Not the love you could actually know about. Merely an old and reflexive love, the way he would inhale deeply, every time, to smell the waft from the biscuits she'd made before picking one up and biting down.

"Maydie," he said.

"Shush," she said. "Now we're home soon and it don't none of it matter a lick to them horses, will it? Nor them kids, nother. Everbody'll be wantin' just to get fed and get to bed. Ain't it?"

"I reckon," he said, abashed.

"But I don't know iffen she can bear it, can she?" Maydie said. She turned and looked at him for the first time. "You reckon she can? Burl?"

"I don't know," he said slowly, deliberately. Now he was looking straight ahead, too.

"Well now," Maydie said. "I reckon she's a woman and she'll bear it, somehow. So you know what's a'troublin' me?"

He didn't speak. He stared ahead, watching the rhythmic flex and surge of the horses' haunches.

"It's how I reckon you'll be the one that ain't a'goin' to be able to bear it. Burl?"

Burlton didn't answer for a long moment. Then he turned and looked at her. She had turned his way at the same time and their eyes locked and held. He spoke now directly into her rounded, liquid pools, and she answered to his small, weather-tightened glints.

"What you mean, me, Maydie?" he said, very softly.

"You," she said. "You ain't no good at goin' where you don't belong. And you'll find yerself a'hung out and hurtin' and wonderin' how it come to happen."

"I ain't..."

"You're a good man, Burl," she said. Her voice was held firm, steady, by what he could tell was an act of conscious will. "Good. It don't matter, no woman. Nothin' can make a good man be a bad 'un. I know that, iffen you don't. That ain't it, Burl. It's that it ain't no place for you, a'messin' around in town, and it frights me to see it. Like watchin' you a'wanderin' around where you don't know nothin', don't know where you mayt tromp up a hive. And you don't know whut mayt happen b'cause you don't know, can't know, even whut could happen. Place like that, it ain't no place for a good man, Burl. Country man. He won't have no chance. That's whut scares me, iffen I got to tell you. And your gal, she don't care nothin' about that. How could she? Because she has done forgot what a good man is. How much trouble a good man can kindly be done. Burl."

"It ain't..."

"It don't matter," she said. "I'm all right, Burl. It ain't a'goin' to kill no stock. But it'll get you, and you're like to not even know it when it does. But I'm all right."

"Maydie," he said.

"Shush," she said. "Let's us get these kids on home."

iii.

Nole was dreaming. He watched himself, engaged in a dreadfully contorted scene, where he ran along a street, naked, amidst a crowd of jeering onlookers. He passed a blurred, anonymous crowd where, every now and again, he would see in stark, clear detail the face of someone he knew: his mother, and Merv, and his father, and Cal Boarder. Donna, wiping a plate. And these, the ones he knew, weren't jeering. They were pointing at him and shaking their heads sadly. Some would call his name, again and again as though insistently trying to remind him who he was, "Nole. Nole. Nole." But their voices were despairing, as though they didn't expect him to respond. And when he did, when he turned and shouted, "Yes? Yes?" they didn't seem to understand him, because he had run beyond their hearing.

He saw his mother, dressed in a long, sheer gown, her body outlined beneath. And now she was stepping forth from the crowd and offering him her breast to suckle, saying, "It's all right, all right, all right." But he couldn't stop, because he had to keep running or the jeering crowd would close in around him. He knew this. And so he went on by her.

Then he was in a dark space. He sensed it was a large, vacant building, but he couldn't see any of it. He was still naked, but now he was finished running, was attempting to hide in this deep space. He moved ahead, trying to find the wall so he could follow it to a corner where he might curl down and remain still. He could feel the wall just out of reach, in front, but he couldn't seem to get to it, no matter how he tried to move further, one slow, dragging step after another. It felt as though the closer he came to the wall, the more difficult it was to move his legs and feet; it was as though he were fighting some internal drag upon his flexing muscles, so that now he had sunk to his hands and knees and was barely able to move at all. He forced himself along, each movement of arms or legs draining his energy, pulling and sucking at his limbs, excruciating.

He stopped, struggled to his feet, and moved obliquely, diagonally, finding this much easier, sliding to the left in the pitch dark. And, at last, he touched the two walls, merging into a sharp corner where he felt he could hide. But as soon as he began to slide into his crouch, he felt a presence in the corner, some small and vicious animal, a flurried snarling and the slashing of small teeth. And now he wanted to get away, back into the room. But he was held by the creature's gripping fangs.

He felt the cold drawing at him, pulling him up through the horror, into the dullness, toward a thick consciousness: first, the roaring throb at his temples, then the taste. The chill earth sucked at his back, the breeze lowering a pinching, snatching chill on his nose, his damp forehead. He lay still.

The voices around him were slurred, drunken. Slowly, he sat up and blinked his surroundings into perception, arrangement: a yellow, smoking lantern-glow and four tattered old men squatting on heels around a wooden carton, throwing cards. Remembering suddenly, he grabbed at his thigh, felt the pistol, and sank back again, relieved.

He was on the mainland side of Nosey Ned's, somewhere on the spit of land around the ferry, Ned's waiting room. He lay among the "residents" while the dry heat of drunkenness on his face and neck did raw battle with the increasing cold. He shivered. It was dark, nighttime. The empty clay jug lay on its side, next to him. He felt very bad.

"Sum bitch," a voice hawked from the card players and there was gurgled, phlegmy laughter from the others.

"You thew the goddamn thing," another said. There was the slurry, smacking sound of wet lips on cold glass. A gurgle of swallowing.

Gradually, like a rising pool, Nole's memory filled into the shallows of his consciousness: Nosey Ned, Spencer, the jug of pulp backings, the taste of bleach and rot. He turned to his side and retched hollowly. He had eaten nothing today—had begun his day with vomiting—and these heaves were frothy, empty.

"Goddamn," he said.

"Hey there, lady luck's a'comin', God hep us," a voice said. "Bless my soul, Mamma, bring us a kinger with you." There was a moment of breathless silence and then, "Shit fire. I'm fixin' to die, right..." and then gurgled laughter.

"Be damned," another said thickly.

The men peered upward, watching Nole blankly as he rose. He had no idea what time it was, how long he had spent here, drinking the stinking jar Nosey Ned had given him. Nor did he know how long he'd lain unconscious. On his feet he felt clearer, as if standing had thinned the nausea and pain. He was all right.

He remembered, now, that he needed money and drink, good drink, and he stood, baffled. He had nowhere to go, no choices, no world at all, within which he could move freely, unconstrained. He felt as though he had been standing on a point of land, some promontory, while the ground around him was being hacked away a piece at a time until he stood alone and empty in spacious nothingness.

He remembered seeing a bear once at a roadside attraction: a kind of permanent mixture of medicine show, general store, and restaurant, standing on the high road up toward Bristol. There had been a sign encouraging everyone to SEE THE

GREAT AMERICAN GRIZZLY THE SCOURGE OF THE WEST. The bear itself—no grizzly, though it was quite large for a native black bear—was atop a painted metal pole, some twenty feet in the air, perched on a platform a little larger than a card table. There, it shuffled an eternal circle, its head lowering at the crowd below, whence young men would throw clods of clay or pebbles or the odd bit of food. They were trying to get the bear to do something, Nole realized, to evoke some response other than this shambled circle, the rhythmic, methodical, deliberate trudging to nowhere.

The bear's expression seemed to display both fear and hopefulness at once. Fear, lest the animal be injured by the flying debris. And hope, lest a piece of food land on the platform. At times, a chunk of cornbread would strike the beast's flank, fall to the tabletop, and skitter over the edge, while the bear whirled and flopped its big paws, too late to catch the morsel. This would please the men enormously, and they took to deliberately trying to skate bits of bread or cheese, peanuts, across the platform.

Nole stared upward at the beast and he felt a twinging cord, a sinking cool sadness, compounded of guilt and sorrow. He had seen the young men laughing and tossing their trivial goads at the animal, who lurched at the food, then instantly regained his lowering mien and resumed his shambling circuit. Nole had seen, too, the bear's keeper, a thickwaisted man in filthy brown overalls, squatting morosely on a low wooden stool, drinking from a blue bottle. Nole had seen this, and he had felt the dropping despair, like a thin wash brushed across the scene, covering the perched, plodding bear and the laughing men and the keeper, and finally spreading over himself. He thought he might cry out, but no sound came. He turned to go.

But it was not in time. Because a young man had approached the keeper, loose and jocular, fresh-faced and handsome.

"How in hell you get him down from there?" the man asked. The keeper swung his head slowly and spat.

"Down?" he said. "Ain't no damn down." He gestured to a tumble of gray laddered sections lying a ways off. "I go up to him. Ever damn mornin'. Imagine that? Not too bad for him, hey, nothin' to do but walk around and get waited on hand and foot, so to say?" He swung his head again, spitting amber juice.

Nole had spun round at last, putting his back to the dark, determined pace of the animal, the loutish keeper, the crowd of craning, laughing men. But he moved through a hazy projection of his mind: the huge bear, alone in his ludicrously compacted world, where, each morning, would appear, like the sun, the slack and stupid face of the keeper, rising slowly above the rim of the table, to flop some hunk of flesh down onto this horizontal plane of the bear's entire existence. And would disappear, faster than ever he rose. It was a disquieting image, and it had turbled the sadness Nole already felt into something approaching desperation, an interior panic, completely concealed on the surface, the hard crust of expression and gesture he held out to the world.

And so within three hours he had gotten drunk and was fumbling grubbily at some young mountain girl, wheedling and demanding.

Absurdly, ironically, Nole turned a full circle, looking for the way up the towhead, out to where his horse was tethered, up under the holding tank. He gradually oriented himself, drawing his sleeve heavily across his face, and began to stumble toward the rise. In the deep cold night, he had trouble finding the place where the underbrush opened out into a trail, and so he fumbled laterally along the low-lying swamp willow and sassafras, working his way along until he felt nothing—only empty space—the lack telling him he had reached the trace. He stepped into the blackness.

Almost immediately, someone grabbed forcibly at his shirt, pulling him off-balance and sideways, and he fell, overborne by the pull of this invisible hand. He felt the scrubbing, harsh blow of the ground where he landed at the same instant the trail was illuminated by a globe of light, moving rapidly toward his face.

A man threw himself onto Nole's prostrate body, letting the lantern land heavily by his side. The man smelled overwhelmingly of stale flesh and alcohol, and he spread himself over Nole in a grotesque similitude of sexual embrace. It was one of the "residents," his eyes livid and crazed in the lantern light. He grasped Nole by the hair, lifting his head from the ground, then letting it fall back. Nole felt the man lower himself entirely, pressing body upon body, felt the man's cheek next to his, the rough scrub of whisker bristle. He heard a liquid voice, the lips moving wetly against his ear.

"My name was at the top," the man bubbled in a singsong tremor. "And many sins below." And again: "Many sins below."

Nole struggled against the clutching embrace and surged into a sidewise tumble, turning both bodies, like lovers rolling, the man beneath him now, still burbling.

"I'll not forget the book, with pages white as snow," the man said again and, struggling now himself, raised his voice from a wet whisper to a drawn groan. "I went to the keeper and settled," he keened, fearfully.

Frantic and repelled, Nole kicked himself free and jerked to his feet. But the man's hands followed, grabbling at his pants, pulling himself upward, the crazed face and the voice rising along the length of Nole's body, climbing him.

"Many sins below!" The man was nearly shouting now, frenzied. "Went to the keeper and settled! I settled long ago!"

Nole flung the man away, crashing him into the brush. He turned and scrambled up the trail, back into blackness, feeling relief and disgust. When he reached his horse, he stopped, grabbing at his thigh for the Colt. Reassured, he mounted and kicked the animal into motion, up toward the road, the high road, out of town.

He listened, within, to a rising swirl of voices—the crazed man and the others, the card players. And before, the sneer of

Nosey Ned, Spencer's heezing laughter. And earlier yet, his mother resisting him, calling his name, and the mocking hilarity of the men at Donna's, Janey Gill's syrupy petulance. And back around: John the Revelator and Spencer's oily exordium, *Go see your daddy. Go see your daddy.* And at last, his father's voice, too: *I b'lieve even you could set up such a little thing as that, don't you? Even you?* And he felt a pillar of outrage and vicious, brooding anger arising within, and saw his father's sneering face. His father had started it all, all the fury and shame and regret. One man.

I went to the keeper and I settled.

He wondered a moment, how long had he lain unconscious at the landing. He had no idea how late it was.

iv.

Janey Gill lay in the bed, watching her sister's naked form shivering in the thin light of the lantern. Janey drew up the feather tick, over her breasts.

"Sarie," she said, syruping her voice, wheedling. "How 'bout you do the milkin' t'morra?" She stretched her legs, feeling the stiffness of the wagon bed, the cold boards on the ride home. "Huh?"

"I ain't, Janey Gill," Sarie said. She ducked into her gown and ran for the bed, hopping lightly in. "I done your milkin' for you last Sundy. Ain't a'goin' to do it again."

"I'll give you a nickel."

"Nickel for the plate. Good's a nickel on a Sundy? Aunt Maydie just makes you thow it in the plate. 'Sides, Janey Gill, you ain't got no nickel."

Janey was quiet. Sarie was right; she had no money at all. She warmed for a moment, thinking of Nole Darlen's promise of money and a ring. *And no Octagon Soap ring, nother*, like Paulson had tried to give her last year. *No more of these low-down hillbillies around me.*

"Have, too," she said. Sarie said nothing, tucking herself up and closing her eyes.

"Don't let no cousins come a'boundin' in here, wake me

up," Sarie mumbled.

"You look out for your own self." Janey felt frustrated and impatient. She was going to meet him tomorrow night at the revival. But then, he had been so strange today. Crying like that. She'd never seen him that way. And now it would be a long week before she would feel his lank body pounding at her, the sweated cries. *Lessen we can squinch off at the meetin' have us some fun. 'Sides, I wouldn't be struck dumb iffen they ain't another little bit he's a'goin' to have to mind, right soon.* She smiled, secretly, pondering.

It would be a cold night and a cold morning's milking. Janey turned and drew her knees up. Sleep would be fine.

Burlton had put the horse up and was walking slowly in from the barn. He was thinking of Rosary, her curved hands on him. He saw Maydie's bulky form standing in the door watching him, and he felt a pall of gloomy indecision. He wouldn't have called this *lovesick*, wouldn't have used the word at all in conjunction with either woman, but it was, in fact, a kind of lovesickness he was feeling. He suddenly found himself doing battle with his own life, his own history. *Whyn't I meet up with her years back?* He thought, and then, *It ain't fair to Maydie to be so strong held here and all the while me a'wishin' I was yonder.* He would not choose to be the man he was, or had been, but there was no other man, no other version of Burlton Hobbes. A farmer, smelling of horse sweat and wagon grease, clomping his way to his rickety house, his broad, plodding wife waiting for him, not to see him, to talk to him, certainly not to touch him, but merely to have the opportunity to blow out the lights and go to bed. While Burlton has a beautiful and sensitive companion lying by herself, fifteen miles away, a universe away from the tobacco gum and the Cloverine salve. And was it reward or punishment, pleasure or pain, to have known her, touched her, spoken—talked—with her? To return home and still be the farmer, still the gum and the barbed wire?

"You comin' in, Burl?"

He hadn't noticed that he had stopped walking. He lowered his head and tromped onward in the thick, heavy brogans.

CHAPTER EIGHT

NIGHT

i.

So it was well past midnight when Nole turned down the narrow lane along Blair's Creek. The fresh, chill air of the spring night had sobered him up, though he felt a constant internal tremor, linked as though by wires to the dull thud in his temples. He descended until he heard the creek just to his left, slapping and turning through high banks along the lane. To his right, a wall of damp clay rose and curved inward, almost overhead, where the branches reached across from one side of the lane to the other. He reached along his thigh and felt the hard barrel of the pistol, inside his pants, the cylinder cutting into the bend of his waist as he rode.

He had a tune running through his mind—it had been playing over and over, since the crazy man at Nosey Ned's landing, but now he became cognizant of the lilt and turn, listening to the notes and the voice in his mind, singing,

There was a time on earth, when in the Book of Heaven,
An old account was standing, for sinners unforgiven,
My name was at the top, and many sins below,
So I went to the Father and I settled, I settled long ago.

An old song like hundreds of others, of sin and redemption, in the rounder's mode, the rough, tough drinker and fighter who's seen his account in the book on high.

For I was always sinning, and never tried to pray. He realized he was humming, timing the lines to the horse's sideways rocking as it ambled along the trail. The ground had leveled for a moment and opened out on both sides so he could see nothing in the darkness, no cut of clay or fence post and, though he could still hear the creek, it no longer echoed against the rise to his right, and so it sounded thin, distant. *But when I looked ahead, and saw the page in gold.*

He'd been quite a guitar player for a time, before the drink took over most of his interest. He'd even played in a string band, in town, when he was younger, picking out the long, looping bass runs he'd heard Riley Puckett play, curving and stepping up and over the chord while the fiddle played its wild, outlandish sallies, his right hand striking the guitar like the steady footbeats of a man chasing a colt—excited, exuberant, but still in complete control—knowing precisely when to throw out the circled line. He had met Merv Craishot when he was playing, and she had been drawn to him by the music, turning her head to cast her eyes on him as she spun and twirled along the dance floor. *Do you know the Wildwood Flower?* But that had all passed. He felt a fine glow of regret. The music had been a part of him, a trusted haven, and now it was gone. He never played for long anymore. He always got drunk too soon, and the music 264aveled out of his hands. He couldn't even recall where he'd left his guitar last. *Went to the keeper and settled.* He halted the horse and sat in the silent, sightless open.

He used to stop sometimes, in the middle of playing alone, at home—the old home, where he would sit on the back steps, looking out over the farm, making music for hours when his father was away. He would stop and tip the guitar up and look at it: the flat, ochre top, stretched wide, with his smeared handprints flattening the finish, and the huge round hole that smelled of felled trees and damp, a pool of air opening to the dark cave inside. But the part that seemed most alive was the fingerboard: the black, deep ebony crossed by narrow rails of bright metal, all of it shaping his own left hand into a springy curve, as much a part of the instrument as of him, as much extension of fingerboard as of wrist and arm. Stopping to look like that, in the midst of the fast, smooth, bending play, was like stopping time itself, or like reaching out and shutting off the dripping of cane juice from the rollers, the individual curved drops forming a pattern, random and unreal, but expressive of the growth, the weight of the cane, and the plodding, circling horse turning the mill, the vats and cookers and the dark smell of the molasses itself, all stilled in the suspended, abstracted droplets.

He sat the horse, listening to the music ringing in his mind. Everything else was quiet except for the creaking of the saddle leather and the running of the creek. He felt the air drop into a deeper chill, and he cupped his hands and blew on them. It was too cold to sit still and, for a moment, he considered turning back, riding for town. But he found he was already *chikchikking* the horse, already continuing down the lane, and so he let the tune carry away his thoughts *In my happy home*. And he let his initial intention carry him further along toward the huge house that had seemed suddenly to signal everything he had lost. *My Father's home above*.

Fifteen minutes later, he passed the Hobbes house on his right, the stream still carrying itself along on the left. But from here, the lane rose along the humped flank of a larger hill, while the stream cut away lower, into the ravine. He knew this, and he saw it through hearing and proprioception—the heaving push of the horse's backside and a shift from the side-by-side swing of its forelegged gait to a forward-and-backward slew as its big hips drove the hind legs into their climbing pace—the fading crinkle of stream water and the closed smell of the tangle on his left, the sassafras and scrub and swampwiller marking the ravine. He was moving up the rise that would turn and ease downward to the mansion. *In just five minutes*, he thought, as though the horse was standing still and it was time that curved the rise, the elapsing minutes that climbed toward the brow of the lane, cut against the higher slope on the right, turning and easing, the slow seconds drawing lane downward to looming housefront. Time alone, as though he had never moved from that murky blind pig where he had found himself snatching up the pistol, never moved at all, only the ticks of the clock pulling aside the walls and buildings, shifting the scenery—Donna's and the laughing men, and then the same room, empty as a grave, Janie hearing his weeping, and Mamma with that man, and Nosey Ned's and the imperative goad *go see your daddy*. And then that tune: *I went to the Father and I settled*. Until the hours had dragged onstage this pitched lane, had grasped and heaved terrifically to bring the huge edifice into the foreground, where it stood, blacker than the black of the night.

Nole recalled the first time his father had struck him. He had been quite young, and he could not recollect whatever trivial offense had merited the whipping. What he did remember in an excruciating evocation of drawn, dragging suspense, was the torturous wait. Because his father had not discovered the crime and meted out the punishment at once, in a surge of feeling, with anger on the one side and guilt on the other, to justify, explain the action—so the whipping might seem a natural consequence of both his offense and the father's anger, or disappointment, or sadness. No. Instead, the father determined the punishment, announced it, and sent the boy to the shed to await the actual whipping, which would come only at the end of the father's day's plowing, or setting, or suckering.

And this was the terrible thing: the afternoon alone in the planked shed, waiting for day to end and blows to fall. And, young as he was, he could barely stand the suppression of feeling, emotion, pain. He felt overwhelmed by the negation itself, distracted by the conflict between wishing the time would pass quickly—so as to get on to the actual punishment—or hoping the elapse would extend, elongate, so as to delay the stinging blow on which all of this waiting was already focused. He found himself frantic with fear and longing, and more lonely than he had ever imagined was possible anytime, anywhere.

He found himself standing at the door of the shed, terrified to step across the threshold, because whatever punishment might come from disobeying this sanction must be horrific in its unimaginability. So he would stand at the door and call, "Daaa-ddy, Daa-ddy" to the silent lot. And he would begin to weep, tears of sad longing and outraged frustration, still calling, "Daaaaa-ddy."

It was the worst he had ever felt in his life.

His father had appeared at last, sweated and grimy from his day's work, but exuding an air of calm satisfaction as he administered the whipping, while his hand induced its thin, stinging pain. And, even then, the boy could see that the father took pleasure, actual physical satisfaction, in remaining calm, methodical, indifferent, through the execution of the punishment. And so there was not even a final resolution, no release for the boy, who had waited all day in agony, anticipating the cathartic climax, the emotional summing up and expiation of the guilt and anger, the fear and longing, and the dreadful aloneness. And, instead here was the dispassionate father turning the entire terrible day back on itself, fixing the awful waiting into a permanent absence of feeling, an excruciating, unresolved tension through which the boy would meet and interact with the father forever, forever crying *Daaa-ddy* to the empty field, to the vacant, pleased, unfeeling face.

ii.

Listening to the echoes of his own childhood cries, he thought, *The shed, yes, the shed.* And so he rode beyond the house, watching its huge, bulking nothingness on his right. He reached the second gate, where he could look in and see the fuzzy darkness that was the smaller building, some hundred feet or more beyond, beside and behind the house, where his father lay sleeping. He dismounted slowly and led the horse across the lane, away from the gate, where he looped the reins around a sapling. He reached and tapped, twice, at the gun in his pants, feeling the weight against his groin and thigh, the way, sometimes, he'd cup himself in the night, in his bed, feeling the soft weight of his own flesh between his legs, not a caress, not sensual, so much as a completion, circular, meeting himself in the touch of his own body.

But tonight he had wedged the heavy Colt between his circling hand and those soft nether parts, and it was the gun he cupped and soothed, in place of himself. And this may have been the turning point, the gesture that determined all his subsequent actions. Because from this moment on, it seemed as though it was the pistol that willed and directed the flesh. As though the touch of smooth, hard metal had short-circuited the summing completion of hand against body. As though he had become instrument to the pistol's agency and control now, striding back along the lane to the main gate and swinging through its sprung tension, onto the flagstone walk leading to the wide porch steps.

There was another time, too, a day he had forgotten until this moment when the memory found its way to him, stepping with him into the deep nothingness around the house. *There was another time, another day, and he sent me there, too*—to the shed, to wait out the day in torment, so the father might feel the gratification, the pleasing pulse of his own cool, passionless control. And, again, the boy waited in a suspension of yearning and guilt, afraid to move beyond the bounds of that shed, and feeling alone, and crying out for his father. And he was genuinely shocked and hurt anew when the man didn't answer, didn't appear at the sound of his own child's agony, even though the boy knew he wouldn't, hadn't the first time—knew the waiting was the thing, prerequisite to the man's orgastic apathy—and so the hurt and amazement was the thing, too.

But this time, my mamma heard, and come to me. Knelt on the sill of the barn and took the weeping little boy into her arms, against her warm breasts, where he was no longer ever allowed to press his face in joy and love, though he still could in pain and agony, for a little while longer. Only then, in shame and guilt, could he embrace his mother's body. And soon, not even that; soon, he would never again be permitted to press his face to her pulsing curve.

And she stayed there with him as he held to her and wept. And the father appeared, ready to complete the day's punishment, in the cold, ritualistic whipping. And Mamma said, "Carl, he's done suffered enough. Why not let's just let it go at this, and let's us all go in and eat some supper?" And his father looked at her and made a jerking motion with his hand, and so she stood up and walked away, leaving them there, the suspended day still hanging over the scene, the dusted soft light of late afternoon slanting into the shed, the little boy looking upward at the calm, still, narrow face, the father directing his glance downward, toward the boy, but not looking, not seeing. Listening, still, to the woman.

Because his father said, "Goddamn her," and made that same jerked gesture. And only then looked at the boy. And said in a strained tone, "I reckon she's right, son," his tight voice not even barely tinged with caring, forgiveness. "I reckon you done had enough trouble today. Let's us go eat." And he took the boy by the shoulder and turned him toward the door and walked him out of the shed, his hand light and cold between the child's shoulder blades, moving along toward the house.

And the boy hated him at that moment—thinking, *He's afraid of her, ain't he?*—with a hatred beyond his own childish capacity to accommodate, absorb, even comprehend the surge of loathing that swept over him. *He's touchin' me like this because he's got to, because he's afraid not to.* Because a little boy can't name "hatred," or "revulsion," and so he has no place to put it, to learn how to handle it. He can only wait. *Wait. Like I waited in that shed, for the time that was a'comin', the time all this was just a'fixin' to lead to, all of it, just makin' ready, gettin' set, for the time that'd come. Merv and the reward that the sonofabitch set me up to and kept to hisself. Not no more. Not this time. Now. Tonight.* He knew he had made a decision at this moment, though he couldn't have said what: He only knew it was going to end, this interminable waiting, at any rate.

Nole had reached the wide wooden steps and he pounded heavily up them, hoping to wake the man. *So he'll have to wait to see me comin' into the room yonder.* He thudded across the porch floor and flung open the heavy front door.

"'S'at?" his father said from the side room. The son couldn't see anything, but he felt the shape of the hallway, the rising curve of stairway, still smelling of the hand-rubbed oil finish the man had demanded, required. Felt the presence of the open door to his father's small room, where the man had actually lived, celibate and hermit-like, for these three years, allowing his son the use of the remainder of the house whenever the younger man saw fit to visit. It was always a visit, even when he came once and remained for a period of months. Because he never moved in, never actually *dwelt*, which would have meant molding the house or even a room of it to fit his form, to reflect his character in some way, even if only in the way his clothes hung in the closet, or which post of the bed he dropped his hat onto when he entered the room. No. For all the impress of *dwelling* created by the son's habitation, this may as well have been a hotel—not even a boarding house—a room paid for and interchangeable with a dozen other bedchambers under the same roof.

Nole saw the white flare from a match, and then the pale orange flicker of the lamp, creating monstrous, oozy shadows in the hallway. He headed for the lightened square and into the father's room.

As if in alien opposition to the the huge empty house, the small room had all the marks of a dwelling, so much so that it appeared far older than it was, as though the man must have resided in it for a considerable time, to have shaped it so closely to his own life, and not the paltry term of three years. It looked like him: the set of the furniture, the neatly—even primly—arranged toilet items on the polished and unmarked dresser. Even the three photographs, the lovely woman, and the girl who would have been pretty except for a straitened quality, some coldness around her features. And the boy, his wide forehead and narrow, curving eyes, with an expression that was almost a smile, but was too tentative, puzzled perhaps, too equivocal at any rate, to have been an expression of any feeling as simple as a smile. The three photographs, in chestnut frames patiently and scrupulously hand-carved by the man himself, and hung above the bed.

The older man was sitting up in the narrow spool bed, blinking away the match-blindness. The sharp, pinched smell of the sulfur. Carl Darlen peered toward the door, picking up the moving image of his son.

"'S'at?" he said again. "'S'it Nole? That you?" He settled back as he recognized his son. "What you doin' out here this time a night?" His hand scrabbled along the small bedside table. Found the cigarette case and picked it up.

"Don't bother," Nole said.

"What? What did you say?"

"Put it down. You ain't got time to light it. Come on, Daddy, we're a'goin' out to the shed." Nole knew exactly what he was going to do now. He could see it perfectly, and he felt a kind of calming release, like the aftermath of some lifelong internal storm suddenly blown out and past. He drew the revolver and hefted it in his palm as though tossing a ball up and down.

"What you got there?" his father said. *He still talks that way. Like he's the big man and I'm the little 'un. Like ain't nothin' he can't handle, nothin' he can't wrop up and put it in his pocket. Like he got it all took care of.*

"Well I'll show you somepin," Nole said.

"What? What're you jawin' about?"

"Wait," said Nole, remembering. "Get some money. You give me some money."

"I ain't got no money."

"Where is it?" said Nole, raising his voice and scanning the room with the pistol, as though looking for something to shoot at, then leveling the barrel and his eyes upon the man in the bed.

"I told you, Nole. You know I don't keep no money around here. Got ten dollar on the dresser yonder. I told you, you don't get no money from me. Not yet. I die, you'll get your share. Not that you ever done a god damn thing to deserve none of it. Money's in the god damn bank, Nole, and you ain't gettin' a bit of it."

Nole reached his free hand back to the dresser and felt around. When he felt the bill, he crumpled it and brought it to his pocket in a single motion.

"Ten dollars," he said.

"Sawbuck's more'n you deserve from me," said his father.

"Besides, I told you. You got plenty money a'waitin' on you, once I don't have to watch the way you spend it."

"Well then I reckon I'll get my share," Nole said. He laughed, thin and mirthless. "I got somepin here for you," he said. "Git up. We're goin' to the shed. Git up, Daddy, you son of a bitch." He laughed again, without amusement or pleasure. "I b'lieve even you could do such a little thing as that, don't you?" He held the gun up, showing it, then leveled the barrel, pointing it at his father. "Git up."

"We goin' to the shed, huhn? What in hell we goin' to the shed for, this time a night? What did you call me? Would you put that gun away? What you after, anyway?" His father got out of the bed and faced him across the room, uncertain about how serious the situation was, or whether it was serious at all. His son was pointing a gun at him, to be sure, but there was no one in the world he was less afraid of than his son. So he refused to believe it, even as he found himself clambering into his overalls, picking up the lamp, and walking out of the room, waved out by the son's pistol hand that made rolling "get-along" motions. Refused to consider that there was any meaning to this strange midnight visitation at all, any threat embodied in the weapon. Refused, even to reflect upon what sort of emotion might have driven his son to take the pistol and ride it out fifteen miles from town in the middle of the night to point it at his father. Refused, even as he found himself stepping out the front door onto the porch, ushered there still by the wagging gun.

And the son wasn't thinking either. He was still operating under the strange intimation that he was submitting to the will of the Colt revolver, and so he, too, found himself moving in concert with his father, without any mulling or contemplation. It all seemed laid out for both of them, and each felt as though he were stepping off paces, meaningless and routine, from room to porch to steps and down to the front ground.

"Jesus Christ, boy," his father said. "It's cold out here. Let's just turn around and go set in the house, hey?"

"Git on," the boy said. "I done told you, we're a'goin' to the shed. I b'lieve even you could get up such a little thing as that, don't you? You remember that, Daddy?" The boy laughed, short, dry, and inflectionless.

"What in hell you talkin' about?"

"Well, I reckon you'll find out in a minute," Nole said.

"It's cold enough to kill hogs. What you fixin' to find in the shed you can't have anywhere's else?"

The boy laughed again. The same flat sound, without smiling. "Cold enough for killin' hogs, you say?" he said. "I reckon."

They walked on, and now the father was silent as his son pushed the sharp, hard barrel of the gun into the man's back, between the shoulder blades, drilling him forward, along the side of the black house and into the mud of the real place, the farm, no longer polished and curved, but sloppy, turgid, and dank. There was no sound, now, but the *skleech* of their boots in the mud, the smell of manure and new-thawed muck. They walked in the fuzzed halo of the lamp, which darkened everything beyond into a deeper pitch, a darker-than-darkness, so they seemed to be walking entirely alone through a squishing slough of air, into black, redolent nothingness.

Stepping into the shed was like coming aboard some cozy platform after a night alone in trackless water. The light threw itself onto the gray planked walls and bounced back, turning their faces pale blue in a yellowed glow from the elliptical flame of the lamp. The father set the lamp on the slatted table and reached to turn and draw up the chair.

"Don't set down," said Nole. "I want you just a'standin' here, just lookin' and waitin'."

"Waitin'?" the man said, his voice ringing a pitch higher, a note of concern or impatience. "Waitin', what for?"

His son laughed, again that dry, cold, meaningless sound. "Waitin' for killin' hogs, I reckon. Damn sure cold enough, ain't it, Daddy?"

He had used to ride into town on his mamma's lap, sitting in the wagon next to the serious, silent father, who spoke only to *gee* or *haw* the team. And his mamma would sing, quiet and slow, from deep inside, and he could lay his head against her chest and hear the full, chambered sound, not of her voice but of her own self, her body, filling with music. And he would drop into sleep hearing the deep, pulsed *thrum* of the song through his mamma's breast, hearing it into his sleep and through the rocking depth, so that the sound and the sleep seemed to be the same thing, the same state of being, some strange peace partaking of the swell of his and her breathing, the skim of warm dampness on her and his skin. And he would wake and roll his head just a bit, against her soft swell, and he would believe that everything could be full and pulsed and beautiful.

And he didn't even remember when it was they made him stop doing it, stop riding on her lap. But they had, of course, and now he could only remember that there was a time before—with the sonorous soft flesh—and a time after, with the jolting harsh rattle of the wagon bed. And he could remember the before time distinctly enough to feel the searing pain of loss, the lack of comfort, the parting, forever from the last safe place.

But it wasn't that loss, he knew as much. He'd become inured to solitude, to the lack of the warmth and the pulse. And he knew what he was, even if he didn't like who he'd become, out in the world, alone, on his too small piece of space. No. It wasn't that; wasn't even the loss of his mother again, today, the naked woman still carrying the weight of that man's hands on her flesh, where Nole was never allowed again. No. It wasn't that. It was Merv and the shame of betrayal, the loss Nole had suffered at his own hands. And it was all because this person—this "father"—had made him do it.

He levelled the pistol, pointing it at the standing, bemused man, who still didn't understand or couldn't believe that this night had any significance whatsoever. Even when his son slowly thumbed back the trigger and held the gun, unwavering, and waited.

After some moments, the father expelled his breath, relaxed. Put his hands to his hips.

"I knew you wouldn't dare," he said to the pointed pistol.

"Ha," the son said, smirked. "You say."

"You wouldn't dare."

The son's wry smile was caught up in the flash from the barrel, as though he had been posing for the photographer's shot. And the gun recoiled terribly upward as the man jumped and crashed to the ground.

iii.

Burlton Hobbes lay in bed, staring upward into the darkness and wondering how it had all come to pass. Before Rosary, he seemed hardly to have been a thinking being at all. He realized now that his surprising connection to this slim, passionate woman had for the very first time roused thought and feeling as functions of his life. Before, he had known how to raise a crop, how to tie a hand of tobacco, how to drive the wagon into town without having to consider options or reasons or significance. *Thinking* would have seemed entirely inimical to *knowing*: If he had to think about a task, that meant he didn't know how to do it. And, like instinct, the knowing-how and the actual doing seemed identical—laying barbed wire onto the locust fence stakes he had hewn himself, stretching and knackering the clawed strand, ratchet in one hand and pliers in the other, knowing precisely when to take first wrap and then to ratchet one more notch before wrapping the wire once more, and on to the next angled gray post—a smart, capable farmer precisely because he didn't think or wonder. He just knew.

But now he lay in the dark silence and wondered how it all could have happened, and he realized that thinking had become the entire ground of his existence. Because everything else just *happened*. Everything else was just something you found yourself involved in, discovered it was happening, without any choice or volition on your part. So that left only the thinking, the pondering. *How could it all have worked out to this?*

And he wondered about that day he had climbed the hill, Hoover scampering and wagging by his side. How he had looked down and seen the strange, lithe woman and been struck by her presence. And what if he had never gone up there? What if he'd gone to the barn and soaked down some oats for his mare, sick with heaves? Or what if she'd never come into the warehouse that snowy day in the autumn? There were other possibilities, other things could have happened, and he found he could mull these over, consider the might-have-beens, weigh their outcomes.

But not the actual case: because it had snowed, and she had passed him the crinkled scrap of paper wrapped around the key to 123 Pineola, and the strangely compelling woman had become his very life, it seemed, the touching and the sighing and the long talk. All of it, something that had happened and no longer could bear the thinking. Only the wondering *How? How?* And he remembered Maydie telling him, "it ain't no place for you, a'messin' around in town," and how he might "tromp up a hive." *Without even knowing it.* "Place like that, it ain't no place for a good man. Country man." And Burl remembered Jem, the bewilderment on his frightened face as he sat shaking in this very house, almost three years back, and asked, despairing, "How did I come to be a killer?" Saying, with a kind of anguished certainty, "I never wanted to kill no one." Or before, when he shot that sheriff in Mississippi and started it all, turning to fire at the sound of a snapping pistol—because he knew how to shoot without thinking, knew how shooting had to be instinctive, the way Burl knew when to release the bind on that barbed wire. And so even Jem was left with the wondering, because he could only know for certain what couldn't have happened, that he couldn't have killed as a deliberate action. And so he shuddered and wept and asked Burl the question no one could answer, because it wasn't even a question any longer.

Because it had happened: Jem had become a killer.

Now Jem was dead, and Merv, too, gasping out her life because she had happened to attend a dance a year and a half earlier.

And Burl himself? Burlton Hobbes, fallen in love with a woman from another world, and he knew there was nothing to ask about this, either. So Maydie had said, "It ain't a'goin' to kill no stock," and Burl reckoned that was about right. Unless it did.

He recalled a visiting minister, a circuit rider, who had led a brush arbor meeting, back around the time of the shoot-out. Burl hadn't much liked the man. He was the sort of preacher who seemed to be trying to insist upon something he knew wasn't true, as though he had a job selling you a defective product of some sort. At any rate, the man's theme had been "acceptance," and he had said, "Brothers and sisters, we don't revere Christ for deciding to go out and die for us. We revere the Son for accepting the burden the Father had already placed upon him. The decision was the Father's, and the acceptance was the Son's. And that acceptance, that's what makes Christ a model for us humans to live by. He carried out the Father's plan that had already been written indelibly into the holy Book of Heaven."

Hogeye had said, "It don't sound like he had a hell of a lot of choice in the matter."

And now, musing in the darkness, Burl thought, *I reckon that's about all there is to it. They ain't much choice in the matter.* He lay still.

It's a'goin' to be a cold night, he thought and let slip his mind into sleep.

He dreamed he was walking along a straight, narrow waterway, like one of the sluices cut from the riverway in Roalton, only now the canal was out here, in the rolled and wooded foothills.

And across the water, he saw Hoover, running back and forth along the bank, barking at him, trying to tell him something. And suddenly it wasn't Hoover, but Rosary, standing on the far bank and waving *Come on down.*

But he was afraid of the roiling dark water. So he stood and watched her wave.

And then he realized that Jem was in the water, and was trying to swim, struggling to move in the surging water, against the slapping current. And Rosary and Hoover, both, across the way, stood impassive, now, in the shadow of an enormous edifice, like a temple. And he realized suddenly that Merv, too, was in the water, fighting to stay above the surface, going under once, then twice, then crying out for help calling, "Jem, Jem." And Jem turned, in a single motion, raised an enormous pistol, and shot her.

Burlton awoke and sat up, abruptly, realizing he could still hear the echoing report of the gunshot. "Maydie," he called. "Wake up."

iv.

And so, the explosion ringing, too loud, Nole had run out the crude doorway, panicked. He had turned back again, back through the mud and into the shed to fetch the pistol, and run out again, across and down the ravine, where he tripped and fell, outstretched, and where he lay still.

While Nole lay stretched out on the pebbled pathway, Burlton Hobbes climbed the hill in the darkness, looking for the source of the gunshot he'd heard. But he found nothing and went back to bed, asleep in the sharp, cold night.

And, after a long time, Nole was up again, and again to the shed, as though all elapse, all motion, all feeling had been strung to this one place, where as a boy he had waited in desperate suspension for his father to appear and to enact his soulless punishment. And where, now, Nole had come back to erase the cold, indifferent power that his father had always wielded. And had blotted it out in a sudden, bursting flare of acrid sound.

"Deader'n hell," he said, standing over the crumpled corpse, the shattered chair, the pooled, black blood. "Deader'n hell."

And the younger man had dragged the body back into that small room, with the family portraits brooding over above the bed, where the son now flung his father's lifeless body. Then walked out of the house and settled himself impassively on the porch steps where he had sat earlier, after laying down the pistol that seemed still to be ringing with the explosion.

And some hours later, at first light or a little after, he didn't know, he had risen and walked deliberately out the gate and along the lane to his horse. Had mounted the horse and ridden slowly away, back up the rise toward Hobbes's. Into the pearling dawn.

The brow of the rise shimmered before him, as though it would engulf him in nacreous splendor as soon as he crested the slope. But when he did so, the glorious coloration fled instantly, to coat the higher knob a half mile away. And he sat his horse in the thin air, looking down onto the Hobbes's dim, hazed, olive-tinted farmscape. It looked smudged and faded in the grainy light. To the right, the creek was obscured in billowed gray mist. But the rise upon which he sat grew clearer and sharper with each passing second, so that, looking over his horse's startlingly apparent head—he could see the tiniest hairs on the dark skin edging the animal's perked ears—he felt as though he were floating in some transformed state over a world gone faint and muted.

But he knew he must descend again, out of this keen transparency and back again into the heavy depths. So he *chikked* his horse and rode down the slope toward the misted farm.

Janey Gill had left the house in a flurry, hearing her uncle shouting at the dog, *What in the world you got into, Hoover?* The sound of his voice merely quickened her pace. Wrapped up as she was in her own body, her own teenaged narcissism, she cared for nothing whatever in the world of aunt or uncle. *Good Lord. Hoover! Git on outen that!* She entered the dark, chill barn.

In the kitchen, Burlton was holding up a gnawed length of

wood and staring at his dog. "Well, I be damned," he said. He stood, amazed, for a moment, his gaze sweeping the corner where Hoover had slept last night. "Looky here," he said. "Well, looky here."

In the barn, Janey Gill slung her milk pail from its nail on the wall and headed toward the stalls, bouncing the thin tin bucket on her thigh. She entered the stall, which seemed to be all cow—sight, smell, the damp slew of straw at her feet—all of it a part of and all of it linked together into her own years of experience milking, the absent, semi-conscious drawing and pulling. She knew that if she thought of anything at all, the task would prolong itself, because she would lose the dense, stupid rhythm of push-up and let-down, as though the motions of her hands were the actual ticks of time and the task's completion depended on time alone. And so she felt no glow, no sense of participating in and with the animal in this miraculous giving down of sustenance through their living, breathing bodies.

And so she squatted beside the cow and milked stupidly, listening to the squirt of liquid in the pail, the way she might hearken abstractly to the ticking of a clock. No more than that. While, in the house, her Aunt Maydie came into the empty kitchen to begin making breakfast biscuits and frying ham, and stopped short, staring at the dog.

"Ye gads," she said. "What's all this mess? Burl. Burl?" But he didn't answer, was nowhere to be seen. She gave out a sigh and turned toward the back hallway. "Where is that man?" she asked herself.

V.

Nole Darlen rode his horse down over the side of the hill toward the Hobbes place. As his mount stepped a stiff-legged gait, picking its way as horses always wish to do when they're moving downhill, he saw rise before him, like a figure in the gray creek-mist, the image of his father's body, already dead, its entire weight flung upward by the force of the bullet. He saw it elongate for a split second—the torso seeming to draw out so that it appeared to pull the feet upward off the floor—then crumple back on itself, crashing, as though thrown down by an enormous hand, over and through the chair, as the fog from the creek on his right whorled and turned in the first breath of the day's breeze. He saw the body, curled over the shattered chair, the pools and streamlets of black blood.

He shook the sight off, forcing himself to think systematically. *How many more hours now? How long before I can throw my own self onto a bed, the way I flung his body, and get some damn sleep? Two hours or so, anyways, ain't it, if this here's all the fast this here horse has got to fetch. Because I'm plumb wore out with of all this,* he thought, suddenly recognizing how tired and saddle-weary he was. *Because I didn't get no sleep last night, out to all hours and up sick and shakelin'. And all that tussle with Mamma and then that jug and you wear your-*

self plumb out thataway. Then to ride out here and shoot him. Hah. "Killin' hogs," he done said. And what'd I say? "I reckon." Hah. His eyes were dry and grainy, and his hands felt cold and raw like scrubbed paper. He could hardly bear the thought of the interval that must elapse between now and his rest, again thinking as though it were time and not distance he had to traverse.

The lane was curving into a leveled stretch just before Hobbes's place, but Burlton was not there to see Nole swing slowly and stiffly along on the walking horse. Hobbes's wife was calling for him from inside the house, her voice a muffled, untuned reed, disembodied and barely distinguishable: "Burl. Burrell! Where in the heavens air you, Burl?"

Nole heard the barn door *clatch* and *skeenge* open, and he turned to look, expecting to see the man responding to his wife's rounded call. But, instead, Janey Gill emerged, carrying her full pail, her other arm outstretched to counter the weight, and walking with a jerked-hip rolling, as though the pail weighed fifty pounds. She saw Nole—but did not at first recognize him—mounted in the lane, and she stopped, set the pail down, and straightened her body. Then she slung her pelvis forward and leaned further back, stretching the tight muscles, flexing her body into a convex, bowed arch. She recognized him suddenly and straightened herself. Made a hasty wave and ran toward him, leaving the steaming pail sitting, abandoned.

He saw her, and thought, *O my Lord, this ain't no time, no time at all,* thinking, *it ain't felt right since I got up offen that porch, like I done timed it wrong. Got to thinkin' and lost track or some damn thing. Done somethin' out of step.* Because it seemed like it was all so difficult, now, like he was surrounded by some gelatinous medium, through which every motion was a struggle, a pushing, surging effort, with nothing to grab onto, no place to find purchase, no air to breathe, even. As though he had never gotten out of that mud by the shed. *And this part shouldn't ought to be so hard, just the gettin' home.*

Oughtn't to wear me down, just a'settin' a horse. And now here was Janey running up toward him, and her very presence seemed to thicken the gel through which he tried to move.

"Haddy, Nole," she said. "You uns is up and about right early this mornin', ain't you?" She put her hands behind her back and swung her hips in a gesture at once childish and brazen. "Don't you forget, now, you uns is a'fixin' to come find me tonight to the camp meetin', ain't you?"

He cleared his throat, thinking, *It's like I got somethin' wrong, like I done set there too long or got up too soon.* Saying, "We'd best not let your folks catch us out here a'talkin' in the first of the mornin', Janey." He wanted her to be gone so he could shake the clock back into motion, begin ticking off the paces of his horse, toward home, toward some sort of rest. "Oughten we?" He ran his hand nervously along his thigh.

"I know it, Nole," she said. "But it's important. Tonight. I got somepin I got to tell you. So don't..."

It had taken a long moment, stroking along the flat, tight curve of his thigh, thinking, *Now what is that? What is it? Somethin'...* But when it came to him, it came in a flash, a roar. And now the clock was ticking too fast, suddenly, so he couldn't stop to piece it all together, feeling his palm riding the empty stretch, where his own body shouldn't be, should be blocked by the round, hard cylinder, or the barrel, that was not there. Not there at all. *Wait! Where! Where in hell is the pistol? Where in hell? Wait! Wait!* He jerked up, rigid in the saddle and glared down at the girl, whose mouth was still moving, chattering, though he couldn't hear a thing, nothing at all, for the pounding, roaring shock. *Where's that damn gun? Wait!*

"Well Nole, I weren't a'meanin' to make you mad," she was saying, though he didn't hear her. He just glared down at her, while his hands scrabbled around, like small, nosing animals, scooting around his body, the saddle, searching. And he could feel the thunderous heat of panic, beginning to beat at his ears, while he still thought, *Wait! Wait!* Because everything was tocking off the time too quickly now, and he couldn't move in any purposeful direction because the entire scene—the flexing and coquettish girl, and the Hobbes place, and the fenced lane itself—was swirling madly around, and his hands couldn't stop their varmint scrabbling to grasp any logical, sensible purpose.

"Goddammit," he said to the girl, whose mouth was still moving, talking. And then, "Goddammit!" shouted now, frightening her into stillness, though he had not heard a sound she had made.

But he did hear the noise of his own cursing, and this seemed to throw him into action. He grabbed at the reins and pulled, fierce and hard, jerking the horse around in the lane, as though he were trying to yank the animal out from under his own body. The horse whinnied a complaint, but danced itself around a tight circle, crouching back on its hind legs, so he had to tilt his body forward, as though the animal had lunged suddenly up a steep incline. Then he dug his heels into the horse's flanks and bawled, "Giddup, damn you." And the horse drove itself ahead from the haunches, hurtling instantly forward and leaving Janey Gill alone and stricken, looking young and thin and frightened now.

He leaned his face into the wiry mane as his horse took the rise in a series of lunging rushes, as though the earth, the lane itself, were breathing hard, forcing horse and rider upward on the huge curve of intake and respiration. He heard the same old song again—*the old account was settled*—only this time in a manic jangle, as though some hand were turning the crank on his mind's music box faster and faster, the grotesquely painted doll tucked inside the box, coiled and tensed and about to spring forth as the music wound crazily faster and faster: *Namewasatthetopandmanysinsbelow...*

Over the crest of the rise, the horse shifting from the lunging uphill surge to a loose, clattered, downward careen, nearly out of control, and he knew he should be leaning back over the haunches, but he found himself pitching forward over the animal's ears, and then pushing himself backward by main strength, against the downward draw of horse and slope and gravity itself, to arch backward like some frenzied rodeo cowboy, as the horse skidded its way tumultuously down the grade.

IwenttothekeeperandIsettled...

Now the silent house was clear and bright, the sun picking up its details and etching them in the morning's byplay of light and shadow, so the front porch seemed sliced diagonally into two planes: the steps coped on an oblique angle of yellow and lavender, half in sun, half in shadow, the hatched triangle of daylight widening as the steps ascended, then spreading fan-like over the flat surface, the planked floor of porch. The day was still young enough for rayed brightness to peek under the near end of the porch roof, so that, sitting on the top step, Burlton could look to his left and see the white ball of the sun drilling its ray between the narrow aperture formed by hilltop and porch roof. When he stood up, his face was in chill shadow, and the roof appeared to have closed down over the hill, shutting off the thin strip of sky like an eyelid closing.

Nole Darlen had not seen Burlton stand up, had not seen him at all. Because Nole was sawing at the reins, dragging his horse to a halt as though he were pulling not merely on bit and horsehead but on the entire force of hill and gravity and panic and maniacal music. *Hold it hold it hold it!* The horse appeared to be completely unaware of the dragging rein for a matter of seconds. Then it came to a sudden and complete standstill, as though it had been transformed at once into a statue. And now Nole, who had appeared to be sitting still, dragging the taut reins against the surge of his running horse, was propelled forward, over the immobile horse's ears, his buttocks rising completely out of the curved saddle, his chest landing hard against horse's curved neck and mane, his arms splayed out, like a man who has run full-tilt into a tree trunk or a phone pole, only here the camera has been turned forty-five degrees, the man's body slammed, leaning and sliding a bit along diagonal pole or trunk. Burlton watched as Nole pushed himself upright again and sat the horse, animal and rider both breathing hard, the one from the exertion of running, the other from the force of stopping. They had passed beyond the first gate, the horse's initial momentum carrying them nearly to the second, so Burlton saw Nole's face from an angle behind and lateral to him: the flat curl of his right ear, the thin, sharp line of his cheek, just the final turn of his long nose. *He looks a mite like her*, Burlton thought, gazing out at the sunlit tableau of man and horse, his own brow feeling cold and metallic in the swath of shadow.

Nole slid and settled his buttocks into the saddle and drew his left hand outward, turning the horse away from the house and into a close circle, around in the lane. *He looks like a feller playin' for a fish, a'workin' his line back, but he's a'goin' to lose that fish, tuggin' on it that way*, Burlton thought. *And he looks a right smart like her.*

As soon as his horse had realigned itself on the lane, facing back east, Nole saw the man on the porch, ahead to his left. The face was in shadow, and the sun was in Nole's eyes, so he wasn't certain at first that he'd seen anything. He rode the horse slowly along, back to the first gate, the porch now off directly to his left, the sun no longer glaring in his eyes. At first, again, he suspected he'd conjured up the image himself, to startle himself, after the panicked ride, the frenzied worry. *No. Nossir. It's a man, sure as hell. It ain't HIM, is it? Ain't him.* He shuddered. *God a'mighty.*

He turned his head away, looking over the landscape, the dropped ravine across the road where the creek rattled and slapped. Then he turned his torso fully toward the gate, leaving reins hanging, horse lathered and still. He resolved to speak first, trying to put the man in the wrong, or at the least to intimate that this was his own first visit to the house today.

"What you a'wantin' hereabout?" he said, looking at Burlton.

Burlton stepped down into the light. He held the pistol barrel-down, straight down along his leg.

"I b'lieve you forgot somepin, Nole," he said. "Or two thangs, both."

"What're you a'doin,' my house?" Nole said, recognizing Burlton too late, but now thinking, *Hobbes. Hobbes. Janey's uncle. Mamma's...What in hell's his name? I can't remember his goddamn name.*

"I tole you," Burlton said. "You left you a gun and your daddy, I b'lieve. You come back to pick 'em up? B'cause I got the gun right here, and your daddy's right yonder in his bed where you done left him. But no, I didn't come over the hill to find them. I came lookin' for you, Nole. And here you is."

What in the hell's his name? Nole thought. And only then did he see the pistol pointing down along Hobbes's overalled leg.

"I heard the shot last night and come out to see what's what. But you know? Weren't nothin'. Nothin', that is, until this mornin'. I couldn't tell it last night, in the dark, but my dog, he's a right smart dog. And I reckon he found it, all that blood. And brought a mess of it home on his fur, all in the middle of the night. Brushed it on the kitchen floor just like a feller'd paint a picture. And a stick of furniture, looks like it mayt be offen a chair, all bloodied-up, too. I didn't see none of it last night, but this mornin', well it's all over the corner of my kitchen. Ain't that a thing? So I come back now and found what I'd been a'huntin' last night but didn't know it, kindly." Burlton hefted the pistol. "Found this here gun, this mornin'. So I mayt not be as smart as Hoover, but once I get the hang, I'm a right quick learner."

Nole began to speak, then checked himself before he had emitted any sound. He settled his weight back into the horse and looked at Burlton.

"I reckon we'd best to get you offen that horse, and then we'll try'n get holt of Sheriff Simmons. So whyn't you just come on down to the groun' and holt them hands up?" Burlton raised the pistol and pointed it at Nole.

At that moment, Nole spurred his horse viciously and dragged the reins over hard. He felt as though the animal would never turn, as though he were trying to pull the entire landscape around, and he kicked, hard, again.

The animal spun and lunged forward as the pistol detonated, loud and final.

EPILOGUE

DARKNESS

Sinner, run and hide your face,
Sinner, run and hide your face,
Sinner, run to the rock and hide your face,
The rock cried out, "No hiding place."

Cryin' holy unto the Lord,
Cryin' holy unto the Lord,
Well if I could, I surely would,
Stand on the rock, where Moses stood.

—Carter Family, 1930

i.

Me, I wonder when he'd had time to work it all out. Can you see that feller tryin' to wratch hold of that horse, that'd got to of been ready to run off from the sound of the gun and all. And him a'grabblin' with one hand at the rein and kindly tryin' to holt on with his legs and get that horse settled down and not to fall off her and all. But he's got to get out of there, too, and fast, or he's just as like to get shot again, so he don't want to slow that horse too much, does he? And all the while, he's just done got a bullet in him, and no little flesh-graze, nor the bein' so scared when he thought they'd done shot him that time where it's likely they hadn't even shot *at* him. Because this time he'd took a forty-caliber what-have-you slug right in amongst his shoulder bones, so he's tore up right smart. And tryin' to stay on a spooked horse at the same time. How'd he ever get around to figurin' it all out?

Ain't that the way? Here you know that boy's nothin' but a coward. He's done proved that much to you right to your own face, kindly. And you'd reckon he wouldn't be able to do much more'n fall off the damn horse and that'd be the end of it. But he'd fool you, this time. Because he not only stood that horse and got her settled down enough to carry him all the way up to Campbell's without her gettin' a snuff of all that blood he's covered with and taken to boltin' off and thowin' him any minute along every step of the damn way. No. He not only has got that horse pulled in enough to carry him four mile with his shoulder turned into chippin's and souse meat, but he's got enough left to kindly cobble up the whole story enough so you ask most folks today what happened out there that night, and they'll tell it to you dezactly the way he said it happened. You never would've thought a feller like that could've done it.

But folks swallered ever bit of it. Well, I reckon he was a pert convincin' sight when he done rode up to Campbell's that mornin' and said "Haddy" to little Hillie. I reckon she must've thought the cabins had falled. She was just out from the milkin' and she was fixin' to hunt eggs, she said, when up rode this terr'ble lookin' feller and says "Haddy." She said she thought he was already dead and was a'talkin' from the grave. Well, no such kind of luck. And Hillie, she says the next thing he says is about how some feller had done killed his daddy and tried to kill him too and did they have a telephone because somebody had got to call the sheriff before the durn killer mayt get away or make up some cockeyed story and try to get outen it. And then he done fainted and finally fell off that horse at last.

Well, so they called Sheriff Simmons to come out quick and they said Darlen was off his head for a piece whilst they was bidin' on the law. But I reckon he weren't much outen his head. Not enough to forget what all he'd kindly cooked up. Because when the sheriff got out there about noon, Darlen ups and tells him the same story, how his girlfriend's uncle has done shot and killed his daddy and tried to kill him too. But had only blowed a big hole in his shoulder. And then he faints again.

And it worked. Worked slicker'n a rat skin. They took and went out there to Hobbes's. And Burl was a'saddlin' up his horse. Said he'd been a'waitin' on 'em, figuring they'd turn up, but then decided he best to go get 'em. Somethin' to that effect. But, of course, what with Nole's story and all, it looked a right smart like he was tryin' to get away.

And they charged Burl Hobbes with killin' Carl Darlen and

with the 'tempted murder of poor little Nole, you know. And Hobbes says he didn't do nothin' but that he'd almost caught Nole Darlen for 'em, and they says that's a pert crackpot story and they done carted him off into town.

Ain't that somepin? Everbody knowed Nole Darlen was a coward and a sneak, but they done went with everthing he told 'em, like a possum in a deadfall, easy as that. And how he ever got it all worked up, I'll never know.

Because it was all a pack of lies.

They found Carl Darlen's body lyin' on his bed shot through the heart with a forty-caliber slug. He had been killed in the shed, they says, and drug back into the house. And they had Nole Darlen who is got his shoulder blowed to Jerusalem by a forty-caliber slug. And they got that forty-caliber pistol a'settin' on Burl Hobbes's kitchen table with two shots fired and blood all over the kitchen floor that had somehow got all the way there from over the hill to Darlen's. So it sure enough looks like Burl Hobbes is got a sight to do with it, right from the start.

And Nole, he starts in to talkin', once he's up out of his coma. And he says Hobbes is havin' relations with his momma, Raferty Darlen. And he says not only that, but Hobbes is mad as hell about him—Nole—a'callin' on that niece gal of his'n—Janey Gill—she told in court how Hobbes went over the hill to the Darlen place that mornin' and she had done heard the gunfire. And so now it looks like Hobbes'd sure enough like to get shed of both Darlen fellers, Nole because his galfriend is Hobbes's niece, and Carl because he's married to Hobbes's own secret galfriend. So it looked a heap like Burl had got one of 'em and just missed with the other'un.

So there weren't too much Burl Hobbes could say about none of it. He stuck to his own version of what went on out there, and I reckon that's just about what happened, but you could see ain't nobody believed a word he said. The prosecuter, he'd get to laughin' and mockin' the whole thing. He'd say "The DAWG," right loud and sarcastic like that. "This man, this here adulterer and murderer would have us to believe that

16

the DAWG done tracked in that blood." And he'd boom out a laugh. Well, it weren't none too funny.

And then somewhere's in there it comes out that Janey Gill is cousin to Jem Craishot. And so folks thows that bit of information into the hopper, and it comes out as Burl Hobbes is Jem's uncle. So they figures maybe Burlton Hobbes is got wind of that ambush set up a few years back that got Jem sent off to prison for life, and about who kindly set that ambush up in the first place. So here comes another one of them motives for why Hobbes mayt of wanted to gun down them two.

So they has the pistol with Hobbes's fingers all over it, and I reckon they has the whaddyacallit 'stranged wife with his fingers all over her, too. And they has all that blood over to Burl's kitchen, where they'd found him fixin' to ride off on 'em when they come to pick him up. And he had just kindly set that pistol down on his own kitchen table. And they has them a eyewitness with a bullet in him from that same pistol and a galfriend kindly from that same kitchen. And, top it off, they has all that Jem Craishot whatchacallit just to thow in whenever they wants to make everbody right sure he prob'ly done it.

But it don't matter to me. It's all a damn lie, and I know it. Because I know where that pistol come from.

Hobbes had been arrested around noon of the day following the murder. He told his story, simply and methodically, as he stood in the kitchen with the sheriff, who remembered him slightly from the Jem Craishot manhunt of three years ago. Simmons was a fair-minded man, who was not one to jump to conclusions or rush to any sort of judgment, and Burl knew the man would weigh the evidence carefully and considerately.

So Burlton told his story and Simmons listened carefully while he wrapped up the pistol and looked over the blood smears on the floor. The bloody chair rowel Hoover had brought in last night was nowhere to be found and, although the dog himself was there, curious and friendly, he had spent enough of today's hours hunting snakes in the creek bottom that the blood on his coat had been erased, or at least covered over with muck and burr to the point where Simmons was unable to corroborate any of Hobbes's story. There was certainly fresh blood on the kitchen floor and that went with Hobbes's claim that it was the blood, dragged in by Hoover, that had caused him to return to the Darlen house this morning, to find the body of the father, to discover the pistol, and to meet the returning son. But there was also plenty of evidence that Hobbes had tracked the blood back himself from the Darlen place, where, in fact Simmons had found footprints matching Burlton's brogans heading into and out of the dead man's room.

"I'm goin' to have to arrest you, Mister Hobbes," Simmons had said, drawing out a pair of handcuffs. The sheriff didn't like having to take a man like Burlton Hobbes into custody, but there was ample evidence clearly showing the man's involvement in a shooting. And so that was pretty much all there was to it.

Hobbes had a story no one could really believe, although there were many who wanted to, at least at the beginning. But he had, by his own admission, shot his chief accuser—in order to prevent his escape, Burlton said, but it was nevertheless clear who had injured whom. Clear, too, that Hobbes had indeed had the pistol in his hands long enough to fire at least that one shot. He refused to discuss his whereabouts on the day prior to the murder, beyond saying he had been to town, as usual on a Saturday.

When Sheriff Simmons found Rosary that evening, he discovered she had recently been beaten, and he silently chalked that assault up either to Hobbes or to his victim, the husband, although Rosary would say nothing, would accuse no one. Either way, Simmons thought, *no matter iffen it was the adulterer or the adulteree*, it was another evidence of motive. Later, when Burlton was on trial for his life, Rosary would, in fact, testify that her son had attacked her after having caught her and

Hobbes together. The people took this as a naked attempt to cover for the accused, *and anyways, if Nole beat her up, then Hobbes'd want to shoot him for that, too, wouldn't he?*

Hobbes was bound over to Superior Court and was appointed a young attorney, the son of a member of the elite group known as "outsider owners," who had built the city from a backwoods crossroads to a planned, industrial community, the "Magic City of the New South." It must be said that the young man did his best to develop a defense for his client, following the line that Burlton's version of the story was, after all, possible. If it *could* have happened that way, the attorney claimed, then the jury was bound to find his client innocent. But the young lawyer's role in the trial, as earnestly as it was played, worked against Burlton from the start, because the lawyer's very presence in Roalton—his cultivated northern accent and relatively cosmopolitan manners—served to remind everyone that Carl Darlen had been a leading citizen of Magic City, and that it was upon his own land Magic City had grown to become the Wonder of the Mountain South.

Besides, every time the attorney attempted to emphasize the "shadow of a doubt" defense, his rhetoric seemed, instead, to call up the simple truth that there was absolutely no evidence pointing to Nole Darlen as the killer. No motive, not even opportunity, since both Burlton and Darlen agreed that the only time they had set eyes on each other, Nole had been sitting his horse, and Hobbes had been holding the gun. So the more the attorney tried to make Hobbes's story appear possible, the more unlikely it actually seemed.

ii.

Well, I went to the trial, that first day, like everbody else that could get in the door. It was like we'd been cheated out of a trial three year ago, with all that Jem Craishot bidnits. So I went and got a earful, and it didn't make me feel no better about that gun.

Prosecution feller, he outlines all the evidence against Burl Hobbes, and it looks pert bad, I'd say, iffen I hadn't knowed better. Then he calls him his witnesses, startin' with Maydie Hobbes, Burl's wife. And he asks her iffen she'd been with Burl all that mornin' and she had to say she couldn't find him for a piece, there in the early morn. And then Burl's lawyer, he gets up and asks her hadn't Burl gone out the night before sayin' he'd heard a gunshot, and she says "yessir."

But then the other lawyer gets back up and asks her did Burl say he'd found anything earlier on when he'd gone lookin' after that "so-called gunshot." And she had to say no, he'd told her it weren't a dern thing.

Then they calls up Janey Gill, that's a'livin' there with Burl, and she says he's been a'tryin' to keep her and Nole away from each other ever since the start, and that he'd got real mad a time or two about Nole bein' kindly involved with her. She was dressed up in a little schoolgirl's outfit, looked like butter

*wouldn't melt in her mouth. Said she seen Burl had went over
the hill that morning, toward the Darlen's, and then she remembered a'hearin' gunfire. And then Burl's lawyer, he asked her
how many shots had she heard and she said she weren't sure.
And then the other 'un gets up and asks did she hear any shots
earlier, in the middle of the night, like Burlton said. And she
said no, she hadn't heard nothin'. And she got up and tiptoed
off the stand like she was comin' outen a church and was still
a'prayin' to the Lord.*

*Then come the big star witness. Nole Darlen, he got up, all
bandaged and a'lookin' wan as could be, and he told how he'd
got out to his daddy's place, and Burl'd said "Your daddy's
a'waitin' for you inside, dead, and I'm a'goin' to send you to
hell, too." And lifted up the gun and shot him. But lucky
enough, Nole got away, though he was bad shot-up, and rode
clear to Campbell's and told 'em all before he passed out how
Hobbes had done killed his daddy and so Nole had saved the
day for justice and the law.*

And that was the end of the first day. Just like that.

*So I says they're a'goin' to hang this on that poor feller that
never done it, and it looks like it mayt kindly be up to me to try
and get some of it straightened out, about that pistol. You don't
like to go and stick your nose into nobody's bidnits or nothin'.
But this looks like to me it's a matter of this feller's life ain't
worth a supped-out chaw without somebody steps up and tells
about where that pistol come from. And I knowed Ketterling
weren't a'goin' to do nothin' about it, because he don't dare to
get the law involved in his little blind-pig bidnits neither. And
iffen they wait on Sid Stanley to show up and say "That's my
iron that Nole Darlen snatched out of Ket's when I weren't
supposed to be in there playin' no Shoot Red Dog anyhow."
And who knows where Siddy got aholt of that gun in the first
place that he wouldn't rightly want folks a'wonderin' about?
Ain't nothin' some fellers likes better'n to wave a gun of their'n*

around and tell you all about what a fine piece it is and how it'll shoot the shuck off the cob and all that, and make dead sure everbody knows it's their gun. Until they comes a time somebody actually shoots one of the goddamn things and somebody gets killed. Lord. Then all of a sudden you can't find nobody never even saw that gun, nor knows nothin' about that gun, nor any gun ever made this side of Jerusalem.

Meantime, I figure ain't nobody else a'goin' to come up and witness to nothin' Nole done the day before, because he'd likely not been with anybody but folks that stayed away from the law, kindly. Moonshiners and rounders and all wasn't about to come forth and tell nothin' to nobody. I figured.

So I says, iffen somebody's a'goin' to tell about how Nole Darlen grabbed that pistol outen a game of Shoot Red Dog that he weren't even allowed to play in, and I reckon he brought that gun out to Blair's Crick to Daddy's house his own self, and so the only way Burlton Hobbes could of got that gun was just like he said he done, he picked it up offen the porch steps where Nole had kindly set it down after Nole had kindly blowed his daddy's brains out with it; iffen somebody is a'goin' to tell everbody about all that, well I reckon it's just goin' to have to be Hogeye, ain't it? And I says, I'll be careful not to tell 'em any more'n they needs to know. Because it ain't holpen Hobbes for me to be gettin' Ket into trouble with the law, nor Sid neither.

Well, Sheriff Simmons and me, we'd got to be pert well acquainted back during all that Jem Craishot bidnits, so I decided it was a good notion to tell him about that weapon. So that evenin' I kindly wandered on over to his office, and there he was, a sippin' on a coffee and he says, "Hey, Hog, what's the news?"

I told him how it couldn't of been Burl had that revolver, but it was Nole had got it the night before and must've brought it out there, so it had to be the way Hobbes'd said it was. And Sheriff, he perks up and says, "I knew it, godammit, that slick sonofabitch." And he says it's kindly out of his hands now that it's on trial, but whyn't I call on Burl's lawyer, soon as he's got the time, and get him to call me as a witness, fix things right? And Sheriff says he'll get over to the county boys and let 'em all know that he had likely arrested the wrong feller, no matter how much it looked like Burl Hobbes had done it, and there'd be a witness to say so.

So I gone to see the lawyer, after court of a Wednesday, second day into the trial. Up in them new offices across from the library. He looked to me to be about eleven year old, a'settin' up in that big leather chair at that big cherrywood desk. "He don't look real," I says to myself, and then I can see he don't feel right about settin' up there hisself. Like he knows he's s'posed to be a great big lawyer and all, but he don't really quite know how to do it. So maybe he figures if he sets in that swivelin' chair and looks real serious across that cherrywood desk, well maybe he can convince you enough that you'll start to believin' it after all. And then, maybe iffen he can see that you believe it, maybe then he'll take to believin' it hisself. But right now he feels like he must look like that eleven-year-old. And he's right about that. So now it's you got to do some play-actin'. Like you got to talk to him as if he really is the big shot lawyer he's s'posed to be, that you could tell this information to, and he will go out and do somepin about it and change everthing. And so you get to talkin' to him real serious, like he is the big man and not the eleven-year-old. And this time you're a'hopin' he'll believe you, so he mayt start actin' like the big shot long enough for you to believe it and get through the tellin'. You know?

So I says, "I know where that piece come from, and it ain't none of Burlton Hobbes's gun. It's Nole Darlen's gun. Or at least it was Nole Darlen's gun long enough for Nole to ride it to Blair's Crick and shoot his daddy with it." That Nole had done took it from a feller the night before at a card game downtown at a blind pig that don't nobody need to know nothin' else about but that he kindly obtained that pistol at it.

Well that got lawyer pretty excited. You could see he didn't have no kind of a case to talk about, and the trial fixin' to wind *up in a few days, he's got to be a mite despaired. And now here comes a feller out of nowheres says he can put that gun right in Nole Darlen's hand the day before. So it must've seemed like Christmas and payday and the circus come to town all at the same time. So lawyer gives a little squeak and jumps down outen his chair and sticks out his hand and starts a shakin' mine like he thinks he mayt pump water outen it, and says, all fired up, "You mayt of saved a man's life today, my friend. Done your civic duty." And such things as that.*

Well I felt pert good about it my own self, at least until I come out of there and it ain't fifteen minutes before the deputy picks me up and says he's the "actin' sheriff," and says, "The prosecutin' attorney's a'waitin' to talk to you, and they don't mean in fifteen minutes." And I says, "Where's Rick Simmons?" and he says, "Didn't I tell you I'm the actin' sheriff, and didn't I say 'right now'?"

And so he hustles me over there to the county building and upstairs, and there's the attorney, sure enough. He's been around a mite, I'd say, and he don't look like no kid, not like Burl's lawyer. This 'uns got a kindly steely look about him, don't make a country boy like me any too damn comfortable, I tell you. Like he ain't here to ask you nothin' he don't already know, and it's likely what you thought you knowed yourself ain't quite the way it really is and why'nt I set you down and get you straight? And they put me in that chair in front of him and he gets to lookin' serious and a sight more interested in me than I wants him to be.

And he leans back in his chair and kindly makes the church steeple with his fingers. You know? And he says, "Mister Blankenship—it's Blankenship, ain't it?" and he mustles around in some papers and says, "Yum humm, Blankenship. That's right." And he gives me another'un of them steely looks.

And he says, "I understand from the defense attorney in the Hobbes case that you're fixin' to offer some last-minute information about the murder weapon?"

So I got started in to tellin' him the same thing, about Ket's and Nole and all, and he listens for about two seconds and then he holds up his hand, like he's a'stoppin' the mail, and he says, "I also understand you have this information due to your involvement in the illegal whiskey business."

Well that shut me up faster'n a pie safe at threshin' time. I says, "I ain't involved…"

"Mister Blankenship," he says. "Tradin' in whiskey is a federal crime, and we'd hate to have to run you in to the revenue fellers just because you was a'goin' to testify in a trial that the outcome is already pert well done by the time you even come into it."

And I starts in again, sayin, "I ain't…"

And he says, "I reckon my boys could find a gallon or two of white liquor on your property if they was to look hard enough, anytime I sent 'em over to find it. That and your own testimony about consortin' with fellers that's runnin' a blind pig. Which you was plannin' to give under oath in a court of law. Ain't that right? I believe that'd be enough to send you off for a pert good stretch."

I says, "Sheriff Simmons ain't the sort to plant no whiskey on a feller."

He gets to laughin', all sneery and nasty. "I got some news for you," he says, still a'laughin' outen the sides of his mouth, kindly. "Sheriff Simmons ain't no sheriff no more," he says. "Not since last night when he already come to me with the same fool story. Well, boy, he's done been suspended for he's already tipped off too many of you moonshine boys up the mountain, one too many times." He pointed a finger at me. "You think he can protect every one of you ignorant low-bred covites? That and a little matter of a dice game at his momma's house."

"You got to be kiddin' me," I says. "Little old puny-bet dice game? What in hell you tryin' to do?"

"Shut up," he says. "You got no say in this." And he gets a stern look on his face and says, "This here is the city, now, Mister Blankenship. We got us a major factory center here, thanks to

*people like the Darlens. It ain't some low-down tobacco town no
more, for hayseeds like you and Burl Hobbes to spend your time
a'messin' with folks like Raferty Darlen and her boy. And don't
you forget it."*

*Then he changes face all of a sudden and turns all syrupy
and snake-like. "Besides," he says, "Who in hell's a'talkin'
about plantin' evidence? I didn't say nothin' like, did I, deputy?
All I says, if I was to send some of my boys out there lookin'
for somethin' round your place, I reckon they'd find what they
was sent after. 'Seek and ye shall find,' ain't it? And it won't be
the first time somebody got sent up to federal prison jest for
snookin' a little corn liquor, would it?"*

*And then I recalled that this here prosecutor was a cousin of
some sort to them Boarder boys that Sheriff had done had to go
to the tax boys because he couldn't get 'em for killin' that boy
up to Spivy. And that weren't a'goin' to help matters too much,
here. So I ain't quite as slow as I look. I took the point, right off
the bat, that it wouldn't do me no good to get up and tell nobody
about that gun. So I told him so. I says, "I believe I understand
what you're a'gettin' at."*

*And he says, "Well, that's good, Mister...what is it? Blanken-
ship. That's good. Because I wouldn't want a hard-workin' feller
like you to get caught up in nothin' he can't handle. You see? So
I reckon we can just forget about all this mess, ain't that right."
He weren't askin' me; he was a'tellin' me.*

*But I says, "I'm a'goin' to have to think this over." Because
I weren't any too innersted in lettin' a bigshot sonofabitch of a
attorney tell me what I can't say, for one. Besides, I figured I
owed it to Sheriff who'd got hit on the blind side, kindly, just
for tryin' to make sure folks heard what I had to say about that
gun. Well, I says, they can't take no badge from me, can they?
And this here's a man's life we're a'talkin' about and comes a
time, I reckon, when you got to tell what you know whether
it's for runnin' your own traps or another feller's. Seems like to
me.*

"You do all the thinkin' you want," he says. "Thinkin' ain't

like talkin'. It won't bring you no troubles you might wish you'd never of tangled with in the first place."

So I got up next day, and I was pert certain I wanted to go on and testify no matter what that feller was a'tryin' to scare me into doin'. At the same time, though, I figured it weren't a'goin' to help me any to just bash my head through the barn door, iffen I could find somebody to help slide her open. And I figured maybe Sheriff Simmons was out of the picture, but they was still the defense lawyer, and mayt be he could see to it I'd be able to tell it without gettin' run up to Leavenworth, kindly.

So I went to see the lawyer early as I could, to tell him the county boys was a'leanin' on me about the gun and ain't there nothin' he can do to keep me out of leg irons iffen I'm to tell the damn truth after all.

And damned if he don't lean back and make the church-steeple thing with his hands, too. And he stops me a'talkin' and pitches in hisself, sayin', "I'm glad you came in this mornin'. Because, tell you the truth, Mister Blankenship, I believe this is pert much an open-and-shut case as concerns the man's guilt. I don't believe, after all, that your testimony about a gun is a'goin' to make no difference in the verdict at this point, with the trial pert near finished, and it mayt could do us some harm when the sentence gets passed. It'll look like we brung in a new witness with a story we'd cooked up as a last-chance sort of a thing. Wouldn't work against all that other evidence. Wouldn't work at all. We need to face facts: The man will be found guilty, and the best we can do is to try and save him from the chair. Your tale about that gun seems a mite far-fetched, particularly since you're the only person in town who seems to be a'tellin' it."

Well I stared at him for a minute until he got to squirmin' a mite, like that eleven-year-old. Then I says, "I reckon they got to you, too."

Well, that made him upset, though he tried not to show it. He stands up and sticks his hand out to me again and says, "Well, thank you very kindly, Mister Blankenship. We appreciate *your help, even if we can't use it, and are you right sure I can't get you a cup of coffee or somepin, but then you did say you didn't only have but a minute, didn't you?"*

So I says, "Lord, lawyer. They only tried to scare me with a couple jugs of moonshine. What in hell they go after you with? The whole goddamn run?"

And that gets him riled up sure enough. And he says he ain't a'goin' to get involved in tryin' to float a story—that's just what he said, "tryin' to float a story"—about no gun, that could be impeached, he says, as easy as mine, and is just as likely to get Hobbes hanged as it is to do anything else.

So I says, "Don't that all boil down to you just called me a liar?"

And he says, "I reckon so, Mister Blankenship. I reckon so."

So they ain't no doubt about it, they have done convicted and hanged a innocent feller. I don't care how much of what they was callin' "carbureting evidence" they found, and I don't know how all that Darlen blood got up to that Hobbes house. Or how Hobbes got aholt of that gun. I reckon it was all just dezactly like Hobbes said it was. It don't matter how cockeyed it sounds. And I don't care how much of whaddyacallit, motive they was for Hobbes to kill any a one of them Darlens. He didn't do it, and that's flat. And they have done went and hanged the wrong feller, and that's all there is to that, as the duck says to the drake.

Burl Hobbes got hanged right quick, just a month or so after that trial. Actually, they give him the chair, roasted him, down to Nashville. And I told everbody I could that they was a'hangin' the wrong feller. But wouldn't nobody listen to me.

Nole Darlen, he left with that Janey Gill. He weren't in much good shape, couldn't use his right arm nor nothin'. Not that he ever used it for much anyways, 'cept drinkin' and such. Last I heard, he was bootleggin' up to Danville or somewheres, a'gettin' rich. I don't know what become of his mommy. Raf-

erty. *Sid says she moved out into that big old house and is livin'*
out there with the daughter, Mary. Says Mommy left the room
where the body was just the way they found it. The bloody
sheets and all. But you can't always go by what Sid says. I'll tell
you that.

Now I sometimes set and think about Merv Craishot, that
poor gal that Nole done got in trouble, and about Jem. Both of
'em dead while they's still so young. Well, at least Jem done
killed him a mess of folks, to deserve what happened, maybe.
Some could say. But old Burlton Hobbes, he didn't do nothin'
but walk in the door, kindly. And he's deader'n a ham hock.

It ain't right, but I reckon it's the way it is. Me, I'm goin'
back home, up the mountain. I believe I've had enough of all of
it. The whole damn show.

But then I got to thinking, about that woman, Burl
Hobbes's wife? How she come into that courtroom ever day
quiet as a mouse on Sunday. And she set there and watched 'em
get ready to convict her husband. Her husband that she
knowed was a'runnin' around with that city gal. But she'd set
there all day, in her country woman's dress and her big country
wife's shoes. And at the end of the day, she'd sit whilst everbody else was a'filin' out. She'd sit and watch 'em take Burl out
of the room, and then she set for a piece more and watch the
door he'd gone through.

And come her time to testify, she got up and said what she
saw. Straight out, with no frills or nothin'. Just what she saw.
And that prosecutor'd try and tell her what it all meant: that
Burlton had done gone over the hill to shoot that man. And
she'd shake her head and say, "He'd heard the shot. He went to
see." And the lawyer, he'd say, real slick-like, "Of course that's
what you'd say." And he'd threaten her: "You know what the
penalty is for lyin' under oath?" And she'd say, "I know what I
seen."

So they convicted him, and she watched them deputies take
him out the last time. And then I saw her come out of the
courthouse and walk down to where she'd tied the wagon. And

I saw her take a hanky outen her pocket and wipe her eyes. Then she went cross the street, to the dry goods, and come out a few minutes later with a big ole wash board, a flashin' in the sun. And got back into the wagon and geed up that horse and headed back home to work the farm. And I says, "Well, Jesus Christ."

So I was a'goin' to go back home, up the mountains, get shed of all this. And then, like I say, I got to rememberin' that woman. And I says, "Hogeye, it's a mean old world, but it's the one you got." And I decided I weren't a'goin' to try and run away from it, but stay here, tell folks what I seen, and keep on with my life, like that woman done. Maybe even ride out there, see if she needs some help with that crop.

Because, just like her, I know what I seen. And it mayt not do a chicken liver's worth of good, but I'm a'goin' to keep on tellin' it. Because if you can't say what you seen, you'll find yourself startin' to believe what folks'll tell you you're lookin' at. And that ain't the way to go. Not in a million years.

ACKNOWLEDGMENTS

This novel is based-in true events that are a part of my family history in East Tennessee. I am very lucky to have my father, Glay, still around (age 101), and his older sister, Opal (age 109). They are a storehouse of information on the region and the period, as well as the specific stories in question.

Thanks to Jen Conley, a fine writer whose work is published by Down & Out Books, as well. I met Jen in 1987, when she was my student at Elon College. I sent her this manuscript, recently, and she introduced me to this wonderful publisher.

RICHARD HOOD is a musician, photographer, and writer, living in Greene County, Tennessee.

BOOKS

On the following pages are a few
more great titles from the
Down & Out Books publishing family.

For a complete list of books and to
sign up for our newsletter,
go to DownAndOutBooks.com.

Rose City
A Teller County Novel
Michael Pool

Down & Out Books
March 2019
978-1-948235-67-9

When Cole Quick returns to his estranged hometown of Teller, Texas for his alcoholic father's funeral, it doesn't take long for old debts to drag him back into the criminal underworld he tried to escape thirteen years earlier.

To escape Teller County with his life intact he'll have to solve an old friend's murder, resist powerful forces conspiring to pillage his birthright, and crack open the debutante town's sterile shell to reveal the dark forces of racism, classism, and corruption operating just beneath the surface.

WARREN C. EMBREE
THE ORNERY GENE

The Ornery Gene
Warren C. Embree

Down & Out Books
April 2019
978-1-64396-012-8

When itinerant ranch hand Buck Ellison took a job with Sarah Watkins at her ranch in the Sandhills of Nebraska, he thought he had found the place where he could park his pickup, leave the past behind, and never move again.

On a rainy July night, a dead man found at the south end of Sarah's ranch forces him to become a reluctant detective, delving into the business of cattle breeding for rodeos and digging up events from his past that are linked to the circumstances surrounding the murder of Sam Danielson.

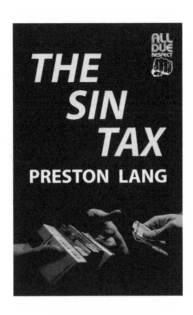

The Sin Tax
Preston Lang

All Due Respect, an imprint of
Down & Out Books
978-1-948235-45-7

Everyone knows that cigarettes will kill you...

Mark works the overnight in a grimy deli in the Bronx, selling gray-market smokes and bad meat. His hot-headed manager Janet pushes him to help her con their boss into paying cash for a truck full of tax-free cigarettes. Soon he finds that Janet is willing to do nearly anything to grab the money, and what they're up to is a lot more dangerous than three packs a day.

The Hollow Vessel
An Errol Coutinho/Big Island of Hawaii Mystery
Albert Tucher

Shotgun Honey, an imprint of
Down & Out Books
978-1-946502-93-3

Everyone wants a piece of wealthy young Rhonda Cunningham, which dooms her plan to disappear into the rainforest of the Big Island of Hawaii.

Detective Errol Coutinho needs to find out how her expensive tent ended up on the Kona side of the island.

And is that her blood in it?

It's getting crowded in the rainforest, and the shakeout will be murder...

CPSIA information can be obtained
at www.ICGtesting.com
Printed in the USA
LVHW091003170320
650292LV00001B/150